Puffin Books

THE TWENTY-TWO LETTERS

Aleph had no objection when his father, Resh, the master mason in Gebal, sent him up the mountain to see how many trees had been felled. It was a kind of punishment for playing at writing with his sister Beth – just a game they'd invented, but Resh was disturbed to think a *girl* might have learned something about the priest-guarded mystery that Aleph, as an apprentice scribe, had permission to delve into. Still, it wasn't a hard chore: the climb was pleasant enough, and Beth gave him food for the journey and one of her homing pigeons to keep him company. Aleph might have seen his task differently, though, if he'd known how long it would take him to get where he was going, so that he could release the bird and let it fly back to its mistress.

Meanwhile, Aleph's eldest brother, Zayin, General of Gebal's small and rowdy army, was off on a scouting expedition. And Nun, his second brother and a master mariner, had put to sea with a cargo of cedar-beams, a fair wind behind him, and a mysterious passenger on board. But they too failed to return when they were expected, and Beth, left alone with her father and with no path of her own to adventure, could scarcely contain her longing to know what had happened to them. Yet there was plenty going on in the city of Byblos – great building works in the Temple, and the Day of Offering drawing near – and Beth's curiosity led her into some daring actions. The momentous day finally arrived, the city filled with the King's subjects bringing him their tributes, and the pace of events began to quicken.

How the threads of the brothers' adventures were tied up, how the news of approaching attack each brought back was capped by an even larger, truly awe-inspiring crisis, and how the end of one chapter of history was also the beginning of another, makes a fitting climax to this exciting, funny, highly satisfying story. (And if the danger Aleph had to warn his people of hadn't spurred him into making use of that odd alphabet with only twenty-two letters, perhaps this book would never have been written!)

Clive King was born in Richmond, Surrey, in 1924. He was the second in a family of four sons. The family moved to a village in Kent when he was small, and this later became the setting for his *Stig of the Dump*. He got an open exhibition to Downing College, Cambridge. During the war he served in the R N V R, and later, after completing his studies, he joined the British Council.

Other books by Clive King

Me and My Million
Stig of the Dump
The Town That Went South

Clive King

The Twenty-Two Letters

Decorations by Richard Kennedy

PUFFIN BOOKS

Puffin Books, Penguin Books Ltd, Harmondsworth, Middlesex, England
Viking Penguin Inc., 40 West 23rd Street, New York, New York 10010, U.S.A.
Penguin Books Australia Ltd, Ringwood, Victoria, Australia
Penguin Books Canada Limited, 2801 John Street, Markham Ontario, Canada L3R 1B4
Penguin Books (N.Z.) Ltd, 182–190 Wairau Road, Auckland 10, New Zealand

First published in Puffin Books, simultaneously
with Hamish Hamilton, 1966
Reprinted 1973, 1976
Reprinted in this edition 1986

Made and printed in Great Britain by
Richard Clay (The Chaucer Press) Ltd, Bungay, Suffolk
Set in Monophoto Sabon

Map and alphabet drawn by Douglas Champion

Contents

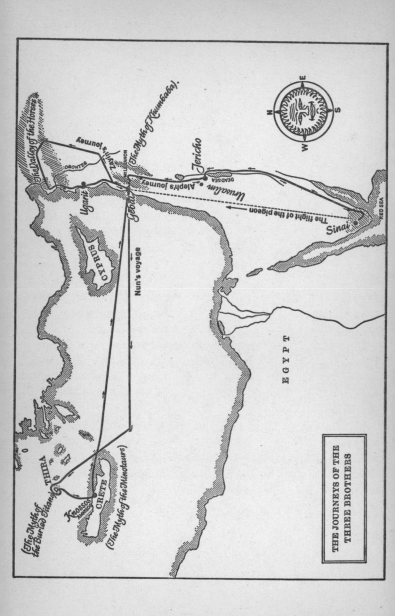

THE JOURNEYS OF THE THREE BROTHERS

(The Valley of the Horses)

Zaru's journey

(The Myth of Kumbaba)

ORONTES

Lebanon

Ugarit

Jordan

Jericho

Winaaim

Aleph's journey

DEAD SEA

RED SEA

The flight of the pigeon

Sinai

CYPRUS

Nun's voyage

EGYPT

THIRA

(The Myth of the Buried Titans)

CRETE

KNOSSOS
AMNISOS

(The Myth of the Minotaurs)

Foreword

When this story begins the world has still to wait fifteen hundred years for the coming of Christ. Europe, Greece, and Rome are not yet names. The War of Troy has not been fought, and as yet there are no Ten Commandments, for Moses has not been born and the writing in which they will be written has not been invented.

But in Babylonia, Egypt, and on the island of Crete people lead lives of civilized luxury. They have highly organized governments and disciplined fighting forces. Each of these nations has its own religion, and also its own system of writing which only a few educated men ever learn.

In the middle of the triangle formed by these three Great Powers stands a small City-State. It is called Gebal – in modern Arabic speech it is still Djebeil. Its people are Giblites. It is to become known to the Greeks as Byblos, 'the place of the book'.

When Resh, the master builder, lived there with his daughter Beth and his three sons, Zayin, Nun, and Aleph, it was already an ancient city where people had been living for four thousand years. The legend is that Time himself built its walls.

CLIVE KING

I

The Mountain of Cedars

The journey of Aleph, the scribe – Mount Lebanon and the myth of Khumbaba, guardian of the cedar-forests – Palestine, the prehistoric site of Jerusalem, and the legend of Abraham and Isaac – Aleph tells of the invention of the alphabet

'Go and count the trees!'

Aleph lifted his eyes from the ground and looked up at the mountains that towered behind the city of Gebal. Above the narrow plain that ran between the foothills and the sunlit sea, above the terraces of olive-orchards, above the pine-woods and the escarpments of bare rock, the cedar-forests stretched from North to South, covering the slopes and valleys with dense green, and reaching up to the bare peaks with the white caps of snow that still lingered on the heights.

'Count the trees, Father?' said Aleph in bewilderment. 'But there are so many!'

His father let out an exasperated breath like the sound of wind through the branches. 'My son,' he sighed, 'I think you have intelligence. I know you are idle! And you are rightly called the Ox, because you are certainly slow. But never before have I had reason to suspect you of actions that may bring disgrace upon your family. No!' he said quickly, holding up his hand to prevent Aleph from interrupting. 'I do not want to listen to your explanations. As apprentice scribe at the temple you are entrusted with knowledge which is shameful and improper to impart to your young sister. You say you have done no such thing, and I hope with all my heart that this is true. I am only saying that it will be better for you to spend your time on a useful errand. And when I say count the trees, do not pretend to think I mean number all the trees in the forest. You are not as foolish as all that. I wish you to go up where the work-parties are felling the trees, find out how many they have cut down, and return to me with the information. Is this too difficult an errand for you?'

'No, Father,' said Aleph. He felt relieved. He was satisfied that he had done nothing wrong, but he had not been sure whether he would be punished. He was glad enough for the opportunity to go up the mountains by himself, and the responsibility was not too great.

As he prepared to leave the house he was waylaid by his sister. 'I'm not to speak with you,' he said. 'Father is angry.'

Beth pouted. 'We were doing nothing wrong,' she said. 'And Father can't mean you to go up the mountain with no food.' She was holding a bundle, and a bird-cage with a white pigeon in it.

'Am I to eat that bird in the mountain?' asked Aleph.

'This is your food,' said Beth, handing him the bundle. 'And this is *my* game, since yours has been interrupted.' She gave him the bird-cage. 'Take him up the mountain with you. When you get to where you are going, let him go. He'll fly back and tell me you've got there. Good-bye, Aleph!' And she darted away.

Aleph walked through the streets of the city to the landward gate, passed through, and set off for the mountains. He was not in a hurry. He was no mountaineer, but not so much of a townsman as to set an impossible pace for the first half-hour and collapse when the going got hard. With the help of his staff he picked his way up the stony ass-tracks through the terraces of olive trees. Above them he came to the pines. The track was now sandy underfoot, but there were thorns to scratch his legs if he wandered off it. In each round pine-tree top the cicadas sang, and Aleph wondered idly what these invisible singers were that made this music. It might almost be the voice of the trees themselves sizzling in the sun, though he was of the opinion that on the whole trees did not sing. But life was too full of things to waste time on a mere insect, or whatever it was.

The track was really steep now, leading over piles of rough rock, and he had to help himself up with his hands, passing the bird-cage and the bundle from one to the other. He was taking a deep breath with each step, and his throat felt dry. He scrambled to the top of a rocky outcrop and sat down to rest, looking out towards the sea. He set the bird-cage on the rock, and felt sorry for the pigeon, a prisoner in the free mountains. But it was not time to let it go yet.

Down below, the town of Gebal was already shrunken by the height he had climbed. The harbour was a little blue rock pool, its rim lined with nutshells that must be boats. The city wall was like something a child might build with sand on a beach, and the palace and the temples and houses were like chippings in a mason's yard. But this thought reminded him that he was indeed looking down on the busy city of Gebal, where traders chaffered over cargoes on the quays, where the priests plotted in the temple, and where his father was in a continuous state of fuss and anxiety as to whether he had enough stone and timber in hand for the King's latest building project. And that was why he, Aleph, was here in the mountains. He had trees to count. He stretched himself. Heigh ho! it was so peaceful up here, with the wind and a nameless bird singing in the tree-tops, but there was business to be done, even here.

He stood for a moment on his rock, suddenly doubtful if

he was going the right way. The mountains looked simple from the coast, a great wall rising straight up along the whole of the eastern horizon. But when you were up in them they were more complicated, made up of ridges and water-courses and deep valleys and false crests. If you did not know the mountains, every now and then you would say to yourself, 'A few more steps and this *must* be the top!' But of course it was not. When you got there it was an isolated outcrop or a minor peak, and above rose the higher ranges and at last the true peaks which held their covering of snow late into the summer. Not even the cedars grew at that height, and so he had never had occasion to go so far. But he had heard that beyond the range there was a flat and fertile valley, and beyond that more mountains, and beyond that the desert, and beyond that – he supposed the edge of the world. Some said a final mighty mountain range, some said merely a precipice into nothing, some said a great sea which poured over in a ceaseless waterfall for ever and ever. He would like to go beyond the mountains, but not perhaps as far as the edge of the world.

He decided that he would have to go along the edge of a slope towards the valley where the timber was being cut, and he set off, walking on the edges of his sandals, glad every now and then of a solid rock to stop him slipping down the slope. He struck a goat-track that showed like a scratch along the thorny hill-side and followed it thankfully, still gaining height. The sun beat down on the exposed slope, the lizards darted away from the stones before him, and though the air was no longer heavy and sticky he felt he was broiling like a piece of meat on heated hearthstones. Then over a crest appeared a dark green feathery shape. It could be a single pine or a scrub-oak – but no, as he approached he could see that it was a cedar. A small one, fighting for its life on the stony edge of the forest. But it meant that he was there.

There was always a special feeling about reaching the cedar-line, and if he had been put there blindfolded he would have known immediately where he was.

Soon he was in the shade of the trees, and he rested again with his back against one of the trunks. Out of the sun the air was cool and fresh again, and the breeze among the needles of the cedars was making its peculiar music. It was only a grove of young trees, or perhaps they were old but had never grown much because it took all their energy to cling to this stony slope, so steep that Aleph had to crawl or pull himself up by low branches to get up it.

He sat and looked out through the dark bars of the tree-trunks towards the sea – the sea that was always with you in this land, whether it was roaring in your ears on the shore or climbing with you as you climbed. As it was now, the straight line of its horizon seemed to be half-way up the sky and truly looked like the edge of the world, so hard and definite was it. And yet he knew that beyond it, to the West, lay islands and coasts where people lived whose kings were even richer than the great King of Gebal. It was difficult to believe, but it was his own brother Nun, the sailor, who had told him, and, indeed, his ship went out loaded with this very cedar-wood and returned with wonderful things of gold and bronze that must have been made by very clever people – unless Nun traded with demons. Aleph liked looking at the sea, but he had no great desire to entrust himself to it.

Cedar-wood! Once again he reminded himself of the work he had to do for his father – trees to be counted. No use starting to count just yet. He had another moment of doubt, as he stood up, whether this was the right part of the range, the right valley, the right grove. If it was, he should be able to hear the sounds of the woodcutters' axes. He stood still and listened. There was nothing but the same sound of the wind in the branches, and somehow it seemed less friendly now; as if it did not care about human matters, about whether Aleph was lost or not. He realized that he was cold, and also that he would have to think instead of dreaming.

It would have been better if he had come up the bullock-track down which the logs were dragged to the coast, but he had deliberately chosen this short cut, relying on his sense of direction. That was his way of doing things. He preferred to keep off other people's tracks. If you knew where you were starting from and what you were aiming at, you usually got there all right. But now the thought came to him that he had been depending on following the noise of the lumber camp for the last part of his journey. Timber-felling is usually a noisy enough process: the shock of axes, the rending of branches, and the cries of the loggers and bullock-drivers can be heard from valley to valley. But here there was silence.

What had happened? Were they all just sleeping in the sun? If so, he would have to scold them for their laziness and tell them they would be punished. His father was always doing this, but he hated having to do anything of the sort. Had the slaves revolted against the overseers and run off? This was a situation for his brother Zayin, the soldier, not for him to deal with. Had they all been carried off by mountain lions, or mountain spirits? He shivered again. A tale came into his mind, told him by a foreign slave from the East he had once known, of the giant Khumbaba who lived on the Mountain of Cedars, whose roar was like the torrent of the storm, whose breath was like fire, and whose jaws were death itself. He was the watchman of the Forest and could hear even the wild cattle stir, sixty leagues away.

Aleph forced himself to stop thinking of such things. He took up the bird-cage, grateful for the companionship of even a white pigeon. He moved off again along the hillside, keeping to the lower edge of the grove. The timber-teams naturally always nibbled at the forest from the bottom edge, so if he continued along at this level he must eventually meet signs of humanity. Unless he should have been going in exactly the opposite direction, and that would just depend on whether this was his lucky day or not.

He skirted along the edge of the trees, often holding the fingers of the great lower branches to stop himself from sliding down the slope. As he came round the spur the whole of the next valley came into view, its upper slopes covered with cedars. On the far side of the valley he could now see the track, scarred by the passage of great logs dragged by the bullock-teams. The disturbed earth and rocks were red compared with the usual greyish-white of the hill-side. Where the track met the forest a great bite had been taken out of the dark green mass of the trees, littered with discarded tops and branches, and by the track were piled the trimmed trunks and usable limbs, the freshly hewn ends showing a rich orange-red in the sunlight. Smoke rose from bonfires of trimmings. But there was no sign of life.

Aleph made his way cautiously round the valley, clambered over the dry water-course at the head of it, and approached the site. The red scarred earth and the severed cedar-limbs made him think of a battlefield, though he tried to tell himself it was absurd to feel that way about earth and trees. He was hoping desperately that there would not be signs of human slaughter when he got there. He was not sure what was best to do – keep inside the forest so that no one could see him coming, or keep clear of it in case someone was waiting in ambush. Both considerations were equally upsetting, so that he went suddenly cold with fear in the hot sun. He thought of turning round and going back the way he had come. But it was absurd, even for him, who did not pretend to be a hero, to run away from an empty space.

He reached the clearing. There stood rough shelters in which the workers slept, thatched with withering cedar-branches. Outside them were a few cooking-pots, some of them broken, and some piles of garbage. He made himself go up to one hut; it was empty, except for couches of leaves and branches. He looked in the others. Nothing but one or two pieces of ragged clothing. By the track was a place where signs clearly showed that the draught-bullocks had been tethered. But now there were none.

They must have gone home. He strained his eyes down the mountain-side, but though the winding track was visible for much of the way down towards the coast, he could see nothing moving on it. Oh well, he could do the job he had been sent to do, count the marked trees and the felled trunks, and go back to town himself and report. And he had better be quick about it: he did not fancy staying the night alone in the camp.

He counted the trunks on the piles. Twenty-nine. He went round the edge of the clearing, looking for the crosses scored on the barks of the chosen trees, and eventually found eleven. Eleven and twenty-nine make forty, the total his father was expecting. Well, that was that. It was all he had been asked to find out. He was tired and hungry, but above all he was thirsty. He could see water in the bottom of the valley, so he would have to go down before he could drink, and then he could eat.

But it was strange, all the same, that the lumber-men should leave twenty-nine trunks by the road, eleven trees still standing, and just abandon the camp. And as he took a last vague look round he noticed something.

The newest tracks of the oxen led away from the tethering place – not *down* but *up* the mountain-side.

He stood blankly for some time looking at the message printed in the earth by the hooves of the oxen, then he wandered around the clearing. True, the ground was mostly stony, but in the ashes of a fireplace, in a soft bank of fallen cedar-needles he read the same sign, though still it seemed to have no meaning. He walked down the main track for some distance until he came to a sandy stratum of the mountain. Here there was no doubt at all. He could see clearly the tracks of men and oxen pointing up the mountain, but not one leading down.

He found that his brain was stupidly turning round the idea that he, Aleph the Ox, the slow-witted, had been left a message by his brothers the oxen, and that it was for him to make sense of it. Well, it was no use neglecting even the dumbest of ox-brains. He needed water, rest, and food. He followed the sound of tinkling water until he came to a small spring, plunged his burning face into a rock pool, drank until he was satisfied, and sat down in the shade of a rock to eat his bread and olives, sharing the crumbs with the pigeon.

As his stomach filled his brain cleared. After all there was no great problem. The lumber-teams had come up the mountain to cut the forty trees ordered by Resh. They had nearly completed the job, and then had abandoned the clearing, and instead of going down the mountain they had gone up.

Why had they done it and where had they gone? There was no way of answering these questions yet. Aleph had heard that it was possible to cross the mountains by continuing upward from this valley, but it was a difficult pass and few had reason to use it. Beyond the crest of the range lived people who were no friends to Gebal. He had heard rumours of armies passing over the flat plains – Egyptians from the South, Assyrians from the East, Hittites from the North. But the people of Gebal were snug in their coastal city, protected by the great mountain wall. Why should they want to cross the pass?

Why indeed? Beyond lay nothing better than slavery. And yet these log-men had apparently chosen to go. Aleph suddenly stood up. He would have to find out. It was no devotion to duty that turned his footsteps up the mountain, it was not heroism. It was just burning curiosity.

If Aleph had known that he was as yet only half-way up to the top of the pass he might not have set off so lightly. The track was easy enough to follow, through the edge of the cedar grove, emerging the other side on to the slopes of a valley from where more and more high peaks could be seen. Skirting the edge of this valley, up another crest, over and down again before climbing steeply up the other side. Many times, as he paused for breath on a steep slope or stood on a crest appalled to see yet more rugged terrain appearing before him, he wondered whether he should not turn back. But as the deeper valleys began to fill with black shadows he knew that even if he did turn back he could not possibly reach the town by nightfall. He was in for a night on the mountain anyway, and he felt that he would rather pass it in the company of the loggers, whatever had happened to them, than spend it alone.

Rather than puzzle vaguely about the mystery of the disappearing log-team, and to save his mind from imagining wild and improbable fates for them, he tried setting himself the sort of problem which he preferred to think about, and it was this. The only clear message that had been left for him at the clearing had been made by the hooves of the stupid oxen. The prints in the soft soil said unmistakably: 'We went this way.' Now if the unthinking oxen could leave this for him to read, why could not Kaph, the overseer, an intelligent and experienced man, have left some indication of *why* they had gone? Because Kaph could not write. Of course he could not. Nobody expected him to be able to write. Writing was a mysterious skill known only to priests and scribes. They spent many years learning the meanings of the hundreds of symbols and their combinations, and once they learned them they took good care that no part of their secret was shared by the common people. The very idea that a simple overseer of a lumber-man should have any knowledge of writing was absurd. Blasphemous, even. Writing was for the stories of the gods, and the affairs of great kings who represented the gods on earth, not for tradesmen's messages. So? So an ox could print in the ground a sign which anyone could read as 'Gone this way'. But though a man had a burnt stick and a piece of white bark to hand, there were no signs that he could make that meant 'Back tomorrow morning'.

These thoughts took Aleph's mind off the tiredness of his legs and the effort of his breathing. But they went no farther. He did not say to himself, 'This is wrong,' or 'Wouldn't it be better if . . .'. Indeed, alone up there among the abode of spirits, he felt uneasy when he remembered what he had told his younger sister. Was that not impious? The gods might punish him for it.

He shivered in the mountain air that grew cooler and cooler as he climbed, and as the sun dropped lower in the sky. He was now coming to a mass of tortured rocks, twisted pillars standing against the skyline. He stopped. He hoped they were rocks. They might equally be the shapes of fiends and demons turned to stone – or at least, the towers and castles of mountain spirits. Or even if no supernatural beings dwelt in this desolate place, wild mountain-men might. Among these pinnacles a traveller would be defenceless against ambush.

Aleph thought of his soldier brother, Zayin. Wasn't there something he said soldiers did to guard against ambush? Send out scouts? Cover their flanks? But there was only himself. And what was it that his sailor brother Nun used to say? 'When in Danger and in Doubt, always keep a Good Look out.' But he was afraid of what he might see if he did look about him among these petrified shapes.

So he shut his eyes, and he felt himself turning to stone as he heard a rough voice shout 'Halt!'

He kept his eyes shut. He was certain that he was petrified, that he had become merely another of the pillars of rock that stood for ever on the desolate mountain-side. That was what they were, petrified travellers. He would never move again.

He heard strange incomprehensible voices – the language of demons – about his ears. Then he jumped. Something sharp had poked him from behind. He opened his eyes and turned round. There stood a strange soldier with a naked sword.

The soldier spoke again in the unknown language. But the gesture of his sword meant 'Move!' and Aleph forgot his state of petrifaction and moved, his mouth dry with fear. As he came round the base of a great rock he came face to face with a number of men. Some of them were soldiers in foreign armour. The others he knew. Among them was Kaph, the overseer, sitting on the ground in an attitude of great dejection.

Aleph's fright turned to anger, and his speech returned: 'Kaph!' he exclaimed. 'What are you doing here? Why did you desert the camp? And – and what are those slaves of ours doing with those chains?' For two of the men he recognized as slaves from Kaph's work-party were advancing on him, carrying chains and manacles.

Kaph spat. 'Ask them yourself. They're the masters now. We're the slaves.' And he lifted his manacled wrists. And as Aleph felt the fetters being put on his own legs, he began to understand what he meant.

That night on the mountain Aleph was more miserable than he had believed possible. He had not been looking forward to sharing a shelter with the rough log-men at the camp. He had dreaded a night alone among the rocks. But here he was, chained to the surly Kaph, hungry, listening to the foreign soldiers laughing and eating round a fire while their captives shivered in the cold night air, wondering what the future held. He almost wished that his fantasy had been true, it would have been better to be changed to an unfeeling pillar of rock.

He could not sleep, but though Kaph, too, was wakeful, it was difficult to get him to talk. When he did, it was little comfort. 'How's it feel then, *Master* Aleph, to become a slave?' he mocked. 'I reckon you must have taken a fancy to it though, following us all this way just to get caught. You and your bird and all.'

Poor bird, Aleph thought. He must let it go now. No reason why it, too, should remain a prisoner. But he would have to wait until daylight, it couldn't fly in the dark.

'How was I to know you were captives?' he said to Kaph. 'I saw the hoof-prints of the oxen, and I followed them. I didn't know what had happened. I still don't. Who are these soldiers? Where did they appear from?'

'Appear's the right word. That's just what they did, appeared like spirits from the forest. There we were, working, and all of a sudden we were surrounded by them,' said Kaph.

'But where had they come from?'

'Over the mountain pass, where they're taking us back now, of course.'

'What are they, though?'

'How should I know?' Kaph growled. 'Foreigners. All I know is, our slaves who used to be log-carriers – good workers they were though – downed tools and started hugging and kissing these soldiers like they were long-lost sisters. Then they have the nerve to come to me and say Pharaoh needs men, and the oxen and the tools and gear and all, and off they march us up the mountain.'

'Pharaoh!' Aleph exclaimed. 'But these men aren't Egyptians.'

'Don't ask me! They're foreigners, and from the South, anyway, they say. What's the difference? I'm a slave and you're a slave now. We can't choose our masters.'

Aleph did not think he could sleep, but exhaustion, depression, and the thinness of the mountain air overcame him and he passed the night somehow in a state of frozen semiconsciousness. He dreamed, or at least he imagined very vividly the warm house by the seashore at Gebal, which he might never see again. But also among his dreams or imaginings were visions of fabulous Egypt. There was, perhaps, a future for him, even a life to live, in Egypt.

The prisoners were roused in the early dawn, while the sunrise was only a faint glow over the crest of the mountain range to the East. The soldiers seemed to have a little bread and water to share round and break their fast, but there was no food for the prisoners.

'One pigeon among the lot of us,' growled Kaph, looking at the bird in the cage. 'Not much, but it may save us from starvation yet.' Aleph clutched the bird-cage defensively, but the march moved off at once. Some of the soldiers scouted ahead, some of them guarded the prisoners and drove them on, and Aleph was too numbed and stupefied by the altitude and the cold to think of anything but the next step up the stony slope.

The sun rose above the crest as they climbed towards it. On the very top they all halted to rest and take their breath. Before and below them appeared a deep broad valley, still in the shadow of yet another range of sawtoothed mountains on the far side. Aleph turned back to look towards the sea and the coast. He was not even to be granted a last glimpse of his home.

He stood there wretchedly, holding the caged bird. If he let the bird go, he thought, it would probably find its way home through the clouds, planing down in almost a matter of minutes. Was not this the time to do it? And yet what had his sister said? His numb brain remembered slowly. 'When you've got to where you're going, let him loose! He'll fly back and let me know you're there.' But he was not there yet. This wind-swept mountain pass was not where he was going. It was not yet time to release his messenger.

The descent down the other side was steep, but direct. Aleph had hoped it would be much easier than climbing, but he soon felt that his leg muscles would collapse every time they took the weight of his body. However, the sun at least was warming, and as they went down the air, too, lost its bite, and they came again to a belt of forest where there was soil and soft vegetation underfoot.

There was a clearing in the forest, and in it were tents and huts, and lumber-men at work, and transport wagons and soldiers. The leader of their guards paraded the prisoners in front of a tent, and out of it came the person who Aleph supposed was the officer in charge of the camp.

The officer looked over the prisoners and the oxen without great interest, until his eye fell on Aleph: then he walked over and stood in front of him, looking him up and down. Aleph's heart turned over. There was no way of telling from the haughty countenance of the officer whether it was in his favour to be singled out from the rest. Perhaps it was because he was the only one carrying a bird-cage! The officer addressed him in Egyptian speech, but Aleph's tongue was slow to reply in the same language, so the officer shouted for a man wearing Egyptian civilian clothes, who came over to interpret.

'The officer says you don't look strong enough to be a woodcutter, and wants to know what is your trade,' explained the civilian, in Aleph's language.

Aleph hesitated and tried to think quickly. If he said he was a woodcutter they might let him work in the forests here, and perhaps he could escape. If he said he was a scribe they might have no use for him, and kill him. But woodcutting was hard work, perhaps he was not strong enough for it, and surely the Egyptians needed slaves with education as well. Better to tell the truth.

'I am a scribe,' he said.

'So young?' said the civilian, and raised his eyebrows.

'Apprentice scribe,' corrected Aleph, blushing. 'I can count, and I know a lot of the signs.'

'What were you doing in the mountains?' was the next question.

Aleph thought there might be a clever answer to this question too, but he answered simply, 'Counting trees.'

The civilian and the officer consulted together, and at length the civilian said: 'If you're a tally clerk, we may have work for you in the South. Join the draft that leaves tomorrow.'

Next morning a column of soldiers and prisoners was formed, and the southward march began. There were plenty of guards and there was nowhere to flee to but the forest full of wild beasts, so the prisoners were not bound or chained and the pace of the march was fairly brisk. In this fertile valley there was no shortage of food or water, and Aleph settled down contentedly enough to the routine of daily journeying and nightly camps. He even took a positive pleasure in looking around at new landscapes every day.

The civilian overseer, Ish, who had questioned Aleph on the first day, was with the draft. As he spoke Aleph's language and wanted to practise it, he sometimes walked beside him and they would talk. Aleph spoke of his family, and of his father who was a master builder, and he began to realize that Ish preferred his company to that of his own countrymen, the Egyptian soldiers.

They passed by the foot of a massive mountain in the

eastern wall of the valley, capped and streaked with snow. Ish told Aleph its name, which was something like Haramun or Hermon. The valley narrowed and the floor of it became crumpled and rocky, and water was difficult to find for a while. One evening they came to a wooded gorge, where the source of a river bubbled up from the base of the rocks and flowed away to the South. After some discussion the escort decided to camp there for the night. The air was chilly and full of the evening cries of frogs and strange beasts in the forest, but the soldiers and prisoners were happy to drink their fill and wash away the stains of travel. They lit fires, and some of the soldiers began to sing, and brought out musical instruments, simple pipes and drums, to which they danced.

Aleph felt it must be a sacred place, as most springs were in that part of the world, and that it was right to celebrate the fact with music and dancing. But he noticed that Ish did not join in, and seemed somehow to disapprove.

'Does this river flow to Egypt?' he asked Ish, but Ish laughed and shook his head and said he wished they could have such pleasant company all the way to Egypt. Then they talked of Egypt and of the marvels Aleph would see, and Ish revealed that he, too, had been a slave; but he was glad of it because otherwise he would not have had such good education and learned to calculate and write.

They followed the river south, skirted a swamp and a small lake, and continued on until they came to a larger lake, almost an inland sea, blue and sparkling among the wooded hills. There were fishing villages on its shores and Ish, who was caterer to the officers of the escort, obtained some delicious fresh-water fish of which Aleph had a share.

Here there seemed to be an argument between the guides and the soldiers as to which way they should proceed. There was much shouting and pointing of arms, and the choice seemed to be between a new westerly direction and continuing south. It was southward they eventually moved: a difficult track where the river wriggled through jungle in a narrow valley, and the air became hot and steamy. At last the valley broadened out again and they came to inhabited and culti-vated land. A copious spring gushed from the foot of an arid mountain, and guarding it stood a walled town. The column halted by the spring, and once again gladly washed and drank, for the air still held the heaviness of the deep valley. The commander of the soldiers was admitted through the gate of the town.

'He's going to pay his compliments to the Governor,' said Ish.

Aleph asked the name of the town.

'Jericho,' said Ish. 'It's a very old town. Look at the stone-work done by the Ancient People! Or some say by the old gods themselves. No one can tell how old those walls are – but we build better than that in Egypt now.'

There seemed to be no hurry to move on from Jericho, and there was little for Aleph to do but see that the pigeon was fed and watered. Aleph and his pigeon were the joke of the whole column. The soldiers were always offering to wring its neck and put it in a stew, but luckily there had been plenty of food for everyone so far, including the pigeon. Aleph was more worried about whether it was taking enough exercise. He still intended to carry out his sister's instructions, and let it go when he reached the place he was going to. But he had no idea how much longer they would have to march, and he was afraid the unfortunate bird would forget the use of its wings. Once he tried the experiment of letting it out of the cage to fly around for a little, and tempting it back with corn before it took it into its head to fly off for good. He wondered whether it could ever find its way back to Gebal now.

Aleph saw Ish watching him with amusement. 'Would you sell me your dove for a sacrifice?' Ish asked.

Aleph felt awkward, not knowing whether he was being teased again or not. 'He's not mine to sell,' he answered. 'He's my sister's.'

Ish laughed. 'Never mind,' he said. 'Perhaps I can get another. I have permission to go with a patrol into the mountains. Would you like to come?'

'If the soldiers need a slave,' said Aleph, 'I suppose they'll pick one. Why ask if I'd like to come?'

Ish frowned. 'You don't have to talk like a slave any more. I told the captain I wanted you as my personal servant to carry my things. Now are you coming?'

'With pleasure,' said Aleph, and he picked up the bundle, and the bird-cage, and followed Ish to where the patrol was waiting to set off.

As they marched across the plain towards the mountains, Ish talked. 'I persuaded them that it would be a good thing to send a reconnaissance patrol this way to see what the hill tribes are doing. But really I'm doing it for my own interest. My people passed through here generations ago. They say there is a place here which is still holy to them, if I can only find it.'

They climbed up out of the oppressive atmosphere of the valley into the clear air of the mountains again. Their guide, a young man from Jericho, led them confidently into the foothills as far as a little village where he was greeted and embraced by his family. Then followed a long and excited conversation in the local dialect, while Ish and the patrol waited impatiently. At last Ish interrupted.

'We have no time to waste here, guide! Lead us on to Urusalim, as you promised.'

'Yes! Yes! At once!' replied the guide. 'To Urusalim. I ask the way to Urusalim.'

'You said you knew the way to Urusalim!' said Ish angrily.

Urusalim, Urusalim ... the word passed from mouth to mouth of the group of peasants as they seemed to speculate upon the existence of any such place. Their eyes and faces showed that the word meant little to them, and their fingers pointed to opposite points of the landscape.

'Well?' demanded Ish of the guide.

'Yes! Yes!' said the guide hastily. 'My cousin, he knows Urusalim. He show us the way!'

The guide took his farewells of his family, and the guide's cousin, a wild, ragged, dark-eyed boy, led the patrol on confidently, farther and farther into the mountains.

But the farther they went the less confident became the leadership of this, their second guide. He began to look uncertainly right and left when they came to forks in the mountain-track, and then he would stop and argue passionately with the first guide, although it was obvious that the first had no useful information to offer.

The corporal of the patrol, whose impatience was beginning to show, cursed the bickering guides and threatened them with the haft of his spear. Then he turned to Ish.

'This Urusalim, sir. If no one's even heard of it, it can't be very important can it?' He obviously wanted to say he thought the whole thing a waste of time. But Ish merely looked at him coolly. 'It has more importance than you may think, Corporal,' he said.

Just at that moment there came round the shoulder of the hill a flock of sheep led by an even younger and wilder boy, who stared wide-eyed at the soldiers as he stood there, his sling and his staff in his hands. The two guides fell upon him with questions, but the boy stood his ground, and when he understood what they were asking he merely pointed with his finger at a distant hill-top and said the one word, 'Urusalim.'

Then he turned his eyes on Ish and Aleph and asked indiffer-
ently, 'Is he going to kill him?'

As this unexpected question sank in, all the traces of doubt
left the face of Ish. 'The boy knows what he's talking about,'
he said. Then, 'Ask him what he will take for one of his
lambs?'

The guides and the soldiers stood boggling at this curious
exchange of words, but after some hesitation on the part of
the boy, for it seemed that the sheep were not his to sell, and
then some haggling about its value, they bartered a lamb for
some of their provisions; the boy and his flock set off down
the valley and the patrol continued on its way towards the
rounded peak that bore the mysterious name of Urusalim.

Aleph could not restrain his curiosity. 'How do you know
the boy spoke the truth, and why did he say, "Is he going to
kill him?"' he asked as they climbed the stony path.

'The second question answers the first,' replied Ish briefly.
He seemed to be sparing his breath on the steep ascent.

'But I don't understand. Is who going to kill whom?'

'Am I going to kill you is what he meant,' said Ish, with a
wry smile.

Aleph walked several painful paces, and his mouth felt dry
in the dusty ravine. 'Are you?' he managed to say at last.

'No,' said Ish.

Aleph felt better. 'Why did he ask then?' he said after a
pause.

'It seems,' said Ish, 'that it is still a place of sacrifice.
Maybe of human sacrifice. That is what makes me sure that
it is the place I am seeking. Many, many years ago my people
passed through this land on the way to Egypt. The leader of
our tribe was bidden by God to sacrifice his own son on the
mountain-top you see before you.'

'What had the son done?' Aleph asked.

'Nothing,' said Ish. 'The son was innocent.'

'Did the father kill the son?'

'No. When he got there, God told him not to.'

'This God changed his mind?'

'That is the story our people tell.'

'Perhaps it was a different god that gave the order in the first place,' suggested Aleph.

'We listen only to one God,' said Ish.

'But you have many gods in Egypt!'

'My people are not Egyptians,' said Ish quietly. 'Under the former kings some of us were people of importance. But now we are of no account.'

They walked on in silence as Aleph puzzled over these sayings. The day, much of which had been wasted by following wrong tracks in the mountains, was drawing towards evening. As dusk fell they came to the little settlement of Urusalim, on the side of a steep hill that fell away into a deep gorge. The soldiers commandeered rooms for the night, and Aleph slept deeply.

He woke with a start to see Ish standing in the doorway of the little room they shared with a knife in his hand that glinted in the moonlight. Beyond the doorway black peaks showed against the starry sky.

'Don't be alarmed,' said Ish. 'It is not yet dawn. But I must prepare to do my sacrifice.'

'Do you wish me to help?' Aleph asked.

'No. This concerns only me,' Ish replied. 'Sleep while you can.' As Aleph fell back into sleep he could hear the lamb bleating on its way to the high place.

When he woke again the sun had risen, the soldiers were preparing breakfast, and Ish was back and giving orders for the return to Jericho. Soon they were retracing their steps down the mountains. They kept up a good pace all the morning, and it was not until the noonday halt that Aleph had the opportunity to talk to Ish alone.

'Have we done what we came to do?' he asked hesitantly.

'We have,' said Ish.

'But –' Aleph hesitated. 'But why have we come all this way to a place you've never been to, and nobody's ever heard of? I don't understand.'

'Many things are hard to understand,' Ish smiled. 'For example, you have not explained what a young scribe from Gebal was doing in the mountains with a bird-cage.'

Aleph was embarrassed that the conversation should be changed to his own affairs. He looked at his feet and shuffled them in the sandy soil.

'It was the writing,' he said.

'I understand even less,' said Ish.

'Not the real writing,' Aleph said hurriedly. 'I would never dream of teaching the priestly writing to my sister. I *should* deserve punishment for that. This was more of a game we invented between us. But my father was angry, so he sent me on this errand to the mountains.'

'I am still puzzled,' said Ish. 'What is this writing, that is not writing?'

'We thought of it only as a game. It seemed so simple and harmless. But I suppose being taken into captivity is my punishment for it. Do you think so?' Aleph asked.

'You will have to tell me more before I can answer that question,' said Ish.

Aleph looked around. In that remote mountain spot there were only the soldiers of the escort dozing in the shade, and the two guides. But he lowered his voice as if afraid of being overheard.

'You're a scribe in Egypt, sir,' he began hesitantly. 'You know the signs and symbols of the priests, which it is forbidden to teach to outsiders, or to women, of course?'

The other nodded.

'I was learning them,' Aleph went on. 'But I'm slow. That's

why they call me Aleph, the slow ox. I hardly knew the first
hundred letters. So I couldn't have been teaching them to
anyone, could I? But Beth wanted to know about the writing.
Beth's what we call my sister. It means "House" really, and,
well, poor Beth does have to stay around the house rather a
lot since our mother died. I was sorry for her, so I invented
this game. We chose letters that màde sounds, and then
made words with them. It's strange – we found twenty-two
letters were enough – so you see how childish it was, not a
thing to concern the priests at all. But my father caught us
playing it on the sand, and he was frightened and angry. And
so here I am. Do you think I was wicked?'

'The priests of Egypt might well be angry at such disrespect
for their mysteries,' said Ish gravely, 'but I cannot think it
was a sin. Show me though, these twenty-two letters which
you have invented.'

Aleph blushed again. 'They're of no interest to you, sir,
surely?' But Ish gently insisted, and Aleph squatted in the
dust and took a thorn twig, and began to trace shapes on the
ground.

'Here's my sign, the head of the ox – horns, ears, mouth:

or Beth used to draw it quickly, like this:'

'And that signifies?' queried Ish.

'Well, that's just it, sir, it doesn't signify anything. I told
you there's no mystery to it. It's just a sort of noise A-A-A-.
The first sound of my name, that's all. Then there's Beth's
sign too, the little house with the door:

or this way up if you like, it makes no difference. It doesn't *mean* house, of course. Just the sound, B-B-B-'

In the heat of the afternoon, in the middle of nowhere in the mountains, Aleph became absorbed in the game he had played at home with his sister. Then he suddenly became embarrassed again that he should be wasting the time of this educated stranger, and he stood up and said sadly: 'It was like this that my father caught us, and sent me up the mountain to count the shipment of forty trees he was expecting from the loggers. And Beth gave me the pigeon in the cage, to let go when I got to the lumber camp. That was her idea. She keeps pigeons, you know, sir . . .'

But Ish was still poring over the signs Aleph had drawn in the dust, and the words he had made up with them, with grave concentration. At last he spoke.

'You must teach me these signs of yours, Aleph, my young friend. I find them very interesting indeed. But now we must return to Jericho, or they will wonder what has become of us.'

And Aleph blushed with pride, but wondered if Ish were not really mocking him.

2
The Valley of Centaurs

The journey of Zayin, the soldier – Talk of the centaur-myth on the Syrian plains – In the Taurus mountains – Man-horses or horse-men?

'Call yourselves soldiers!' Zayin jeered. 'I've collected eggs in the farm-yard from creatures with more guts than you! I've seen them clip wool from animals with as much sense! Why I bring a dismal pack like you along with me I don't know – I'd be better off by myself or with a dog on a lead!'

Zayin was in his element. Eldest brother of Nun, Aleph, and Beth, he had always been a leader and he felt it his due that he should now be leading the army of Gebal. And to be many days' march away from home, far away from everywhere on the Syrian plains, followed by his men who looked unquestioningly to him to lead them on – what more could a soldier want?

His little army, now standing round him with blank faces, were satisfied, too, in their own way. They were enjoying this speech from their commander. There was no pleasure and precious little sense in marching over the empty interior with nothing but dry bread in their packs, not knowing whether a day's march would find water or not. But their comfort was that they had a leader who seemed to be sure of what he was doing, and could spur them on by strong and scornful words when they felt faint-hearted.

The expedition had started off happily enough up the coast from Gebal. So long as they had the high mountain on one side and the sea on the other the men of Gebal were content. The water-courses that cut the coastal strip into sections were dry, or shallow and easy to ford; the few fishing villages were honoured to accommodate the Giblite soldiers and provide them with food for their next day's march. But then they had come to a place where the mountain range fell away. A wind from the interior seemed to be eternally blowing through the draughty gap: there was no longer the snug feeling of being enclosed by the mountains. The inhabitants of the miserable villages of black stone were sullen and suspicious. When Zayin turned inland, and the friendly sound of the sea receded, the men wondered uneasily what strange destination they were headed for. But, as long as their leader knew, it was not theirs to worry.

But, in fact, Zayin had little idea where they were going. It was simply not in his nature to worry. He was a soldier and a leader because it suited him and he liked it; Gebal had an army because every little state had to have an army; the soldiers were soldiers because they could not stick to any other job, and the King had sent them on this expedition partly because they had been behaving so badly at home, and partly – well, there had to be expeditions. There had been times in the history of Gebal, so their annals told them, when they knew exactly who their neighbours were and just what their relations with them should be. But now new rulers were rising in Egypt, or some said the old ones were coming back, and in the North and East entirely new nations were coming into being. Zayin's army had been sent to see what it could see.

He remembered the King's words: 'We live in a time of change. The birds of the air tell me that Babylon is not what it was, and that Egypt is ruled by a woman, and who knows what barbarians may next appear from the North? Go, Commander of Swords, take your men who do nothing but play dice and trouble slave-girls, go and find out what in the name of Horus is happening in the world.' So he had gone.

He felt differently from his men about leaving the coast and turning into the interior. The mountains made him feel shut in and the fretting of the sea irritated him, but the wind from over the endless plains gave him a feeling of freedom. No obstacles now between here and Babylon! And if he journeyed on and on, all the nations of the flat world lay before him.

So Zayin was happy, but all the same his military experience made him cautious. It was a very little army of foot soldiers that he led, merely a reconnaissance patrol, compared with the great masses of men that Pharaoh could send on his expeditionary forces, or with the well-drilled battalions of Assyria. He had watched from observation-points in the mountains as these had passed along the broad valley beyond the range, filling it like a tide with spearmen, chariots, and baggage trains, or strung out through a defile in an endless line. The Giblite troop was not sufficient to carry all before them like that. Old men remembered when chariotry had been quartered on Gebal, but now he had none. It was not for him to sweep up to the gates of Babylon. They would have to avoid all but the smallest towns, where they could frighten the inhabitants into giving them food and shelter.

So it was that they had turned north up the Syrian plain, and every day's march was like the one before, rolling empty country littered with rocks that made every step uncomfortable. Beyond each rise you felt *something* must lie on the other side, but it never did. The men straggled over the rough plain, picked wild flowers and put them in their helmets, and did nothing but grumble when the time came to bivouac at night.

But an advance scout had just returned to say that he had sighted a town in the distance, and it was the difficulty of getting some sense out of his report that had provoked Zayin into his outburst at the troops.

'You say this town is right ahead? How far ahead?' Zayin questioned the scout.

'Who can tell, sir? The sun lights it, like a ship on the flat sea. It may be a day's march, may be an hour. There's no knowing on this cursed plain.'

'Well, then, how big is it? Is it a great city, or just another wretched village of the plains?' Zayin persisted.

'Same thing, isn't it, sir?' the man replied. 'Can't tell till you get there. Remember that clump of rocks yesterday? Some swore it was the walls of Babylon, one fellow said it was a few packs of wool dropped by an ass. I bet them anything they liked it was a clump of rocks, and most of them owe me their next week's ration, though I don't suppose –'

'Never mind your bets,' Zayin interrupted. He turned to the troops. 'Listen, you rabble of fishermen! There's a habitation ahead. We don't know how far or how big it is, thanks to the efficiency of our advance guard. We're going to find out. But remember this. They don't know how strong we are either. For all they know we're the vanguard of Pharaoh's thousands. If we march up in a smart and soldierly manner with an air of confidence, they'll bow in the dust before us and it'll be feasting and soft beds for all of you tonight. If you straggle up like a parcel of tinkers they'll set the dogs on you and the children will pelt you with stones. So just try and look like soldiers for once. All right?'

A surly sergeant spoke: 'Aren't we going to put them to the sword?' Some of the men grunted approval. Zayin looked at them and smiled.

'Thirsty for blood, are you, you dogs? Not today though.

For me, I'd rather get a comfortable night's rest under a good roof by peaceful means than wade in blood for the fun of it. Make yourselves at home – but even at home you don't burn down your father's house and slaughter your grandmother just because you need exercise – or do you? It wouldn't surprise me with some of you.'

This raised a laugh at the expense of the troublemakers. They re-formed ranks and marched off in good order. After they had breasted a couple of rises the township came into sight, first a cluster of cones on the horizon. They marched on through the afternoon, the soldiers muttering bets as to how many cooking-pots awaited them with appetizing suppers. Every now and then it would disappear as they advanced into a hollow, and each time it came into sight again it seemed a little nearer.

It was two hours before they got to it, and when they did they were not greatly impressed. A huddle of mud-built beehives, perhaps a hundred in number. But still, it was civilization of a sort. And coming out towards them was a party of men dressed in saffron robes. As Zayin had predicted, it was the elders approaching to make peace.

'Come on, then, men!' called Zayin. 'Close ranks! Square your shields! Spears erect! Swing those arms!' The soldiers swaggered with martial vigour, Zayin strode out in front, and the white-bearded, saffron-robed elders prostrated themselves in the dust before him.

'Halt!' cried Zayin, and with a clash of arms the battalion came to a more or less simultaneous stop.

Later that evening Zayin was reclining at ease in the living-room of one of the beehive huts. It was clean, and good smells were coming from a cooking-pot near by. The headman of the village, who had not ceased from murmuring, 'Welcome, welcome,' ever since they had arrived, was squatting opposite him. Zayin had been relieved to find that they had a language in common that served well enough for conversation.

'I don't suppose you have guests like us very often, old man?' asked Zayin.

'Oh, welcome, welcome!' answered the old one eagerly. 'Your words are indeed true and full of wisdom. And yet armies come and armies go not infrequently over these plains. Only yesterday it seems we had a great multitude of spears passing by!'

Zayin sat up with a jerk. 'Yesterday? What multitude?' This might be serious news for him and his small army.

'Yesterday, did I say?' the old man went on hurriedly. 'Oh, it may have been a month back, a year, who knows? Nothing much happens between the passing of armies. It *seems* like yesterday.'

Zayin relaxed; this old fool was not to be depended upon for accurate military information.

'Whose army was this, then, Grandfather?' he asked. 'What country did they come from?'

'Oh, you are welcome, welcome!' muttered the old man distractedly. 'Your lordship would know all these strange tongues and strange nations. I am but a simple villager.'

'Well, say, old muddlehead!' Zayin persisted. 'Did they come from the North or the East? Did they speak of Pharaoh or of the Lord of Babylon?'

'By my beard,' answered the old man, 'I understood not a word they spoke. But they came from the North.'

'From the North?' Zayin repeated. This was interesting. The North was a zone of mystery and myth wrapped in clouds and darkness. No one knew all the tribes and nations that lived there. South was Egypt and the desert, East was great Babylon, West was the sea and the great kingdom of

Crete. But from the North came things and people that were strange and new and frightening.

'Yes, from the North,' affirmed the old man. 'And there were creatures among them that had six limbs: four legs like an ass, but much stronger, besides an arm for a spear and an arm for a shield and a human head with a mane like a lion.'

Zayin laughed shortly. 'I am a soldier, old man,' he said. 'Not a fanciful scribe to write down marvels. I shall believe in your six-limbed man-beasts when I see them.' But at the same time a chill ran down his back. What horrors had these plain-dwellers seen?

'I saw them,' asserted the old man doggedly. 'I saw them with these good eyes of mine, and so did many of our village, though we hid at a distance in the desert.'

'They are ignorant and fanciful peasants,' Zayin told himself. 'They have looked at their reflections in the water and seen donkeys.'

They continued their supper in silence, and then spoke of other things, but that night Zayin dreamed of warlike man-beasts with four legs and two arms. And next morning he re-formed his troops and marched northward.

After a few more days Zayin became aware one morning of a change in the behaviour of his soldiers. Ever since they had launched out into the open plains they had been depressed and uneasy, but now they seemed to be laughing and smiling again, and even singing. Zayin spoke to one of the sergeants marching near him.

'The men seem happy this morning,' he said.

'Sir,' said the sergeant.

'Getting used to the plains, eh?' said Zayin.

'No, sir,' said the sergeant.

'What do you mean, "No, sir"?' said Zayin.

'They don't like the plains, sir,' said the sergeant.

'What's come over them, then?' asked Zayin.

The sergeant hesitated. 'Don't know, sir,' he said at last. 'Some foolishness, I reckon.'

'What is it, man?' Zayin persisted. 'Something I don't know about?'

'Reckon it's nothing, sir. But it makes 'em happy,' said the sergeant curtly.

Zayin was mystified. 'Come on, man, out with it!' he said with some sharpness. 'If you know something, or the men know something, it's your duty to tell me at once.'

The sergeant continued marching, looking straight ahead. 'If they see a bit of cloud on the horizon, and it makes 'em sing, it's nothing to bother you about, sir, to my way of thinking,' he said.

'Cloud?' repeated Zayin. 'What's remarkable about a cloud? We see them every day, don't we?'

'Nothing remarkable, as I told 'em, sir. Take no notice, I said. If some of them like to think it's mountains, well, it does no harm, does it?'

'Mountains!' exclaimed Zayin. 'Sergeant, if someone's sighted mountains and not reported the fact to me – there'll be trouble!'

'Yes, sir,' said the sergeant stolidly. 'Just what I said, sir. If it's mountains the general will want to know. If it's a bit of a cloud that *looks* like a mountain he won't. He'll be able to tell the difference right enough, when he sees it with his own eyes.'

Zayin was about to explode with anger, but he kept silent. He remembered what he had so often said to his men about believing his own eyes. He strode without speaking to the top of the next rise and halted, scanning the horizon and shading his eyes with his hand. Just above the skyline to the North was a line that might have been a low dark cloud, but he knew that it was not. It was the jagged peak of a range of mountains. And he had the feeling that they must hold the secret of something he wanted to know, and he resolved that he alone would be the one to discover this secret.

It was in the afternoon a day or two later that they came to the foothills of the mountains. Zayin gave the order to pitch camp a little earlier than usual: the end of the empty plain was as good a place as any to halt, and exploration of the mountains would have to wait until the next day. But in spite of the day's long march he felt restless as the soldiers went about their work, erecting the tents and preparing the evening meal. There were still some hours of daylight left, and the feeling that he himself must discover the secret of the mountains was too strong for him. So, calling his under-officers together, he told them to see to the posting of sentinels for the night, and announced he was going alone up the nearest hill. The sergeant who was his right-hand man offered to go with him, but Zayin insisted that no escort was necessary, and set off up the slopes.

It was a pleasant change to be back in the mountains. Of course, the view from the first low crest revealed only a higher crest beyond. But there would be no harm in going on alone a little farther to see what lay on the other side. He went down to a shallow ravine and scrambled up the other side among great boulders.

To his surprise, when he reached the crest he found that the ground fell away before him even more steeply and swept down to the floor of a broad valley. The setting sun flooded it with light, and shone, too, on innumerable objects in the bottom of the valley, white, brown, and black, that cast long shadows on the green pasture. What were they? Boulders? No, some of them were moving. Men? No, their movements were like those of animals grazing. It was difficult to tell size or shape from that distance. Heedless of the lengthening shadows and of the distance from the camp, Zayin let himself go over the edge of the valley, slipping, sliding, catching at shrubs as he could, sending showers of stones trickling hundreds of feet below him to the bottom. He arrived at the foot of the slope in an avalanche of rocks and soil, uncertain whether he was on his head or his heels, and as he crashed into the bushes that grew there a great creature leaped out of the shadows and bounded snorting across the turf. When it came to the groups in the distance they, too, plunged and tossed and fled away to the other end of the valley.

Zayin picked himself up, shaken and dizzy, and strained his eyes after the retreating creatures. What had the old man of the plains said? That it was 'like the running of gazelles and the dancing of young women'. The movement of these beings was indeed a beautiful sight in the evening sun, though all he had seen was their rounded hind-quarters and flowing tails. But what of the rest of their bodies. Had he seen a human face and arms? What a fool he had been to disturb them in such a clumsy manner. Whatever they were, they were nervous, timid creatures, easily scared. He must follow them, quietly, and show them that he came in peace.

The valley was much longer than he had thought, and it would soon be quite dark. But Zayin kept on. Soon the foot of the valley walls were in shadow, then the shadow-line crept up them and the dusk gathered. The stars came out, and at length Zayin was walking over the smooth turf in darkness. And it seemed that as he walked, the creatures he was looking for returned softly to surround him. He could hear snorts and stamping hooves, and could make out dim shapes, a little darker than the darkness. One, apparently bolder than the rest, was approaching him, step by step. Zayin stood quite still.

'Come,' he said quietly. 'Come, we are friends.'

The creature came nearer in the darkness. Zayin held out his hand until he could feel its breath. His other hand was on his sword, but somehow he felt that the creatures were friendly, whatever they were. But they kept their distance, and they would not speak.

Zayin kept walking. He must find somewhere to spend the night. Through the gloom he thought he could make out a shape that was too square and too big to be an animal. He approached it warily: close to it seemed to be some kind of shelter with one open side. Was there something stirring in it?

'Ho there!' called Zayin, firmly. There was a sudden movement in the darkness.

'You in there!' he called. 'Come out so I can see you!' Part of the darkness seemed to bunch itself together and launch itself upon Zayin. He side-stepped and lunged with his sword. Whatever it was swerved past him, and as it did so dealt him a powerful blow on his sword arm, making him drop his sword and curse. Then it thundered away into the night, with a sound as of more than two feet. Zayin felt around for his dropped sword, rubbed his aching arm, and decided that these creatures had little sense of hospitality. He went into the shelter, satisfied himself there was nothing there but a pile of soft vegetation, laid his sword on the ground and lay down himself. He was very tired and there was nothing to do but go to sleep like this.

No time seemed to have passed before he sat up in the morning sunlight and looked around him. Horses! they were grazing on the dewy grass, or just standing looking at him inquisitively.

They were, after all, animals with four legs and curved necks that ate grass like cattle. And yet Zayin could not feel disappointed. He had heard of horses, certainly, and had seen them, harnessed to chariots, when he had watched Pharaoh's army from the mountains. But he had never been so close to them before, or seen them running free. He was charmed as he watched the colts gambolling in the sun or nudging up to their dams. How much more pleasant their company was than the grumbling soldiers.

But Zayin suddenly felt a twinge, or rather two. A twinge of conscience and a twinge of hunger. He had deserted his army, and he could not stay here and eat grass. He would have to make his way back to the camp.

It took him longer than he had expected to walk back over the floor of the valley, and he could see that climbing the sides would be very much more difficult than sliding down had been. He started the laborious ascent, trying to avoid stretches of loose rock. And then, as he climbed, he noticed a figure descending towards him from above. By the armour he seemed to be one of his soldiers. Zayin stood on a rock and waved, and the figure waved back and continued to come down towards him, almost as recklessly as he had himself done the day before. Soon Zayin was able to recognize the man as the sergeant. He glissaded towards Zayin in a scramble of stones and tried to stand to attention and salute.

'The gods be praised,' the sergeant panted. 'You at least are safe, sir!' The man seemed to be at the extreme of exhaustion.

'What's the matter, man? What's happened?' Zayin demanded, suddenly very concerned.

'Ah, sir, it was only too true about the monsters! Your army's scattered. They thought you had fallen into their hands, and without you they were dismayed and panic-stricken when the monsters swept down on them.'

Zayin sat down on the rock, began to say something, and then stopped.

'Sergeant,' he said at last, 'I was wrong to leave you. What have you been imagining in my absence?'

'No imagining, sir,' protested the sergeant. 'There were monsters.'

Zayin heaved a deep sigh. 'Tell me about these monsters, Sergeant,' he said resignedly. 'And then tell me what happened to my men.'

'But, sir!' the sergeant protested, 'they were the monsters you told us of. Four legs to run and leap on, and two arms to wield spears and bows with. Our men panicked and fled.'

Zayin held his head in his hands. 'I, too, have seen the monsters,' he said at last. 'Indeed, I spent the night with them.' The sergeant's eyes became round. 'In the morning,' Zayin continued, 'I saw that they were horses. Mere animals like the ass, only bigger and swifter. One of them gave me a passing kick with its heels in the dark. But they can no more wield weapons than I can eat grass.'

The sergeant looked at him wildly. 'Then perhaps, sir,' he exclaimed, 'you can tell me how I came by this?' He bared his left arm, which had been roughly wrapped in his cloak, and showed Zayin the broken shaft of an arrow that was still imbedded in the flesh.

And at that moment, with his good arm, the sergeant seized his commanding officer and thrust him down behind the rock, flinging himself after him.

'Pardon, sir!' he gasped. 'But there's another lot of 'em!' And he pointed to the valley floor.

Zayin looked down. Galloping apparently straight towards them was a party of four-footed creatures, brandishing bows and spears above human-looking heads. He sat paralysed behind his rock. Could they climb perhaps, like mountain goats? Even fly? But no, they halted on the level ground beneath him. After all they had not been seen, for no eyes seemed to be directed towards them. He and the sergeant could escape up the hill-side again. Keeping low, he twisted round and looked up the steep slope. But, as he looked, a figure appeared outlined against the sky on a crag, almost immediately above him. Then another and another four-legged, two-armed figures with spears held ready. There was no going forward nor back for them, neither up nor down, and it was only a matter of time before they were seen on the stony hill-side.

3
The Island of Giants

The voyage of Nun, the sailor – The secrets of celestial navigation – People that lived on a volcano –The island of Thira and the myth of the buried Titans

'Oars inboard!' ordered Nun, the sailor. 'And hoist the sail!'

The mountains above Gebal were a black wall to the East in the early dawn. Inshore they had cut off the breeze, but the ship was far enough out to sea to catch it now, and the men were glad to pull in their heavy oars and stow them along the bulwarks. They manned the ropes that controlled the single great sail. With a rhythmic chant, following the commands of the boatswain, they heaved the halyard and the spar crept up the mast. The sheets were secured, the sail-cloth filled with wind, and the heavy-laden ship, which had been wallowing gently in the swell, slowly gathered way through the blue water.

Nun, second son of Resh, the chief mason, and the youngest master mariner in the merchant fleet of Gebal, felt a sense of peace come over him, as it always did when he put to sea. All that could be done on shore had been done. The rigging had been checked and worn ropes replaced. The ship had been careened and the weed scraped from her bottom. The timbers had been sounded and the seams recaulked to keep her watertight. A new pair of eyes had even been painted on her bows. The cargo of cedar-beams had been loaded aboard without any of them being dropped through the bottom. He had his passport, inscribed on stone in the name of the great King of Gebal, and the right sacrifices had been made for a fair wind.

The farewells on the quay-side had perhaps been more affecting than usual, for his elder brother Zayin was absent on his expedition to the interior, his younger brother Aleph was overdue from his errand in the mountains, and he could see that his father and his sister Beth were torn to see the last of the brothers go, leaving them to their anxieties. But he had promised them a cheerful reunion soon, pushed out from the quay-side, and now all that was behind him.

The wind was fair. Westward lay the islands. Cyprus they could hardly miss. It was Nun's custom on west-bound passages to make the first crossing blind, though there were still ship-masters who thought it rash to go so far out of sight of land, and preferred to creep round the coast until they were north of the island and then strike south to make sure of hitting its longest coast. In this way you were hardly out of sight of land at all – but once you had left a coast for good what guarantee was there that you would ever see it again, however correct your sacrifices had been?

But Nun's business lay farther west than Cyprus. It would be enough to have a sight of it to the northward to satisfy him that he was on course. Still, he would have to think of a haven for the night. It would be a pity to waste this good easterly breeze – he was impatient at crawling over the face of the water under oars – but one could hardly stay at sea all night.

He looked away from the receding shore and saw his passenger standing beside him. In the distractions of clearing port and putting to sea, he had hardly had time to do more than formally welcome this stranger aboard, and since then he had forgotten about him. It was with an unpleasant feeling of surprise that he noticed him now. What Nun liked about being at sea was the freedom from interruption. No strangers to meet, no news good or bad until the next port. He was vexed now to think that he had with him this man of whom he knew nothing, and to whom he would have to be polite and guarded in his speech.

The passenger smiled pleasantly. 'Are we making good time, Master?' he asked, speaking Nun's language carefully and correctly.

In a hurry? Nun wondered to himself. But perhaps the man was only making a polite remark. 'We go with the wind, sir,' he answered. 'We can't do better than that.'

'Your gods are kind to send us such a wind,' said the stranger.

'Goddess, actually, sir,' said Nun. 'Yes, the Lady of Gebal is keeping her part of the bargain. Since there were no beasts or babies to sacrifice, we settled for a little gold figure I got last time in Crete. And we lugged a stone anchor up to the temple of the God of Battles, to keep him in mind of the navy. Those ought to buy us enough wind to take us there at least, and a bit of luck to keep us clear of enemies.'

'Ah!' said the passenger. 'Let us hope we make good time then. I have an urgent appointment in Crete, or thereabouts.'

'Urgent appointment?' Nun repeated. 'What kind of a creature is that? I've not heard it spoken before.'

'I mean I must be there by a certain time,' said the passenger. 'That is why I took your ship. You have a reputation for swift voyages.'

'I don't like to waste time certainly,' said Nun, pleased by the compliment. 'But as for appointments, and times that are certain, I've very little knowledge of them. The winds blow or they don't; the sea gives you a calm passage or holds you up with storms. All right, we make the best time we can, but there's never anything certain about it.'

'I speak of sun-time and star-time,' said the passenger. 'These are always certain, for centuries ahead. We who watch the heavens in Chaldea know that in a short while certain stars and planets will meet. What this conjunction signifies is less certain, though we expect some great disaster. Nor do we know exactly where this will take place. My calculations lead me to the island of Crete, if Crete lies where they say it does: but it may be that when I get there I shall find it is not the place. I have already completed half my journey from Chaldea, and I trust you will let nothing delay me now. But since there is nothing interesting to see while the sun occupies the heavens, perhaps you will permit me to sleep.'

So saying the stranger wrapped himself in his robe and stretched himself out on the deck. Nun was puzzled and irritated. Who was this overbearing foreigner with his urgency and concern for the future? It was enough to spoil the pleasure of any voyage – having to get there by a certain time, and wondering what was going to happen when you did. A Chaldean, did he say he was? A priest, or a magician, or one of those astrologers, Nun supposed. The sort of person one went to sea to get away from. Nun felt like throwing him overboard to feed the fishes. If there was any trouble with storms or calms he would not hesitate long to do so; but at present all was going well and the stranger had impressed him to such an extent that Nun found himself giving orders in a low voice so as not to disturb his daytime sleep.

All day the east wind drove them on, and there was never even any need to make adjustment to the sail or the sheets. But as the sun sank towards the sea ahead of them, and Nun leaned on the steering-oar and steered a little north of where it would disappear below the horizon, he could see that the crew were beginning to look anxiously around, and he could feel a slight anxiety beginning to form inside his own stomach. Darkness was coming, and still no sign of land.

He had done this passage often enough before, but from Gebal to Cyprus was a good day's sail from dawn to dusk. He sent a man up to the masthead and told him to keep a good look-out on the starboard bow, and it was not long before the cry came, 'Land ho!'

The passenger woke and got to his feet. 'What land is this, Master?' he asked.

Nun was busy altering course towards the land by leaning on the steering-oar and giving orders to adjust the pull of the sheets. He answered the passenger's question shortly, 'Cyprus.'

'Have you business in Cyprus, Master?' asked the passenger.

'No,' replied Nun, 'we're buying no copper on this trip.'

'Why are we altering course, then?'

'It will soon be dark,' said Nun. 'We must find a haven for the night.'

The man from the East looked at the heavens. 'It will not be dark,' he said. 'There is no cloud, and the stars will soon be out.'

'Starlight's no good to me,' said Nun. 'I like to see where I'm going.'

The Chaldean came across the deck and stood close to Nun, putting his hand on the steering-oar. 'Listen,' he said. 'I have travelled many nights across the desert already, under the stars. Why should we waste a night in haven when we have the open sea before us?'

Nun looked at him and thought for a while. Then he said, 'When you are travelling across the desert in the dark there is little danger of falling into the sea. But if you strike land while you are crossing the sea it can be fatal. That's why we like to see where we are going.'

But the passenger continued to argue. 'You have made this passage by day?'

'Yes,' replied Nun.

'Did you strike any land?'

'No.'

'If there is no land to run on to by day, why should there be any by night?' the stranger went on persuasively.

'It's all very well for a landsman to talk,' retorted Nun. 'You don't know how confusing the sea can be at night, with the sea-sprites flashing their lights in every wave and all those nameless stars spinning above your head.'

The stranger put his hand over Nun's on the steering-oar and looked deep into his eyes. 'Captain,' he said, 'would you learn secrets unknown to any other shipmaster? Would you not like to be at home on the sea by night as well as by day? The stars are not nameless; each one has his place and direction. Sail with me tonight and other nights, and I will teach you the names of the stars and the constellations, and tell you how they can guide you.'

No man had ever laid hands on the steering-oar when Nun was manning it, and few had ever argued a point of navigation with him since he had become master of a ship. Now is the time to throw this interfering stranger to the fishes, Nun thought. And yet he did not even feel anger rising inside him, and he wondered why. I should assert myself as captain, he told himself. What would the crew think? And yet, what was it that made the crew respect him? Could he pull an oar better than the oarsmen? No. Could he splice a rope better than the seamen? No. Was it because he could curse them and keep them in order? Not even that, for the boatswain could curse much more fluently than his captain. No, it was because he knew where they were going. He had the whole voyage, out and back – the gods willing – planned in his head. The crew respected Nun for it, and Nun could not help respecting this stranger who seemed to carry in his head not merely landmarks of a voyage but also signs in the heavens to guide him. It might be something worth learning.

Without a word, Nun let the steering-oar move over to starboard under the pressure of the stranger's hand, and the ship's head turned slowly away from the land and towards the open sea and the setting sun.

He saw the startled and outraged looks on the faces of the crew, but spoke to them casually. 'What's the matter, then? You've slept all day, while the wind's done the work. Let's see if you can sleep as well by night. I only need half of you to keep company with me and the stars. Boatswain, the oarsmen on the starboard side can keep the first watch.' And there was enough confidence in his voice to make the men move obediently to their look-out positions as ordered by the boatswain, though not without some muttering.

'No shore tonight?' he heard them remark. 'The Old Man off his head, then?'

Nun did not feel as confident as he hoped he sounded, but part of him felt a surge of excitement at the prospect of the night passage.

The sun sank on to the horizon ahead of the ship, and as it did so it seemed in the haze to lose its roundness and collapse like a pricked bladder. The sailors watched it with long faces. Would they ever see it again in its proper shape, or would they reach the edge of the world in the darkness and be poured over it into nothingness? The last red spark showed above the sea, turned suddenly bright green, and sank. The sailors' hearts seemed to sink with it. But Nun's eyes were already on the zenith, the highest part of the sky where the stars were beginning to appear, and on the darkening eastern sky astern of the ship.

'Tell me!' said Nun impatiently. 'What is the name of that one? And that one, and the bright one alone by itself there?'

'Have patience!' said the Chaldean calmly. 'We shall see them all together soon. Those you see now will not help you with your voyaging, for they are wanderers too, every night in a different part of the sky. It needs many years of study to learn their paths.'

The east wind drove them on, and darkness came quickly. Soon the whole sky was a-glitter with stars, and Nun craned his neck and stared as if he had never seen them before. 'I shall never know all their names!' he sighed.

'Patience!' said the stranger again. 'If a man lived a thousand years and never slept by night, he would still leave many stars unnamed. Learn them by their groups first, their constellations. First of all tell your steersman to steer by that bright group that is now above the horizon. That you may call the Lesser Dog, and it will lead you west for a while until it sinks below the sea. Now look to the North. There is the Great Bear, who is always with us, and the Little Bear, in whose tail sits the North Star, the only one that stays still in the firmament. If you want to steer north at any time, that is your mark.'

'Who wants to steer north?' Nun scoffed. 'It's a region of monsters and barbarians. But if I wish to steer west for Crete, I follow the Little Dog?'

'Ah, but only for the next hour. Then you must look for the stars of the Hydra, the Virgin, and the Serpent as they come down to the horizon before you. And following them will be the Water-Bearer, the Fish, the Whale, and finally, the Giant Orion.'

'I must remember all that?' Nun mused. 'Hydra, Virgin, Serpent, Water-Carrier, Fish, Whale, and Giant? Follow them, and they will always lead me westwards from Gebal to Crete?'

'Aye, but only at this time of year, in the Dog Days. See, to the South, the greenish eye of the Great Dog Star. The sun is between the houses of the Bull and the Heavenly Twins, so the Dog is above the horizon.'

'What a busy life these heavenly creatures lead!' exclaimed Nun. 'How shall I ever follow their comings and goings?'

'What I have so far told you is simple,' said the astrologer. 'You must also learn the sequence of the sun's travel through the houses of the Zodiac, some of which I have mentioned, and others such as the Ram and the Crab, the Goat and the Lion, the Scales, the Scorpion, and the Archer. And you may wish to know the constellations of the North, the Lyre and the Swan, and of the South, such as the Ship which voyages over unknown seas well down on the southern horizon, as you can now see. These all contain the stars that are fixed.'

'I am glad to hear it. They are always there to see, then?' asked Nun.

'They may rise and set like the sun,' said the other. 'And their position in summer is different from their position in winter. But the case of the wandering planets is more difficult, though we can tell their paths among the other stars with reasonable certainty.'

'That must be a great comfort to you,' said Nun, unable to restrain his mockery. 'But the only path I wish to know with certainty is that of my ship.'

The Chaldean ignored the interruption, and continued: 'But then there are the comets and meteors whose paths no man can foretell and whose significance puzzles our understanding. For the direction of a ship by night or of a line of march over the desert is nothing compared with advising a king in decisions of state, or reading the meanings of celestial conjunctions which may foretell events far distant in time and space. And it is for this that I have been sent with you to the most western point of the civilized world. Something is going to happen which concerns the House of the Bull, and as you must know, both Babylon and Crete are much concerned with the Bull. A little before dawn the constellation of the Bull will be in the heavens. That is one reason I wished to be at sea – there is often mist and cloud near land at that time.'

'An appointment with the Bull!' Nun exclaimed silently to himself. 'So it is for that he wants to risk my ship!'

But the Chaldean seemed to read his thoughts. 'Be not anxious,' he smiled. 'If the stars can guide great empires, surely they can steer your little ship through the night.'

So the night passed, with the Chaldean patiently pointing out the constellations and Nun repeating their names, and the same with the greater individual stars, Altair and Deneb and Alphecca and Dubhe and Algol and Mirfak and Aldebaran and Betelgeuse. The watching sailors looked with awe and suspicion at their captain in deep confabulation with the mysterious stranger, and Nun had to detach himself from his studies now and then to see that the look-outs were awake or to give another star to the steersman to steer by; but he could feel already that this new knowledge was giving him power over his men. And he was so captivated by his lessons that he quite forgot he had not slept. But at last he noticed that it was his tutor who seemed to be losing interest, and was gazing fixedly over the stern of his ship.

'The lesson is finished for the night,' said the Chaldean. 'The Bull is rising in the East, and I have my calculations to make.' And not until then was Nun overcome with a great weariness of body and mind, and having given the steersman a last star to steer by until dawn, he stretched himself out to sleep and dreamt of wandering among the Houses of the Virgin and the Twins, and encountering the Serpent and the Scorpion along the Milky Way.

He did not sleep long, but when he woke the sun had risen astern, the easterly breeze still drove the ship through the blue waves, and all around was an empty horizon. Some of the crew were sleeping after having kept the night watches, but those who were awake turned their eyes towards him, with the unspoken question written on their faces: 'Where are we?' They looked expectantly at him, as if awaiting new steering orders or adjustments to the sail – but Nun could think of nothing to do but keep driving westwards. Indeed, he began to regret the absence of his newly-made friends, the stars. The great blazing sun was comforting to see, but the higher he rose in the heavens the less helpful he was in keeping direction. Nun looked at the Chaldean, peacefully sleeping now that the stars were gone, but decided not to wake him. He took some breakfast, doing his best to look more con-fident than he felt, and told the boatswain to find the crew jobs such as splicing cordage and scrubbing planks to keep them occupied.

All day the ship drove on, and all day the Chaldean slept, but now Nun took comfort from his presence and told himself that all must be well if his learned passenger slept so peace-fully. At noon the sun rose so high that the masthead seemed to strike at it as the ship rolled to the port side, and all Nun could do was to keep the wind astern and draw as straight a furrow as possible through the blue sea, trusting that the wind was not playing him tricks but was still coming directly from the East. And after noon, when most of the crew were lying around forward, resting in the heat, the boatswain came aft to Nun and spoke to him quietly.

'Captain, you're running into danger,' he said.

'Danger?' Nun repeated. 'The sea's wide and clear of rocks, the sun shines and we've a fair wind. What's this talk of danger?'

'I daresay there's no danger in the sea,' said the boatswain. 'Not for me to say you don't know where you're going, sir, you and the foreign gentleman. But it's the crew, sir. The men aren't happy, not seeing land for a night and a day. They say we're being driven west to barbarian lands, or worse still heading for the brink of the world, where the water goes over the edge. They want to know where they are.'

'Tell 'em they're at sea,' said Nun curtly. 'That ought to be enough for them. If they don't like it they should have gone for soldiers or woodcutters.'

'Aye, sir,' said the boatswain, still troubled. 'Trouble is, there's some of them *aren't* sailors, and never will be. I tell you, sir,' and the boatswain's voice lowered to a husky whisper, 'it's the big fellow, Quoph, that's the troublemaker. He's no seaman, best of times. Been a soldier, but thinks sitting in a ship's an easier way of getting around than foot-slogging it through the desert. Now he's wishing he'd never left shore. Him and some of the others are saying they'll make you turn around and go back to land.'

'Do they think I can turn the wind round too, so they can sail back?' asked Nun scornfully.

'They say they'd rather row, than sail the devil knows where,' replied the boatswain.

'Tell 'em never mind what the devil knows, their captain knows where he's going,' said Nun angrily. 'And I'll alter course when I see fit, not when they do.' The boatswain looked at him, as if still uncertain that the captain did know where he was going, but said no more and went forward again. Nun looked after him, saw him speaking to a knot of men, among whom he recognized Quoph, the monkey-faced ex-soldier, saw the boatswain leave the group and the rest of them continue to wave their arms in argument. Then he saw Quoph coming aft down the ship towards him. A few steps behind him was a small group of men, looking equally surly but not quite so bold.

'We're going back to land,' said Quoph roughly, halting at the beginning of the poop-deck.

'Good-bye,' said Nun, just as curtly, leaning lightly on the steering-oar and eyeing the waves. 'Enjoy your swim!'

Quoph flushed angrily. 'We're not joking,' he growled. 'Turn the ship round!'

Nun noted Quoph's rising rage, and also that the rest of the group were hanging back. I can deal with this one alone, he thought. Aloud he said: 'No ignorant soldier gives orders here. I'm in command.'

'If you won't turn, we'll make you,' Quoph snarled. He pulled out a copper seamen's knife from his dress.

If I provoke him, he'll rush me with the knife, thought Nun, judging the lift of the swell from astern. He turned to Quoph, and putting all the contempt he could into words, sneered, 'Get forrard, you scabby ape!'

That did it. Red with rage and without looking to see if he was followed by his supporters, Quoph launched himself with a shambling run across the deck. At the same instant Nun put all his weight on the steering-oar. The ship yawed, a swell from astern caught her on the quarter, the deck tilted, and Quoph's rush took him straight over the ship's side into the sea. Only then did Nun hesitate for a second, seeing a coil of rope lying handy by the bulwarks. But his second thoughts made him pick up the coil and fling it towards the man floundering in the water. Quoph grasped the bare end and hung on. Nun took a turn round a post with the other end and held it, then turned to the other members of the crew who were still holding back at the other end of the deck.

'Your friend would rather swim home than stay with us,' Nun called to them. 'Anyone else like to join him?' The men shook their heads.

'I'll let him go alone, then?' asked Nun, letting the rope run out a little round the post as he turned the steering-oar again and put the ship back on course.

'Save me, save me! I can't swim!' came the plaintive voice of Quoph from the sea. The ship was moving so fast through the water that it was all he could do to keep hold of the end of the rope.

The men flinched as the line ran out, but one of them muttered, 'Best let him go. He only makes trouble.'

'The rest of you are content to stay with me and obey orders?' Nun asked them.

'Aye,' said another man. 'Reckon you care for your own skin too. We'll be better off with you than with that ape on the rope's end.'

'Right,' said Nun, making his end fast. 'I'll get you there and back, never fear, if you do what I say. As for our shipmate here, he can follow us for a bit if he wishes.' So while the men went back to their stations and he settled the ship back on course, he left Quoph trailing astern, his cries getting more and more waterlogged. When at last he gave orders for him to be hauled aboard gasping and trembling, there was nothing left in him but sea-water and the despairing resolution that had kept him grasping the end of the rope. Nun saw that Quoph would cause no more trouble.

Then Nun perceived that the Chaldean was awake and watching him.

'Congratulations, Captain,' said the passenger. 'I see you are a man of courage and resource.'

But Nun felt a burst of anger towards this man who had got him into the present situation. 'Thank you,' he said curtly. 'But where are we?'

'I was about to ask you that,' the passenger said calmly.

Nun took him by the arm to the side of the ship, away from the seaman who had now taken over the steering, and spoke low but angrily. 'You don't know where we are?' he expostulated. 'After all your magic with the stars! Perhaps the men were right, and I should have thrown *you* overboard.'

'Be calm, Captain,' said the Chaldean mildly. 'This is a matter of mathematics, not sorcery. If your ship were a camel

I should know how far we had travelled in a day's march over the desert, but I must confess that this thing of wood and rope and canvas is strange to me. Let us reason calmly. This passage, coasting along the mainland and the Isle of Cyprus, takes you how long, usually?'

'Four days.'

'And that is going north a little, and south a little, and sleeping in haven every night?'

'Yes.'

'We have been at sea for a day and a half, with a good following wind,' mused the Chaldean. 'Even so, we can hardly be nearing Crete yet, let alone the edge of the world.'

Nun was torn between feeling irritated at his passenger's air of superior intelligence, and being soothed by his calm approach to the crisis.

'Let us wait till sundown again,' said the Chaldean. 'Maybe the stars, or perhaps the moon, will tell us a little more about where we are, and maybe we shall alter course to the North, and to the islands.'

Then darkness came again, the stars reappeared, and the Chaldean noted the height of some of them over the northern horizon. He observed the rising of the moon, and questioned Nun closely about the running of the ship. Then he was silent for a while, and Nun was aware of things going on inside this stranger's head that were quite new to him. Calculations, to Nun, were a matter of fingers and toes or pebbles, or beads on strings; but the stranger seemed to be able to perform them instantly.

A little before dawn, as they still forged ahead on the same course, the constellation of the Bull rose again astern, and the Chaldean gazed at it in rapt contemplation. At last he spoke, and his voice seemed troubled by uncertainty, but his instructions were clear.

'Captain,' he said. 'If you were to alter course now towards the sign of the Lyre, by noon next day we should sight the islands.'

'Is this sure?' Nun asked. 'You sound doubtful.'

'Finding the islands is a little thing,' said the sage. 'The doubt arises as to what we shall find when we get there. I must confess that I am troubled. Some great disaster is what the stars foretell, but what its nature is I cannot make out.'

'My men will be happy enough to see land,' said Nun. 'Disasters can take care of themselves. If what you say is the quickest way, we'll alter course.'

They did so, and reset the sail, and as morning came they continued on the same course. Sure enough about mid-day the joyful cry went up 'Land ho!' And everybody was jubilant – except the Chaldean.

The crew were chattering excitedly, and the old hands were wagering as to what part of the land it was. When they were near enough for one of them to recognize it as the island of Kasos, off the eastern point of Crete, they were amazed. In just over two days they had completed a voyage that usually took five or six, coasting from point to point. They looked with admiration at their skilful captain, and with awe at their strange navigator.

But the Chaldean took Nun aside. 'Master,' he said, 'this is your ship and I am a mere passenger –'

'How can you say that?' Nun exclaimed. 'You have taught me secrets no other sailor knows. My ship is yours.'

'You feel I have saved you a day or two's weary coasting?'

'Indeed,' said Nun. 'I don't know where I'd be without you. Still up some mainland creek perhaps. How can I repay you?'

'I beg only two of the days I may have saved you on this voyage,' said the sage.

'They are yours,' said Nun, puzzled. 'But what do you mean?'

'Your business is with Knossos, I know,' said the Chaldean.
'And so I had thought was mine. But now the stars tell me
differently. You know the islands well, Captain?'

'I can tell where I am among the islands by the taste of the
water over the side,' Nun bragged.

'Is there an isle about a day's sail, from dawn to sunset,
due north of Knossos?'

'That would be Thira,' Nun replied.

'Then if you can spare me two days from your enterprise, I
shall be grateful if we might go there first,' said the Chaldean.
'I do not know what we shall find, but, whatever it is, I
believe it is of grave enough importance to affect you and all
who live in the known world. So it is not only for myself that
I ask it.'

'But don't your stars tell you more precisely?' asked Nun.
'They brought us to Kasos at the time you predicted. Why
are you doubtful about the other thing?'

'It is of a different kind,' replied the sage. 'This knowledge
of disaster is within me. The stars merely help me find the
time and place. But I can say no more. May we go?'

'You have my promise,' said Nun.

So once again there were looks of outrage on the faces of
the crew as, instead of heading west along the northern coast
of Crete, they continued on their north-westerly course after
clearing Kasos. Here there were lesser islands strewn over the
sunlit water to guide them by day, but they would be treacher-
ous hazards by night. So before sunset they found a little bay
in one of them and made fast for the night. Nun was glad
enough to sleep the night through without responsibilities,
while some of the crew stretched their legs on the barren
islet, grousing freely at being deprived of the joys of port. But
the Chaldean stayed awake all night and communed with the
stars.

Next day it was only a short run to Thira, and they neared

it in the early afternoon. Indeed, they were aware of it a long way off, because of a thin plume of smoke that seemed to be coming from the pointed top of the island.

Nun and the Chaldean gazed at it from the poop. 'You have landed there before, Master?' asked the passenger.

'No,' replied Nun. 'I have seen its burning mountain times enough before now. But I've never had business there – and who'd go to such a place for pleasure? Though they say . . .'

'Yes?' the Chaldean prompted.

'I don't know,' said Nun. 'It has a certain reputation . . .'

'Indeed? What kind of people live there?'

'One hears strange stories, that's all,' said Nun. 'I've never taken much note of them, and I can't even remember what they're about. But we shall see for ourselves now, shan't we?'

Suddenly, as they gazed, the wind failed them, for the first time since they left Gebal. The sail flopped heavily against the mast as the ship rolled in the slight swell, not a breath of cooling air touched their bodies, and the distant shore of the island shimmered in the afternoon heat-haze. At Nun's command the sweating sailors furled and secured the sail, got out the heavy oars and sat down on the benches. The boatswain gave the beat, and the ship forged sluggishly ahead as Nun steered a course round the steep shore of the island, looking for the harbour.

The island stood like a pile of white bones in the blue sea, reflecting the heat and the glare of the sun. Here and there were patches of silver-green olive trees, and dried-up wisps of vegetation that might be vines, and they had to look hard to make out the scattered houses built of the same white rock as the island itself. From whichever way they looked at it, as they slowly coasted around, it looked the same – an almost perfect cone, with a blackened top and the sinister plume of smoke now rising straight into the heavens. But of life there seemed to be no sign.

They had made a complete circuit of the isle, and the sun had dropped down the sky very little in that time, before Nun decided that a little jetty and a cluster of buildings on the eastern side was the main harbour. He turned the ship in her tracks and headed back to it.

'Not much of a haven,' Nun murmured as they approached the apparently deserted quays. 'But it will do in this calm.'

Even when they were near enough to see rows of sealed wine-jars standing waiting in the shade of a rough ware-house, there seemed to be no human guardians of the place. The only sound was the regular plop, groan, and splash of the oars, beating now at a dead slow pace, just enough to keep the stem gently cutting through the water. Nun raised his hand to halt the rowers, and there was only the gurgle of water along the keel and the drips falling from the raised oars. Nun looked at the Chaldean, and the oarsmen looked at each other, and no one seemed capable of breaking the silence – until the boatswain startled them all by letting out a sudden roar:

'Ashore there! Are you all dead, or drunk?'

One of a stack of empty jars seemed to come to life and a human figure got to its feet, grasping clumsily at a spear and rubbing the sleep of his siesta out of his eyes. The harbour-guard stared stupidly at the approaching ship, and then shouted something over his shoulder. Other figures appeared from patches of shade and moved confusedly here and there; but though the boatswain, using various shouts and signs, tried to get them to indicate where they should come along-side, there were no helpful gestures in reply. So Nun ordered the oars to be drawn in, manned the steering-oar, and there was just enough way on the ship to take her smoothly alongside the jetty, where two of the crew jumped ashore and made fast.

The harbour-guard had now got itself into some sort of

military order and Nun noted that their helmets and armour were of Cretan pattern, though the bronze lacked the well-known Cretan spit-and-polish. Yet still there was no offer of help: they stood stolidly across the end of the jetty as if barring the way to the land. Then, just as Nun himself jumped from the poop on to the jetty, the soldier standing nearest to him lifted his hand in the gesture of drinking from a jar and said one word: 'Water?'

'So you do speak a known tongue!' Nun remarked. 'Thank you, the supplies in *our* water-jars *are* low.'

The soldier looked into the hold of the ship, looked again at Nun, and repeated with a query in his voice: 'Water?'

'Yes, we need it badly,' said Nun. 'Where can we get some?'

The soldier looked blankly at Nun, seemed to search in his mind for words in the language that was obviously difficult for him, and at last found four words: 'You give me water?'

'*I* give *you* water?' Nun repeated. 'What do you mean? We have come a long way, been at sea for days. How can we give you water? Have you none on your island?' He looked closely at the soldier: certainly it didn't look as if he had washed recently. The soldier shrugged and looked away.

'They don't seem very glad to see us,' said Nun to the Chaldean who was standing patiently on the poop. 'Come ashore, sir, and we'll see if we can get some sense out of this island.'

He held out his hand to the Chaldean to help him over the ship's side. The soldiers looked with some show of curiosity at the outlandish dress of the stranger as he stood poised on the wooden bulwark. And as the Chaldean's foot touched the stone of the harbour a hollow rumble seemed to come from the very core of the island and the ground trembled until the stacked wine-jars rang one against the other. Nun felt a sudden chill of terror all over his body in the hot afternoon. The sailors who stood by the ropes fell weakly to their knees muttering incantations, the Chaldean stood in thought with a stern set face, and the island soldiers behaved as if nothing had happened.

'Our welcome has been spoken,' said the Chaldean at last.

At that point there was the sound of a disturbance at the landward end of the jetty: voices and footsteps seemed to be approaching. Nun looked round, thinking perhaps it was someone in authority, and wondering weakly what was the next surprise this strange island would produce.

The surprise was a little middle-aged man in a rather grubby civilian robe, chattering to his military escort in the Cretan tongue and helping his short steps through the dust of the harbour with a walking-stick. The soldiers stood out of his way without much show of respect, and he came up to where Nun and the Chaldean were standing. Taking one look at Nun, the ship, and the sailors, he switched immediately into the Phoenician language without pausing for breath.

'Have you been waiting? So sorry! You must excuse us,' he burst out. 'So unexpected so early in the afternoon – you know our wretched siesta habit. Or perhaps you don't.' Then turning to glance at the ship: 'From the Phoenician coast, aren't you? I've seen your ships in Crete, of course, although you don't often call at Thira. But you're very welcome. In fact, you're here not at all too soon. Things are bad.' He eyed the cargo of cedar-beams under its hide covering with some puzzlement: 'How much have you got?'

Nun hesitated. 'I – I'm afraid we're not here to trade,' he said.

'Trade?' repeated the little man sharply. 'Oh, of course, no haggling. We pay the price. But how much water have you? Where's it stowed?'

'Water?' said Nun. 'We've about enough for our crew for half a day, if they're rowing. I'd be obliged if you'd tell me where we can replenish.'

The man stopped talking for a good half minute and looked amazed at Nun. 'You're *asking* us for water? But they know the situation perfectly well in Amnisos. All ships calling from there are obliged to bring us water.' His face attempted a smile. 'You are pulling my leg, Captain. But it is not kind of you.'

Nun was beginning to understand. 'I'm very sorry, sir,' he said. 'A misunderstanding. We're not from Amnisos. We sailed straight from Gebal without touching land. If we'd known there was a water shortage here, of course we would have brought some. But all we have, I'm afraid, is a cargo of timber for Knossos. We called here for . . .' Well, what had they called for? This worried little man did not seem to have much to do with the Chaldean's grand calculations and predictions. 'Just a social visit,' Nun concluded feebly.

The little man's face, which had fallen into a picture of disappointment and dejection, pulled itself together. He shrugged. 'Oh!' he said, several times, in several different tones of voice. 'No water. I had thought perhaps even a bath . . .' Then he put on a smile. 'You must excuse me again. A social visit you said? One forgets on this wretched island. This really is kind. You mean you've really come to see *me*? You know it's just as good as water to a thirsty man – very nearly – to have visitors. You see nobody comes now, what with one thing and another . . .' He interrupted his thoughts: 'How rude of me. Here I am talking business and I haven't even introduced myself. Ekerawon's my name. How nice of you to come!'

'I'm Nun, from Gebal,' said Nun. 'And my friend here from Babylon –'

'From Babylon!' interrupted Ekerawon, his face lighting up. 'But you mock me, Nun of Gebal, when you say you have come all that way to visit us. You mock our wretched island. What could possibly draw you here?'

And at that moment there came again the hollow rumble from the core of the island, and the stones of the harbour trembled under their feet and the wine-jars chimed again. And the Chaldean saluted Ekerawon solemnly and said: 'The stars have indeed led me to you, all the way from Babylon, O Ekerawon. And I am sure that your island has something to tell me.'

To Nun's surprise Ekerawon burst into happy laughter. 'Oh, *that*!' he exclaimed, waving his hand vaguely towards the bowels of the mountain. 'Yes, of course, my dear sir, we have signs and wonders here, worthy even of Babylon's interest. But it's a long story if you don't know it. Gentlemen, you will be my guests for the evening! Accept my poor hospitality, and my little knowledge is at your disposal. Come!'

But Nun hesitated. 'We must not impose on you,' he protested. 'We have brought nothing. Are you sure –'

Ekerawon laughed again. 'My house is humble, sir, but we are not paupers. We have food, we have friends, we have music. And if there is no water – who cares, so long as there is wine?'

The evening's entertainment was wearing on. Darkness had fallen long ago. Sprawled on cushions in Ekerawon's courtyard, stupefied by the rich dark island wine which his host kept pouring into his cup, but which was doing nothing to quench his thirst, conscious of all the hours of sleep he had missed at sea, Nun was doing his best to keep his eyes open. The Chaldean was sitting in impassive dignity, saying and eating little. A large fat friend of the host, Philaios by name, was gorging himself on stuffed vine leaves and little fish in hot sauce. Four or five slaves kept beating out an insistent, rhythmic tune on drums, cymbals, a pipe, and some kind of stringed instrument. A thin girl with long dark hair, fierce eyes, and few clothes was twisting her body in a dance that seemed to move everything but her feet. And Ekerawon kept on talking.

'. . . an impossible family,' he was saying. 'And, really, one can hardly call them gods.'

Philaios interrupted him, his mouth full of fish. 'How can our young friend follow the story, Ekerawon, if you chatter away like an old woman? Begin at the beginning!'

'Perhaps *you* would like to tell the story then, Philaios,' said Ekerawon with a little pout.

'Very well,' said Philaios, washing down his mouthful with a draught of wine. 'Once upon a time –'

'You'll have to start earlier than that,' Ekerawon interrupted in his turn.

'What do you mean?' said Philaios.

'The story starts before Time was born,' said Ekerawon. 'So how can you start with *Once Upon a Time*? I knew you'd get it wrong.'

'All right, then,' said Philaios, returning to his food with a shrug. '*You* tell the story. But keep it simple.'

'Right,' said Ekerawon, turning to Nun, 'I'll tell the story. As simply as I can. Only it's not a simple story. Such a family! All right, Philaios, I see you looking at me!' He sat himself upright on his couch and held up his hand. 'In the beginning,' he began solemnly, 'in the beginning there was Earth and Sky. We still have our Earth-Mother, of course. If you look south from here you can see the island of Dia: we say that's the Earth-Mother's body, lying in the sea.'

'That's nothing to do with the story,' put in Philaios.

'Am I telling the story, or am I not?' demanded Ekerawon. 'The children of the Earth and Sky were the Giants,' he continued. 'A monstrous lot they were. Some of them only had one eye, some of them had a hundred limbs, and they grew and grew, out of all proportion. They quarrelled among themselves and their parents couldn't control them. One must admit they were a failure.' He took a sip of wine.

'The last of this brood was old Time himself,' he continued, 'Chronos you may call him, or what you like.'

'El,' said Nun. He felt he had to say something, or fall asleep.

'I beg your pardon?' Ekerawon inquired.

'El is our name for Time,' Nun explained. 'They say he settled at Gebal!'

'Most interesting!' Ekerawon exclaimed. 'I was going to say something about this character, but if he belongs to your part of the world now, I'd better not say a word against him. Besides, who are we to judge a demigod for a little thing like mutilating his father and devouring his own children?' He giggled and drank some more wine.

'You've forgotten the point of the story,' said Philaios.

'What point?' Ekerawon demanded.

'What happened to the Giants,' said Philaios.

'I haven't *finished* yet,' said Ekerawon petulantly. 'Yes, my friend,' he said to Nun. 'The Giants!' He stood up and suddenly became serious. 'This monstrous race, who defiled Earth and menaced Heaven, were shut up for eternity in prisons underground, from which ever since they have been trying to break out and take vengeance on the inhabitants of the world. And here we are,' he concluded, draining his wine-cup.

'Here we are?' repeated Nun, uncomprehending. He couldn't even tell whether it was himself who was being stupid or his host who was being incoherent. And then, for the third time since they had set foot on the island, there came the hollow rumble from underground, the floor of the courtyard shook, pieces of twig and insects came raining down from the vines overhead, and the crockery danced on the table. This time, instead of dying away, the tremor was followed by a stronger one, which Nun felt like a blow through the couch on which he was lying. He sat up, no longer sleepy; the music of the various instruments tailed off, the girl-dancer stood contorted, her eyes wide and staring. There was silence while Philaios downed a whole cupful of wine and nearly choked himself, but Ekerawon was on his feet quivering and storming at the musicians and the dancer.

'What have you stopped for?' he screamed at them. 'Do I keep you to stand and turn pale every time the earth shakes? Play on, you miserable white-livered geese! Dance, girl – it's all you're fit for! More wine for the guests! Scatter rose-leaves! Gentlemen of Babylon and Gebal, your cups are empty, you put me to shame. Your health, my old friend Philaios! Be merry! We are not afraid, are we?'

Yes, thought Nun, we are: and you, my host, are more afraid than anyone. But he did not speak his thoughts. He was stone-cold sober, and wished he was anywhere but on this unhappy island.

An unreal smile was pinned on the face of Ekerawon, and he turned to Nun as the music started up again and the wine began to circulate.

'What were we talking about, my friend?'

'You were saying,' replied Nun, 'the words "Here we are!" And then the earth shook. I am afraid I still do not under-stand.'

Ekerawon sat down. He was still trembling. He drank again, and said weakly: 'You have heard the voice of the Giants and felt their struggles in the earth beneath us. Did you know that it was here they were imprisoned for their revolt?'

Nun was silent for a space. 'All of them?' he asked at last.

'Oh, some here, some there, no doubt,' replied Ekerawon. 'They say there are other burning mountains under which some of the tribe are pent. But we have enough here, eh,

Philaois? Sometimes they sleep for years on end. Sometimes their rage to escape shakes the island for days. Just recently they have been very wakeful. It has been almost impossible to sleep. And, on top of that, no rain and no water. It is very trying, is it not, Philaios?' and now Ekerawon was sitting weeping tears into his wine-cup.

'Why do you live here, then?' asked Nun.

'I don't know why,' sniffed Ekerawon. 'Why do we carry on, Philaios? I'm too old for this kind of life, and yet where else have I got to go? I have my vineyards here, and the wine is good. These animals,' he sniffed, pointing to the slaves, 'they know no better. They've always lived here. They're just as scared – I mean the cowards are afraid when the Giants roar, but next moment they forget about it. But my family's from Crete. My father came and planted the vineyards. Very special wine we make here, a favourite with the court of Knossos. But no one knows how I suffer from the strain of living here.'

And then the Chaldean spoke, for the first time in many hours.

'What would happen, think you, Ekerawon, if these Giants were to escape?'

'The end of the human race they say,' replied Ekerawon casually. 'That's the story – that the Titans have vowed vengeance on all other creatures, gods and all, once they get loose.'

'Does the thought not appal you, Ekerawon?'

'Yes. Yes, appalling,' agreed Ekerawon gloomily. 'But they say it won't happen.'

'What if the stars tell me that it *will* happen?'

Ekerawon shrugged. 'What could I do about it? Sit on top of the mountain and hold them down? Maybe it will happen. *When* though no one can tell. We may all be dead long before. Have some more wine, you are drinking nothing.'

'What if I were to tell you the exact date when it will happen, as foretold by the stars, and well within your life-time?'

Ekerawon got to his feet, holding out his hand in a gesture to stop the Chaldean speaking. 'No! No, no, no! No dates! That's the last thing I want to know, even if you *know* it. What, sit here waiting for the end of the world? There's no pleasure in that. Drink man, drink! Why I've never met such a solemn fellow.' And turning to the musicians he shouted: 'Some really gay music there! What's this dirge – are you all half asleep? Have you seen me dance? I feel like dancing. How's this, eh?' And the little man sidled away over the pavement in a ridiculous caricature of the girl-dancer's steps.

The Chaldean was also standing. 'I was about to ask you, sir,' he was saying to the retreating back of Ekerawon, 'if you would excuse my absence while I go to study the stars. It must be but a short time before dawn.'

'Stars?' said Ekerawon dreamily, spinning on one foot. 'Yes, of course. Take as many as you like. Make yourself at home. My stars are yours. And give my compliments to the celestial bodies, but don't bother me with their predictions, just now, there's a good fellow. I'm dancing . . .'

The Chaldean bowed courteously and stepped from the light of the torches into the shadow. Nun saw that Philaios was asleep on his couch, his face flushed with wine. He gave up trying to fight sleep and sank back on the cushions. The music played on. Ekerawon was holding the dancing-girl by the hand and spinning her round. Nun's eyes closed. The couch he lay on seemed to rock – was it wine, sea-weariness, or the subterranean struggles of imprisoned Giants? Until dawn, Nun lay in a nightmare-haunted sleep.

4
The Walls that Time Built

In Gebal, the town that Time built, time passes – Beth spies upon the Egyptian mysteries of the priests and scribes – Chosen by the King as a Temple Maiden

'Be off then, shooo, you lazy birds!' Beth cried, and flapped her arms at the pigeons. 'Go off and find food for yourselves!'

The pigeons took their time, waddling and strutting over the flat-topped ramparts of Gebal, near the house of Resh, the chief mason. Then they suddenly took off together with a flutter of wings, wheeled round in a flock, and rose up into the blue sky. Beth watched them climb up above the sea horizon, round against the green of the mountain-side, then gradually lost sight of them as they set off up the coast.

Beth sighed. They fly away and leave me, she thought. But usually they all came back by evening, though sometimes there might be one or two missing, and then she would wait and wait and at last have to give up waiting, and wonder what hawk or falcon had attacked and struck them down.

Her brothers, too, had gone away and left her. Zayin, the strong, the man of weapons, he had gone first. But she was used to Zayin going off on hunting or warlike expeditions. He would come back: it was unthinkable that he should come to harm. As for Nun, the resourceful, the serpent of the sea – he always came back prosperously from his ventures, though he sometimes had tales of pirates and sea-fights to tell. But what of Aleph, the unworldly scribe, the slow ox? What had happened to him?

It was many days now since Aleph had gone off on his errand to the cedar-forest and disappeared. The white pigeon he had taken with him should have flown home within a few hours to show that he had reached his destination, but that had never come back either. A messenger had been sent to the lumber-camp to ask after him, but had failed to find Aleph or the woodcutters. And now a search-party had gone up the mountain with orders to report back after a certain number of days. Today it was due back! Beth would perhaps get some news when her father returned from the palace.

Beth knew that her father was as worried as she was – but he at least had his work to think about. At home, she had too much time to sit and worry. And her conscience was uneasy. It had all begun with that writing game they had been playing. Absent-mindedly she traced the ox-head sign in the dust with her toe, then looked guiltily over her shoulder and rubbed it out. Her father had been shocked to see Aleph teaching her the signs – yet sending him up the mountain had not been a severe punishment. But had the Gods been offended? And was Aleph's disappearance their retribution?

Beth paced restlessly along the ramparts. She could not go back to the house and sit with her thoughts. But where else could she go? She turned to the sea and her thoughts flew to Nun, steering his ship over the sparkling waves. She looked up the coast to where the headlands receded into the blue haze, and thought of Zayin at the head of his army. She faced the mountain and felt that at least she might have been allowed to join the search for Aleph. She turned towards the palace – and she made up her mind.

A little later she was making her way through the narrow streets of Gebal. This was not much of an escape from the confinement of the house that stood under the great walls. The city was crowded on to a little promontory on the coast: the palace and the temples took up the best sites with their courtyards and sacred pools, while the houses and markets had to make do with the space left over, huddling side by side and one above the other on the slopes. Beth jumped back quickly as a large ass came round the corner, driven smartly by a boy with a stick and loaded with panniers that stretched right across the street. She nearly dropped the dish she was carrying.

She threaded her way through the crowds of porters, water-carriers, fishermen, and strange sailors from the port, towards the palace yard where she knew that her father was directing the work. Now and then she felt eyes looking at her, for she was tall for her age and even her brothers sometimes told her she was pretty. But nobody made way for her.

Between the temple and the palace soldiers stood on guard. One of them stepped into her path, but without bothering to lower his spear. He was tall and handsome and his bronze helmet shone in the sun.

'Where might you be going, girl?' he asked contemptuously, with a glance at the poor dress she was wearing and the dish she was carrying.

Beth's heart thumped a little, but she kept her eyes cast down and muttered tonelessly: 'Dinner for Resh, the chief mason.'

The soldier looked her up and down as she stood there determined not to blush, and at last he said with a slight grin, 'Pass, slavey,' and stood aside. Beth went on, still keeping her eyes down and her face expressionless. It had worked. She had passed for a slave-girl.

The courtyard of the palace was ringing with the sound of bronze chisels on hard stone and the air was full of fine white dust. Masons were chipping doggedly at the faces of half-

squared blocks; slaves were hauling on ropes attached to a
vast monolith while other slaves thrust rollers underneath it;
a tripod of beams stood over a pit, holding a pulley and rope
on which more workers heaved, raising rubble from a deep
excavation. Beth blinked in the drifting dust and looked
round for her father. There he was, talking to some priests.
She went up to the group, keeping her head lowered, and said
in a low voice, 'Your dinner, chief mason.'

'Set it down, set it down,' said Resh, and went on talking
in an agitated voice to the priests. 'It shall be done as you
say, Your Reverence, it shall be done, I assure you.' He
bowed and the priests turned aloofly away. Resh looked
after them in an abstracted manner, and said in Beth's
direction, 'Well, girl, what are you standing there for? Is
there any message?' Then he turned his head and recognized
his daughter.

'Beth!' he exclaimed in a shocked voice. 'What are you
doing here? And dressed as a slave-girl?'

'I've come to ask if there is any news, Father,' said Beth. 'I
couldn't bear to stay at home any longer, waiting.'

'News? News?' repeated her father. 'What kind of news?
Explain yourself, girl!'

'Oh, Father, news of Aleph, of course. Has the search-
party returned?'

'No it has not. And the best thing you can do, young
woman, is to return home yourself. We have enough trouble
here already.'

'Do you think Aleph will come back, father?'

'It looks as if none of them will come back,' said her father
distractedly. 'Our best lumber-team, twelve yoke of oxen, the
search-party, forty baulks of timber needed for the new
palace ... And why are you dressed like that?' he asked
again, as if he had noticed her for the first time.

'I thought people wouldn't notice if I dressed like the slave

who comes every day. I know you don't like me coming here
but –'

'Of course I don't. Women are not allowed here.'

'Except slaves, Father.'

'Yes, of course. But they don't count.'

But they have more freedom than I do, thought Beth.
'Good-bye, Father,' she said aloud. 'I'm sorry there's no news
of the workmen.' She turned to go.

'Beth!' she heard her father call as she walked away from
him.

She looked round and said, 'Yes, Father?'

'What was that you said the other day about a pigeon?' her
father asked.

'A pigeon, Father?'

'You said Aleph took a pigeon with him. Has that come
back?'

'No, Father. That hasn't come back either.'

Resh said no more, but Beth could see that he was thinking
of her brother as much as she was.

As Beth moved off towards the gateway her eyes wandered
round the courtyard, and she wondered what secrets were
here that women were not allowed to see. Stones being fitted
to make a wall – no great secret about that. A great tapering
obelisk with a pointed top, lying on its side, but empty of any
decoration or inscription. The hole in the ground seemed
more interesting: judging by the length of rope needed to
haul up the baskets from the bottom it must be deep. She
edged towards it and peered down the square shaft through
solid rock. A well? What was secret about a well? Now what
were the veiled hints she had heard in her family, about the
old kings of Gebal being buried in deep shafts in the rock,
with all their treasures? And in secret, so that no impious
hand would ever be able to desecrate the place where they
lay? That might be it. Did not they also kill the slaves who

dug the burial chambers? She shivered a little and slipped away unobtrusively towards the gate, passing on her way something that looked like an unfinished drinking-trough for a giant ass.

She was glad when she got back to the house, and felt safer. It was better, perhaps, not to be a slave. She changed her dress and combed out her hair only just in time, because her aunt looked into the room.

'Where have you been all the morning, Miss?' asked her aunt suspiciously.

'Oh, dressing, and looking after my pigeons,' replied Beth carelessly, plying the Cretan comb decorated with dolphins, a present from Nun after one of his trips.

'Is that all?' sniffed her aunt, still suspicious.

'Oh, I saw that Father got his dinner.'

'Well, now,' exclaimed her aunt, 'I do believe you are beginning to grow more thoughtful! As long as you don't take it into your head to go off in the street alone.'

'Auntie!' Beth protested, making round eyes. 'As if I would!'

Her aunt left the room. As if I'd take it into my head to go into the street, thought Beth. As if I'd take it into my head to climb the mountain! As if I'd take it into my head to lead an army across the desert! As if I'd take it into my head to go to Knossos and see the Queen! As if I'd take it into my head to fly away like my pigeons! As if I would! She threw her little hand-mirror on to the floor, but the polished bronze merely clanged and bounced, and she picked it up and put it on the bed with her comb.

She went and joined her aunt and cousins at the midday meal, and listened to them chattering on about who had just had a baby, and the troublesome ways of slaves.

Beth slept in the hot afternoon, awoke still feeling cross, and occupied herself with some little pots of cosmetics Nun had brought her from Egypt. But she soon got bored with altering the shape of her eyes and climbed on to the wall again. It was empty of pigeons. She looked around the sky. There were flocks of birds over the sea that might be hers, or they might be seagulls. There were others circling high in the evening sky. She picked up a long bamboo wand with a piece of rag on the end and began to wave it to attract the pigeons' attention. How she wished she could whistle like the man across the road who also kept pigeons. Several flocks of different sizes were coming in from the coast and circling over the city, and she tried to make out her own flight with its pair of pure-white birds. Then she remembered, there would only be one white bird. The other was still in the mountains with Aleph. One flock circled lower, and she went on waving; then she stopped to scatter some grain over the roof – just enough to lure them home. They were supposed to find their own food among some country bumpkin's crops: her father would not allow her a lot of good food to be spared from the kitchen.

The birds were fluttering around her and settling on her shoulders. She pushed some off, and offered her favourites palmfuls of grain, speaking to them as they cooed to her. 'There you are, Midnight. Had a nice day?' she asked the black one. 'Get off, Rocky!' she said to a brown one. 'I fed you yesterday!' The white one came and perched on her hand. 'Ah, my Lady Snowy, where is your husband? Still up in the mountain with that foolish brother of mine? What are they up to together, eh? Well, why don't you go and fetch him back? You've got wings, you can go where you like! If I were you I'd be searching the mountains, right up to the peaks where there's snow the colour of you. Coo? Well, what's the use of *you*?'

The red sun was dropping towards the sea, the birds were settling on their perches, and it was time for her father to return for his evening meal.

Resh was cross and silent at supper. When Aunt asked him why he was not eating he snapped that he felt something was eating *him*, and when Beth asked him sympathetically what it was, he said it was worry, worry, worry, and nothing but worry. He said it had not been like this in the old days; you just got on with your job then and work was a pleasure. But now it was rush and bustle all the time, finish a new temple here, make a tomb there, enlarge the palace somewhere else. And you could not rely on anyone either: the workmen were lazy and incompetent, timber got lost in the mountains, and even the stone they worked was not what it used to be. He Did Not Know What the Times Were Coming to!

'And to cap it all –' Resh began to say, before a mouthful stopped him (Help! Beth thought, he's going to tell Aunt what I did this morning), 'To cap it all there's going to be an offering.' The women were silent, wagging their heads sympathetically.

'What's an offering?' Beth asked.

Her aunt told her not to ask silly questions, everybody knew what an offering was.

Resh turned to her aunt. 'Perhaps you'll tell us what it is then!' he said.

'Well, dear, it's – it's a thing the priests do,' said Aunt vaguely.

'If it was a thing the priests did, would it worry me?' demanded Resh. 'It's a thing everyone in Gebal has to do. Every man jack of us.'

One of the cousins clicked her tongue. 'Oh dear,' she said, 'you'll have to tell me what to do.'

'I don't mean *women*,' said Resh quite rudely. 'I've no shortage of *them*.'

'Yes, Father,' said Beth sweetly. 'Aren't you lucky to have us all to look after you?' Aunt and cousins looked at her with alarm, but she went on, 'What do the men have to do, then?'

'It's a counting, you might say, as much as an offering,' her father said. He was usually prepared to explain things to Beth, though she did not always listen. 'All the men of Gebal have to come before the King, to be numbered, and of course they have to give him something to show what sort of men they are. In this way the King knows how powerful his kingdom is.'

'He gets some nice presents, too,' said Beth, but her aunt told her not to be frivolous.

'But why should you be worried about a thing like that, Father?' Beth persisted. 'You're quite rich, aren't you? And you're clever at carving and things. You could make something nice for him, I'm sure.'

'I think the King knows what I'm worth to him. It's not that.' Resh brooded in silence for a while, then burst out, 'But how am I going to look as a family man, with no sons at my side? There'll be my own foreman with seven sons – and me, what have I got to show?'

'You have three fine sons, dear,' said Aunt soothingly.

'But where are they?' cried Resh, banging the table with his fist. 'What can I say to the King? "One's gone off hunting in the desert, one's flirting with the women of Knossos, and another's simple in the head and got himself lost in the woods"?'

'Oh, Father, that isn't fair,' said Beth, and flushed. 'I'm sure Zayin and Nun and Aleph would come back if they knew you wanted them.' But her father went on muttering: why couldn't he have a family that stayed at home and supported him. Beth could see that he was really worried.

'Oh, Father,' she sighed, 'I wish I was some use instead.'

At that her father looked hard at her, then hid his face in his hands and said in a muffled voice he hoped it would not come to that. It was not in fact a very happy meal.

*

The summer days passed in Gebal and still there was no news of the sons of Resh. The search-party had returned after combing the mountains and forests and finding nothing. The days and nights became hotter and stickier and more breathless. Whenever she could, Beth got up on to the city wall to catch what air there was. She envied the people who lived outside the walls, though most of them were poor, or foreign. Her father said that not long ago even good Giblite families could live outside the walls and feel safe, but these were troubled times and it was better to be inside. From the walls, Beth could see the ragged boys splashing in the harbour. How cool it must be for them, she thought. When she had been small, she had run about with the children who lived near the port. She was not allowed to do that any more – whether it was because her father was richer and more important or because she was older and more of a woman, she wasn't sure. But what *was* there for her to do?

One morning of oppressive heat she found herself putting on her old shabby dress again and tying her hair with a cloth. She had not really thought what she was going to do, and she had not even the excuse for going to the palace that she had had the last time. But she had got to the point when she had to get out of the house on her own again. She told the slave-girl that she was going to carry the master's dinner to the palace, and the girl was quite happy not to have to make the journey in the heat.

The guards seemed more vigilant than last time when she approached the palace yard. A soldier in armour lowered his spear and pointed it at her, and asked what her business was in a stern voice. She did as she had done before, standing with lowered eyes and muttering: 'Dinner for Resh, the overseer.'

But the sentinel merely replied, 'No one allowed in,' and stood there. Beth flushed with anger at such obstructiveness.

'Is my fa — is my master to go without his food?' she burst out.

The soldier merely looked at her curiously, said it was not his business and she had better move along.

Beth turned away and stood in the shade on the other side of the open space by the palace, holding the dinner bowl and not knowing what to do. She felt like crying with frustration. Then she saw another soldier marching up to the one she had just spoken to. The guard was changing. She heard the first say to the second something like 'Same orders', and the soldier marched away. Beth looked at the relief guard. It was the handsome young man who had let her in before. She waited until the first soldier was out of sight, then she went slowly up to the other. She did not bother to wipe the tears of frustration out of her eyes, but looked up at the soldier.

'Good morning, Sergeant,' she said. She knew he was not a sergeant.

'Hullo, girl,' said the soldier.

'I am the servant of Resh, the overseer.'

'He knows how to pick them, then. What's your name?'

Quickly she thought for a name. 'Aina,' she said. 'I am a slave, a captive. But I was not a slave in my own country.'

'You don't look like one,' said the soldier gallantly.

'I must see my master,' said Beth.

'Impossible,' said the soldier. 'No one's allowed in. Special orders.'

Beth was going to ask 'Why?' but decided against arguing. Instead she turned away sorrowfully. 'They will beat me if I don't carry out my errand,' she said.

The soldier looked uncomfortable. 'They flog me, too, if I disobey orders.'

Beth turned back quickly. 'Oh no!' she exclaimed. 'Would they? Then I must go away. It is better for me to be beaten than you.'

The young soldier had been made to appear less than heroic. 'I'm not afraid what they'll do to me,' he said. 'Look, maybe there's no harm in you just nipping in and out again. I'll take the responsibility,' he added proudly.

Beth gave him a look of gratitude and admiration. 'Oh, thank you, Captain,' she said. 'You *are* kind,' and leaving him a smile, she darted past before he could change his mind. *That* worked, too, she thought to herself, pleased with the success of her wiles, though what her father would have said . . .!

Things in the palace yard seemed quieter than they had been last time. The gangs of labourers were not there. The great stone had been set up on end and there was a handful of men working on it, perched on wooden scaffolding. Beth crept closer to see what they were doing. There was no clanging of heavy stone-mason's tools now, only a tapping and tinkling of little hammers and fine chisels. The men who were working were not muscular slaves but priestly looking men with intent faces. On one surface of the stone an elderly man was working with a pen and black ink. On the other sides, men were following the outlines he had made, cutting them into the stone. Beth stared, fascinated: there were birds and bees and beetles, snakes and fishes, little men walking and kneeling, and other signs which meant nothing to her, all neatly arranged in lines and columns. How she wished she could join them, and pass the time usefully drawing little creatures! But she knew that was impossible: this was the sacred writing of the priests, the secret of kings and gods. Aleph might learn it some day, if he was still alive. But she never could.

The men went on working without speaking or looking up. But as she stood there one of them dropped his mallet, almost at her feet. Without thinking, she picked it up and handed it back. The man muttered a word of thanks, then gave her a look of outraged astonishment. He had not expected to see a girl there, Beth thought. She glided away as quickly as she could without attracting any more attention.

She could not see her father anywhere; indeed, the whole place seemed strangely deserted. The paved court, too, looked as if it had been swept and tidied for some important occasion. And what was that great square object, standing half in the shadow of the wall, half in the dazzling noonday sun, wrapped and swathed in heavy cloth?

Beth heard measured footsteps approaching round a corner. Suddenly afraid, she ran and hid behind the swaddled Thing that stood against the wall, pulling a loose corner of the cloth round her. She heard voices coming nearer.

'And what,' said one voice, that seemed to be weary and strong, gentle and cruel at the same time, 'is That?'

'That?' came another, rather pompous voice. 'That, your Most Sublime Majesty, is a Stone. Wrapped up, as you see, to – ah, to protect it from the Weather.'

'Hmm!' came the first voice. 'How thoughtful of somebody!' And the footsteps passed on, but Beth, stifling as she was in the stuffy cloth, had frozen in terror. 'Sublime Majesty' were the words she had heard. It must be the King!

So that was why the palace yard was swept and deserted: King Abishram was making one of his rare tours of inspection. Beth summoned up the courage to peep from her cloth round the corner of the mysterious block. The procession of priests, soldiers, counsellors and courtiers was passing on into the front court where the stone with the inscription stood. Perhaps that was what the King was going to see. Beth looked again at the back view of a figure at the rear of the procession, which seemed familiar. It was her father! Father walking with the King! – or at least in the same procession.

Well, she couldn't go up to him now and offer him his dinner. But her fear of being discovered was overcome by a great curiosity as to what was going on.

She gave the King's retinue time to pass clear of the great doorway that led into the next court. Then, still carrying the dish, she stole to the doorway and peeped round. The King was standing before the stone of inscriptions, the scribes were kneeling in the dust before him, and the High Priest was holding forth.

'Your Divine Majesty will of course be able to read for Himself the inscription His servants are raising to His perpetual memory,' the priest was saying. 'But,' he went on hastily, 'His humble servants will not expect His Majesty to perform such a menial task as reading for Himself. His Divinity will perhaps permit His servants to expound the text for Him.'

I wonder if the King *can* read, thought Beth to herself. As the voice of the High Priest started intoning, she strained her eyes to follow the procession of little signs that marched across the face of the pillar, and almost persuaded herself that she was reading them line by line. The slim, pointed obelisk became a poem instead of a decorated stone. The words went like this:

I

ABISHRAM

KING OF GEBAL

FAVOURED OF THE

GODS, OF THE LADY

BALAAT-GEBAL, OF

RESHEF, GOD OF

BATTLE, OF ISIS, OSIRIS,

AND RA: I, ABISHRAM OF

GEBAL, COMMANDER OF

MANY ARMIES, COMMANDER

OF MANY NAVIES, EQUAL TO
PHARAOH HIMSELF, ARMED TEN
THOUSAND MEN, SENT THEM
TO THE NORTH TO SUBDUE THE
BARBARIANS. I BUILT A THOUS-
AND SHIPS, I CUT TEN THOUSAND
CEDARS AND SENT THEM TO MINOS
IN EXCHANGE FOR MUCH GOLD.
I, ABISHRAM OF GEBAL, CUT MY
DWELLING OF DEATH IN THE LIVING
ROCK OF GEBAL SO THAT I MAY ABIDE
FOR EVER WITH MY PEOPLE AND MY CITY.
I, ABISHRAM OF GEBAL, COMMANDED A NUM-
BERING OF MY PEOPLE AND MY WEALTH . . .

The voice of the High Priest broke off. 'The work is, of course, unfinished,' he said. 'Does it please Your Divine Majesty so far?'

'I feel flattered,' said the King.

'Your Majesty is most gracious,' said the High Priest, bowing. 'When the Offering and the Numbering is complete, we shall inscribe the details on the pillar. Though, of course, if Your Majesty wishes, and as it is well known all over the world that Your Majesty is Lord of a thousand thousands, we may put that number in immediately, if Your Majesty wishes?'

'No,' said the King shortly. 'Count first, then inscribe.'

The King turned abruptly to go. Beth, suddenly panic-stricken, dodged back towards the pillars of the great door. But at that moment the dish, which she had rested on a projection of the stonework, fell with a clatter and smashed all over the pavement.

Beth saw the horrified gaze of the High Priest, who had been standing on the plinth of the monument and was the first to see her. Then the King followed the priest's gaze, and Beth saw and felt his piercing black eyes resting on her. And now the whole of the royal retinue had turned and were looking at her. She was too petrified to do anything. Two soldiers darted forward, took Beth by the arms, dragged her towards the King, and threw her in the dust before him.

'And *what*,' came the voice of the King, 'is *that*?'

The High Priest looked hard at Beth. 'Only a slave, Your Majesty. She shall be put to death for spying.'

'Deal with the matter,' said the King wearily.

Beth was too frightened to speak or look up. Then she heard a voice she knew – her father's, quavering with agitation.

'If it please you, my lord High Priest, the – the creature was not spying. She was bringing me my dinner. She is my – my slave.'

'Your slaves are badly trained, Chief Mason,' said the priest contemptuously. 'It will be enough to have her soundly flogged. See to it.'

The two soldiers picked Beth up again, but her father was beside her, kneeling in the dust before the High Priest. 'Your Exaltation!' he was pleading. 'She is a tender maiden, not accustomed to being beaten, and free born. She is not a slave, she is – she is my daughter!'

There was a silence, and it was the King who spoke.

'Let us see her face,' said the King.

Beth fearfully lifted up her head, and looked straight into the face of the King, with its curled beard, powerful nose, and the two deep black eyes that seemed to be weighing her up.

'She would seem,' the King spoke at last, 'to be suited to become one of our maidens of the temple. Arrange it, High Priest!'

And Beth looked at her father, and could not tell whether she saw relief, sorrow, or pride in his face.

5
The Court of Minos

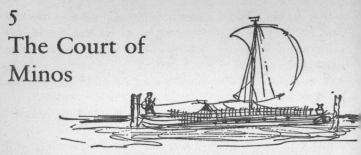

Nun, the sailor, on the island of Crete – The myth of the Minotaur, the bull-monster – Amber-traders of Scandinavia – The Chaldean prophesies destruction

Sunset was colouring the western slopes of Mount Ida as Nun steered towards the harbour of Amnisos, the port of Knossos. His crew had spent as restless a night as he had on Thira, the ill-omened isle tormented by drought, bemused by strong wine, and shaken by the terrible upheavals in its bowels. They were as glad as he was to return to the ship at dawn and push off into the open sea away from the menacing plume of smoke that hung low in the cool dawn air. Though it meant a long day's row to reach Crete, the farther they were from Thira the happier the men were. But the Chaldean was silent, or slept, all the day, and Nun was surprised to see him standing beside him on the poop now.

'That is Knossos?' asked the Chaldean.

Nun was glad to be in the position of a man of experience again. 'Knossos?' he said. 'No, what you see is only the port. The palace of King Minos lies inland, and – thank the gods! – I have no business there. We'll spend a night or two in the port, where they treat foreigners well enough even if they *are* a bit officious. Just long enough to discharge our cargo and for the crew to get drunk. Then we'll buy a few knick-knacks and be off again. The less we have to do with the court the better.'

'But *my* business lies with the court,' said the sage in a low voice. Nun looked at him sharply. As he had feared, his passenger was going to involve him in more affairs that he would rather avoid.

'I don't think I can help you with that,' said Nun. 'I'm not an ambassador, only a simple sea-captain.'

'Is it so difficult to obtain an audience with King Minos?' asked the sage.

'You wait and see,' replied Nun. 'There's not a city wall on the island, they say, but Minos is more difficult to get at than the King of Troy, for all his walls and turrets. And here comes the first obstacle.'

They were still an hour out of the harbour, but from out of the lee of the island of Dia came a ship of thirty oars, manned with armed warriors, heading to cut them off.

Nun gave the order for the oarsmen to easy, and they thankfully rested on their oars. 'No use fooling around with the coast guard here,' he said. 'The first time I put into Amnisos I didn't like the look of them and decided to race them to port. Nearly got rammed and sent to the fishes.'

They waited until the other vessel hove to within speaking distance.

'What is your business with the Kingdom of Minos?' came the hail, and the speaker repeated it in several languages to make sure the visitor understood.

'Cargo of cedar-wood from Gebal!' Nun called over the waves. 'Passport from His Royal Highness King Abishram!'

'Where's the passport, Bos'un? Let's have it ready!'

The boatswain heaved the slab of inscribed stone out of the ballast at the bottom of the boat and held it in readiness as the Minoan vessel came alongside. The oars were shipped on the port side, and the vessels came together. An official, helped by two soldiers, jumped aboard. He glanced at the cargo of cedar-beams and then at the stone.

'What's *that*?' he sniffed contemptuously.

'Ship's documents,' replied Nun shortly. 'Can't you read hieroglyphics?'

'You Giblites!' sneered the officer. 'You've got the insolence to bring out a lump of stone with Egyptian scrawls on it, for His Invincible Majesty King Minos's edification! Your documents are out of date! Anything to declare?'

'No,' said Nun, keeping his temper. He was used to Minoan officialdom.

'What's this, then?' demanded the official, looking at the Chaldean.

'My passenger,' Nun answered. 'He's not a *thing*, he's a scholar and a gentleman. I'm sure he has his own documents.'

With great dignity, the Chaldean produced from his pack a tablet of baked clay, inscribed with writing and sealed with an impression of a lion and a bull. The official looked at it.

'Nail writing!' muttered the official, but he seemed to be impressed.

Without another word he turned and jumped back into his boat, followed by the two soldiers. 'Carry on into port!' he shouted at them. 'You look harmless, anyhow.' And the coastguard vessel pushed off.

Nun, already fuming at this first sample of the vexations of port after the freedom of the seas, gave orders to continue towards the land.

They rowed on in the direction of the harbour. As they neared the jumble of quays and warehouses, Nun strained his eyes to make out how he should approach and where he should tie up. Then he ordered the crew to rest on their oars again, and spoke to them roughly.

'Now listen!' he barked. 'Especially any of you who haven't been here before. Yonder's Amnisos, and that's the island of Crete if you didn't know, and somewhere between the mountains is the palace of King Minos. We're going to be the guests of the Cretans for a few days. You'll find them not a bad lot, even though they *are* Westerners and don't have our way of looking at things. But they're touchy, like all these new nations, see? Lucky they don't understand our language, most of them, but watch what you say about them all the same. And they're fussy about official things. This isn't one of these free-and-easy ports where you can run ashore and get drunk and misbehave yourselves as soon as we tie up. It may take hours before we're allowed ashore at all. Don't misunderstand me – I don't care what happens to a single man jack of you! For all I care any one of you can spend the rest of his life in a Cretan jail – *I* shan't come and bail you out! But I happen to want a crew to take this ship home again. So I'm warning you – watch your step and watch your tongues, or you may find yourselves thrown to the bull-monster!'

The men had been listening to Nun's speech with little enough attention, like most sailors and schoolboys when they're being told to behave, but at the mention of the bull-monster they began to exchange looks and mutter remarks.

'What's this bull-monster, then?' whispered the youngest deckhand, with rounded eyes.

'Aha!' cackled an old seaman. 'Just you be a good boy, sonny, or it'll get you, sure as fate.'

'Don't give us that old story!' said a younger oarsman contemptuously, and spat over the side.

'All right, then,' retorted the older man, 'I had a mate who saw it.'

'I've seen a bull,' said the boy.

'Not like this one. Eats men, it does – specially young lads, my mate said.'

'How did *he* know?' the oarsman put in.

'He *ought* to. He got ate up himself!'

The boy's eyes grew wider and wider. Then he burst out: 'Look, if the bull ate him, how —' But he was interrupted by the captain's order to pull on their oars. The younger oarsman, however, went on muttering as he rowed: 'Don't give us them bull stories.'

Nun did not know himself what the truth was about the famous bull of Minos, or about the people who were taken to the palace of Knossos and were never heard of again. For himself, he would keep clear of it. And the business of entering harbour now took his whole attention.

Another small boat put out from the shore and came alongside. Another official came on board and asked the same questions, and whether anybody on board had the plague or any other sickness. Nun said they were all healthy and hoped they would not catch anything in Crete, but the official was not amused. Only then were they allowed to enter the harbour mouth. The official gave directions, and Nun gave orders to the oarsmen to pull together, to hold water one side, to back water, and at last to ship oars as they came smoothly alongside the quay. Nun heard a sigh of relief go up from the oarsmen as the long voyage came to its end; but he felt little relief when he saw the Cretan officials waiting for him on the quay. It was getting late and the officials did not look too keen on clearing another ship and cargo as the evening fell — but this was Amnisos, and things had to be done properly even if it might take all night. He felt thankful that his cargo was only cedar-beams. The Cretans were great ones for making lists of things, but even they could not take long to account for forty logs. If it had been a load of corn they might have insisted on counting every grain.

Then Nun remembered the Chaldean, and his heart sank further. A captain was responsible for his passengers as well as his cargo. There would probably be endless arguments about this stranger. There he was, standing upright and silent on the after-deck, his baggage at his feet, waiting with dignified patience to step ashore.

'Let's get this done, then!' came the voice of yet another official from the quay-side. 'Unless you'd rather stay aboard all night.'

Nun sprang from the deck on to the quay where the official was standing with two scribes. The scribes had pens and portable ink-bottles, and they were holding large fragments of broken pottery to take down their rough notes on.

'Name?' snapped the official. 'Hailing from? Number of crew? – no, never mind their names, can't expect us to write down all this outlandish stuff. Just make sure you don't leave any behind when you sail. Type of cargo? Quantity? Who's it consigned to? Oh, indeed, for the royal palace itself, is it? Well, you don't expect His Majesty to come down and thank you for it himself, do you?'

Nun did his best to answer the questions, many of which he had answered twice already, without losing his temper. And then the official's eye fell on the patiently waiting Chaldean. 'What have you got there?' he asked suspiciously.

'Passenger, from Chaldea,' Nun replied shortly.

'Oh yes?' sniffed the official. 'And what's *his* business here?'

'Better ask him yourself,' said Nun. 'He wants to see the King.'

'Wants to see the King, does he?' the official sneered. 'And does he think the King wants to see *him*, by any chance? Comes here deck passage with a load of lumber and wants to see the King! I'm a busy man myself, and he'll be lucky if I can spare him a few moments some time tomorrow. But he'll have to be looked into. Here, you! Where's your credentials?' he called roughly to the Chaldean.

The Chaldean said nothing, but once more drew from his

wallet the baked tablet with the cuneiform writing on it and handed it to Nun, who passed it to the official.

The official gave it a contemptuous glance. 'No good showing me that nail-writing either. This'll need translating tomorrow, if we can get an interpreter. Er – just one moment.'

Nun saw his expression change as if his eye had fallen upon something unexpected. The official turned his back, raised the tablet to catch the light of the setting sun, and peered at it closely. Nun, looking over his shoulder, saw that it was the seal of the lion and the bull at the bottom of the tablet that he was examining.

When the official turned to face them again he seemed to be a different person. Holding the tablet reverently in his hands he bowed over it in the direction of the Chaldean, a strained smile on his face. 'Pray tell His Excellency,' he said to Nun, still smiling, 'that he is most welcome to Amnisos, and that the best accommodation we can provide is at his disposal, unless he wishes to proceed immediately to Knossos.'

Nun was amused at this sudden change of behaviour, all apparently due to the mysterious lion and bull seal. He was even more amused when the Chaldean gravely said to him in the same language, 'Pray convey to the servant of King Minos my thanks for his welcome, and say that we accept his offer of accommodation for the night.' It was not only the reflection of the sunset-clouds that made the official's face look red.

After that, the port formalities proceeded with a smoothness and speed that amazed Nun. A guard of soldiers was put on the quay near the ship, and he was told that it would be well looked after and protected from thieves; the sailors were allowed to go and enjoy themselves in the town, and were even given cheerful advice about the best taverns.

And Nun found himself being politely escorted with the Chaldean to a superior guest-house that was obviously reserved for none but the most important travellers. It was built squarely and solidly of stone and wooden beams, and the walls inside were covered with colourful paintings of fish and dolphins. Soon they were being served with food and wine by attentive slaves who carried bowls and jars of fine pottery, and every piece of the dinner service was decorated with designs of octopus or flowers. As he lay back on his couch, Nun began to think that life ashore in Crete was worth lingering for after all – though a Chaldean astrologer was a queer companion for a sailor to spend a night ashore with. And, indeed, the sage seemed to become more and more remote and withdrawn, and made only absent-minded replies to Nun's attempts to talk.

'May I ask what it is that troubles you?' asked Nun at last. 'Here you are, at the end of your long journey over desert and sea, with all the comforts of civilization. You should be thankful and enjoy yourself.'

The Chaldean smiled faintly. 'I fear I must be a poor companion to you, my young friend,' he said. 'But it is all very well for you. This is indeed as far as you need go, and you deserve to enjoy the fruits of the land after your responsibilities at sea. But for me the travelling is nothing. The mission is all, and that is not completed. I have learned what I came to learn. But now I must deliver my warning to the world, if the world will listen. For, my friend, it is a thing of such terrible import that it concerns the ears of kings and rulers. And tomorrow I must seek the ear of King Minos.'

At these words Nun felt a great emptiness in his stomach in spite of the good food and wine.

'What is this thing, then, which concerns the ear of Minos?' he asked.

The sage paused before he replied. 'I cannot tell you, my

friend, because I do not yet know myself.' Then, seeing Nun's mystified expression he stood up and gave him another faint smile. 'I have one more appointment with the stars before dawn tomorrow. So if you will forgive me I shall now go to bed.'

And at that, Nun decided that he was too tired after all his nights at sea to puzzle any more about his strange passenger, so they went to their separate bedrooms, and Nun, free of all his captain's responsibilities, fell into a deep and dreamless sleep.

Next morning they were travelling along the road that wound through the valleys between Amnisos and Knossos. Nun had been glad enough to accept the hospitality of the guest-house for important travellers the night before, although he had not intended to go on to Knossos with the Chaldean. But in the morning the Cretan officials had politely ushered him towards the gaily decorated chariot that waited by the door. He had begun to argue, the officials had become firmer, and at last he had decided that he might as well go. In fact, he was not sure whether he had any choice – he wished he could feel certain that he was an honoured guest and not a prisoner. He still felt that kings were not his business, but if a king wanted to look at him, it was at least a chance for him to look at a king. And it was a change, he told himself, to see a little of the interior of a country. He spent his time between one seaport and another, and each one was not much different from the next.

The road was full of traffic. There were slow ass-trains bringing panniers of produce from inland; even slower ox-wagons with loads of timber from the port; a column of marching soldiers with narrow-waisted shields; and one or two fast chariots driven in dashing style by athletic army officers who cursed angrily at any slower vehicle that got in their way. Their own chariot proceeded uphill at a moderate pace, and Nun, now a mere passenger, had nothing to do but stand and look around him. He tried sitting on the edge of the chariot but the jolting made it too uncomfortable at the pace they were going. He found it was necessary to brace himself against the swaying of the chariot with his legs, and this was not so different from being at sea; but he also had to keep his knees a little bent to take up the shocks caused by the bumps and potholes in the road. He understood now why chariots did not have seats.

They had just come round a corner on a rather narrow length of road when the driver let out an oath. There appeared to be some kind of procession ahead. Nun could make out a column of soldiers, a group of musicians with drums and flutes and cymbals, and a large vehicle that advanced at a snail's pace, if it moved at all. The driver caught up with it and shouted to the soldiers at the tail end to let them through. Nun could tell by the tone of his voice that he, too, thought that his vehicle was of sufficient importance to be given the right of way. But a sergeant of some sort stepped out of the ranks and shouted back at him, and their driver slowed up his horses and fell in behind the procession, still muttering impatiently under his breath.

'What do you think it is?' Nun asked the Chaldean. 'The train of a prince?' But the Chaldean did not even shrug. This morning he seemed too wrapped up in himself to be interested in his surroundings.

After they had crawled on at this rate for a mile or so, the road widened, and the charioteer pulled out again to overtake. The sergeant cursed him again, the driver swore back, apparently insisting on his urgent business with the palace, and, in spite of the protests of the soldier and two other officials, he whipped up his horses and began to overtake them on the other side of the road. There was barely room for the chariot to get past the big cart which seemed to be the most important thing in the procession, and as they drew up to it Nun was surprised to see that it was no luxurious conveyance for a prince or for the image of a god, but a great wooden cage on wheels, drawn by six slow oxen. And from the cage there glared at them as they passed a great animal with wide curving horns – a bull.

'It seems that in this country the men walk while the bulls ride,' Nun quipped to the Chaldean. But the sage did not even smile.

They got clear of the procession and bowled along at a fair speed, but it was not long before they had to stop again at a military post where a bored-looking officer interrogated the driver and looked suspiciously at the passengers. A heated argument followed, both of them waving and glaring towards the strange figure of the Chaldean, until he put an end to it by calmly reaching into his wallet for the baked brick with the lion and bull image. This he showed to the officer without speaking a word and immediately the officer's expression changed; he saluted respectfully and waved the chariot on. There were two more check-points, and each time the same thing happened and the magical brick had the same effect.

And then, round a bend in the road, they came in sight of Knossos. Set in a hollow in the hills, surrounded by terraces of vines and olive trees, it looked like one vast building of golden stone, rising in square-cut steps of parade-grounds and shaded colonnades. Along the edges of the flat roofs on every building were horns, the curved stone symbols of the city of the Bull. No fortification surrounded Knossos, but when Nun remembered the number of times he had been stopped and questioned since making his landfall in Crete, he realized that no enemy was likely to take the place by surprise.

They drove up to the great entrance gate. Sentries stopped

them. They drove on to a guard-room. The brick seal was produced once again and a respectful chamberlain was summoned to escort them up the ceremonial way to the palace on foot. And it seemed that the whole palace had turned out to greet them!

Down the slope of the ceremonial way streamed a motley crowd; swaggering young noblemen with broad bare shoulders and slim waists, a file of black soldiers advancing at the double, led by a Cretan lieutenant, children of all ages running in circles; but it was the women Nun found himself staring at. He had never seen such elaborate coiffures of curled black hair, such boldly outlined eyes and reddened lips, such frilled and flounced skirts and a lot of unveiled body. He felt his eyes popping, and a feeling of panic as these creatures came towards him — but then he realized that nobody was paying him any attention at all. The whole crowd swept past, with one or two questioning glances perhaps at the bearded Chaldean, the men and women chattering excitedly like birds in high-pitched voices, as they began to congregate in an undisciplined but high-spirited throng round the main gate at the bottom of the slope. Nun and his party turned to see what it was that attracted them. There was a lot of pointing and craning of necks towards the road along which they had arrived. Then a cheer went up and more excited waving, and Nun could see that round the corner of the road had appeared the procession which they had overtaken. It was the bull that the inhabitants of the palace had turned out to greet, not the Chaldean philosopher — and certainly not the obscure Giblite captain. Nun suddenly felt resentful that those girls had not even looked at him.

'Why the excitement over the bull?' Nun asked the chamberlain, without pausing to think that he might not even understand his language. But it seemed that the official had knowledge of the Giblite tongue.

'Ah, yes, the bull,' said the chamberlain. 'They make him welcome. He comes to live in the palace.'

'I see,' said Nun. 'I hope I don't have to share a bed with him!'

'No, no, my friend!' said the chamberlain hastily, but without a smile. He seemed a worried little man, not like the light-hearted crowd of courtiers they had just seen. 'We have rooms for everybody. His Reverence from Chaldea will lodge in the quarters of the priests. The bull will be accommodated with the other bulls. And you, my friend,' he dropped his voice to a rather embarrassed murmur, 'you are I understand His Reverence's – er, valet?' He quickly caught Nun's expression of annoyance at being called the Chaldean's servant and hurriedly went on, 'That is to say – er – secretary? Private secretary?' Nun was amused to see the little man looking at his sunburned features and hardened hands, and trying to make up his mind just what he was doing here.

The Chaldean had overheard and came to his rescue. 'This young Giblite gentleman is here as my friend,' he said with some dignity. 'He is neither a servant nor a scribe.'

The little man looked even more worried. 'Of course, Your Reverence. A thousand apologies! You will understand that the palace is rather crowded at this season. The bulls, you know. And we have strict instructions that everybody must be accommodated according to his category. You will forgive me, but we have no schedule for – er – *friends*.'

The Chaldean gave him a straight look. 'So much the worse for King Minos,' he said, 'if he has no place for friends.' The little chamberlain turned pale, looked hurriedly over each shoulder, and his hair seemed to stand on end at this disrespectful reference to the King. The Chaldean continued, 'Surely you have somewhere you can lodge a young foreign visitor?'

And suddenly the chamberlain's face cleared, and he broke

into a smile. 'But of course!' he beamed. 'Pray excuse my obtuseness! How remiss of me not to understand! Your friend is a Young Foreign Visitor. I shall be delighted to give him accommodation with the other Young Foreign Visitors,' and he bowed and led the way fussily along the echoing stone corridors.

'That's all right, then,' said Nun, and he and the Chaldean exchanged a brief glance of amused incomprehension at the working of the palace official's mind. They went up steps and along more corridors, lit only by tall shafts to a roof far above, and they passed on either hand more gloomy passages leading to cellars and storerooms. Nun began to long already for the open air of his own poop-deck and the wide sea horizon. How he would hate to spend his days in the depths of this vast mass of masonry!

They came out again into the daylight of a little sunken courtyard, and the chamberlain peeped into a little office where some pages were lying around playing dice and said something sharply to one of them. 'The page will conduct you to your quarters, Honourable Young Foreign Visitor from Gebal, while I escort His Reverence to the house of priests. Farewell, and good luck!' But Nun was at a loss to understand the mixture of respect and gloating mockery which seemed to make up his smile.

The Chaldean took him aside by the arm. 'Good-bye, my young friend and benefactor. I trust I may once again call on your help to carry me back to your country. But stay, before we part! I am not happy to leave you alone in this great palace. I have my talisman, as you have seen, the message from my King and the imprint of the lion and the bull. You have no pass, but take this! It may help you if things become difficult.' He pressed into Nun's hand a small, hard object, then they went their separate ways. As he followed the strutting page down yet more gloomy corridors, Nun stole a look at the Chaldean's gift. It was a stone cylinder about the size of his middle finger-joint, but it was too dark to make out the design.

After more flights of steps up and down, and many right-angled turns, they reached another open courtyard which Nun saw at once must be the quarters of the Young Foreign Visitors. Nun was very young for a sea-captain, but the others seemed younger still. Some of them had fair hair and pale skins, some were dark and swarthy, and all of them seemed to hang together in groups according to their various colourings and the languages in which they chatted. Those who were not lying in the sun were engaged in some sort of physical exercise. Some were wrestling, some swinging heavy weights, and some groups were forming human pyramids. But the most common exercise seemed to be some form of hand-stand or hand-spring, and the biggest group of all were taking it in turns to do forward springs over a sort of vaulting-horse. But no, it was not a horse – whoever saw a horse with horns? The block over which these young men were springing was fitted with broad curving horns, just like those of the bull he had seen in the cage.

It was a scene of great activity, yet it seemed to be much less light-hearted than the tumbling Nun used to do as a boy. Nun could swing himself around the rigging of his ship with the best of his seamen, but he did not feel much inclined to join this club of grim-faced gymnasts, merely because the court of King Minos seemed to think it was the right thing for Young Foreign Visitors.

The page showed him to a small room, like a cell, with two hard beds. It was nothing like as comfortable as the guest-house at Amnisos had been, but he supposed he could not be too demanding in a palace. He smiled his thanks to the page and the page grinned back and left him. Nun sat down on the bed and wondered what he was doing there, why he had come, and what to do next. Just then a young man came in, breathing heavily, and sat down on the other bed.

Nun looked curiously at his room-mate. His hair was pale yellow and very straight, his eyes pale blue, and his skin seemed to vary from white to brick-red, according to how much the sun had got at it. Nun had never been so close to a man of this colouring before; he realized he was sitting and gaping at the stranger stupidly, yet no words came to him. What sort of language would such a strange creature speak, anyway? The stranger looked at Nun with rather blank blue eyes, then spoke in the Cretan tongue with an appalling accent.

'Too much bull in Crete!'

Nun's knowledge of Cretan was not extensive either, but he felt he should try to make conversation.

'Too much bull?' he repeated rather foolishly. The words did not seem to have much meaning.

'Bull talk,' said the fair young man. 'Bull pictures, bull games, bull dancing. Lot of bull.' He flopped heavily on the bed.

'And the bull monster?' queried Nun, trying to keep up the conversation.

'No bull monster,' said the other. 'Bull stories.'

'What about the women?' suggested Nun.

The other shut his eyes, was briefly silent, and then said: 'Cows.'

Conversation was clearly going to be difficult with this laconic stranger. There was a long silence. Nun was surprised when the other broke it.

'Where you come from?' He still had his eyes shut as he spoke.

'Gebal,' said Nun. The other made no remark at all – presumably the name meant nothing to him. Nun felt he ought to ask, 'And you? Where are you from?'

The young man opened an ice-blue eye at the last rays of the westering sun shining on the courtyard outside, then pointed a long stringy arm towards the North. 'Far,' he said. 'Very far. You don't know.' There was another silence, and then he said, in a distant voice, as if not interested in the answer, 'You have snow in Gebal?'

This was actually a difficult question to put and to understand, because in the language they were speaking 'snow' was an uncommon word.

'Snow,' Nun repeated. 'Why, yes. We have snow in Gebal. We have the sea, we have the mountains, and we have snow on top of the mountains.'

The young man sat up and his eyes seemed to come to life. 'We, too, have sea, mountains, and snow,' he said. 'But do you have this?' He pulled from round his neck a string of translucent golden stones. 'Elektron,' he said, holding the amber out to Nun.

Nun took the strange gems. They seemed to hold the light and warmth of the sun, and they clicked with the gentle sound of wood or bone.

'In my land,' said the stranger, 'much snow, much cold, much dark. But this sun-stone we find by the sea, bring to King Minos. Look!' He rubbed the biggest stone on his woollen sleeve, pulled a twist of wool from the blanket, and held the stone over it. The wool jumped and clung to the stone.

What strange northern magic is this, Nun wondered, but the other made nothing of it, and hearing a movement of feet in the courtyard, stood up.

'Come!' he said. 'We eat!'

Groups of young men seemed to be making for a big hall on the other side of the courtyard. Nun and the Northerner followed. They were all taking seats on long benches at big tables. There was a babble of different tongues. 'Meet my friends!' said the Northerner, and Nun was glad to be introduced to a group.

Not that he felt he had much in common with them. Their very names seemed impossible to catch. His room-mate introduced himself as something like Ag, and the others Nun decided to think of as Eg, Ig, Og, Ug, and so on. They were all much taller than Nun, each one had fair or reddish hair, one had a flaming red beard, all of them had great beefy limbs and massive hands. And Nun wondered that they seemed older than all the other Foreign Visitors, as well as much bigger.

They also seemed unconcerned, while the behaviour of the other groups showed tension or bravado. The red-beard waved a meat-bone at him. 'Come, eat!' he called in bad Cretan. 'We sailors, we like to eat.'

'I, too, am a sailor,' said Nun.

'And he comes from a land of mountains and snow,' said Ag.

'Good! Good!' came a chorus through mouthfuls of food, and Nun shook hands all round with large greasy fists, then sat down and joined them.

The food was good: fancy dishes of fish and meat and vegetables, spiced and sauced, wine, fruits in abundance, all served on the finest painted pottery. 'Bull pottery too,' Nun remarked to himself, noticing that pictures of bulls being hunted, captured, netted, or wrestled with, seemed the favourite decoration.

He had not nearly satisfied his appetite when he heard above the chatter the voice of a page who had just come in, calling something which he at last distinguished as 'Nun the Giblite! Nun the Giblite!'

'Who wants Nun the Giblite?' he called back, raising his voice in nautical fashion. There was a hush, and eyes were turned on him as the page approached. It was the same page who had rather contemptuously delivered him to his cell, but now his bearing seemed very much more respectful.

The page bowed. 'Nun the Giblite is requested to accompany me to the Chief Chamberlain's office.' The other diners exchanged glances and murmurs, clicking their tongues and sniggering.

The young man with the fair hair opened his eyes wide. 'My friend, what have you done?' he asked.

Nun, who had been sitting unnoticed and ignored by most of the gathering, now got up with the eyes of the whole room on him. He bowed, smiled briefly, and walked out with the page.

The page took him along corridors to the chamberlain's office, where another chamberlain, wearing the usual worried expression of the palace officials, took charge of him and led him at an even faster pace through more corridors and up more steps murmuring apologetically as they went. 'An error of the administration – regret the temporary inconvenience – see to your proper accommodation myself – immediate audience with His Majesty . . .'

'Audience with his Majesty!' exclaimed Nun, almost as out of breath as the flustered official. 'But I don't want to see the King.'

'Understand your feelings –' babbled the chamberlain. 'Such short notice – our fault entirely! But you will find His Majesty so condescending, so gracious – especially to his friends – no need for anxiety.'

So His Majesty does have friends, thought Nun. But puzzled as he was to know how he had reached this dizzy promotion, he kept the remark to himself.

The halls and passages through which they were passing were becoming richer and more luxurious. There were paintings on every wall – sea-creatures, birds and beasts and flowers, processions of libation-bearers and throngs of gay ladies. And in the ante-rooms they encountered the courtiers themselves, supercilious young noblemen and bright-eyed, fashionably dressed women who stared at Nun as he was hurried through, and whispered and giggled behind his back as soon as he had passed. At last they came to a living barrier of palace guards with figure-of-eight shields. There was a group of courtiers laughing and chatting to the aristocratic young officer in charge, apparently trying to cajole him into letting them through. The officer was chaffing them in return, but still apparently being quite firm and admitting no more. The Chamberlain led Nun up to him and said in an agitated voice, 'Get your soldiers out of the way, please. We're late as it is.'

'Throne room's full, old man,' said the officer haughtily. 'Orders to let no more in.'

The chamberlain actually began to wring his hands in frustration as if he was trying to twist his fingers off.

'But I have special instruction to bring Nun the Giblite in time for the audience,' he moaned.

'What, this?' sneered the officer, looking Nun up and down. 'He's not even dressed!'

Nun felt he could say a number of things. That he had not asked to come to the palace; that, having come, he had no desire for an audience with the King; and that, anyhow, he was wearing more clothes than the young officer, whose summer uniform seemed to consist of an inflated chest and a narrow kilt. But he was not going to be made a fool of after coming all this way. Without a word he felt in his wallet for the seal the Chaldean had given him. In the light he could see the device of the lion attacking the bull. He held it out between finger and thumb before the nose of the officer. At first he thought that it had not had any effect – he had no idea why it *should* – then he realized that the barrier of guards had melted away in front of him, and with the chamberlain clucking in the rear he walked into the throne room.

Well, this was odd! Nun had never met a king before, but he had heard tales of the grandeur of Pharaoh and the Lord of Babylon, and even King Abishram of Gebal kept a remote and mysterious state. Nun had nerved himself for magnificence: he had been telling himself that he was a man and a seaman and would not be impressed by all the pomp and ceremony of royal courts. But what he saw before him was disconcerting in an unexpected way.

The room was a rather low-ceilinged chamber of moderate proportions. The walls were gaily painted with a design of lilies on a background of clouds, with some imposing but friendly gryphons lying among them. About a score of men, mostly middle-aged or elderly, all dressed in fine linen and exquisite jewellery, were standing in groups or sitting on the upholstered bench that ran round the edge of the room, conversing in soft high-pitched voices. One of the larger groups was centred round the Chaldean: the councillors were obviously trying to put him at his ease with the utmost politeness.

Nun, prepared to be defiant and independent, suddenly felt rude and awkward in this elegant assembly. He moved towards the only face he knew, the Chaldean, who bowed and smiled gravely; and one of the group came forward to welcome him, addressing him in his own language.

'Envoy from Gebal, welcome! They tell me a stupid mistake has been made about your accommodation. They shall, of course, be punished. I beg you to forgive us – most embarrassing! And how is your dear King – er, Abishram?'

Nun felt as a sea-captain does when a sudden squall takes him unawares. He should have had a polite diplomatic message from King Abishram ready – but he was saved from saying anything by the hush that fell over the gathering.

Those that were sitting rose to their feet and those who were standing moved with dignified ease into a circle facing a second entrance to the throne room; and in came King Minos. The circle of councillors bowed deferentially, the King greeted one or two of them cheerfully by name, made his way to a little low throne at the top of the room, and sat down. Then he gave a sign, and everyone else sat down on the surrounding bench, except for one white-haired man, who seemed to be the senior councillor, who addressed the King: 'Your Majesty, the envoy from Chaldea craves audience and speech, on a matter which he claims is of the gravest import to the kingdom.'

'Let him approach,' said the King.

The Chaldean rose to his feet, stepped towards the throne, bowed deeply three times, and waited for the King to speak.

'I trust you had a pleasant journey,' said the King urbanely.

'Most High Majesty,' said the Chaldean. 'The stars spoke to me of Your Majesty in far Chaldea. At their bidding for many days I journeyed across the desert, scarce stopping to rest the camels at night. Rivers I have crossed and mountains, and in two days I crossed the sea from Gebal —'

'*How* many days?' put in the King.

'Your Majesty is most kind to be interested in our journey. Two days we sailed from Gebal, voyaging without ceasing to carry our tidings to the Great King of Knossos.'

'You mean you didn't stop at night?' asked the King.

'There was no need, Most High Majesty. The stars led the way in the night-time.'

'*Most* interesting,' said the King. Then, turning to the councillors, 'Is the Sea Lord here?'

A red-faced man rose and bowed. 'Your Majesty?'

'Two days from Gebal to Crete,' said the King.

'Astonishing!' said the Sea Lord sceptically.

'Find out how it's done,' said the King, curtly. 'I believe the sea-captain is here.'

All eyes turned to Nun, who stood up, bowed, and did not know what to do next. The Sea Lord spoke.

'Er – His Majesty expresses interest to hear that Giblite ships are sailed at night. Is this true?'

Doing his best to give the impression that he was the representative of a powerful naval force in possession of navigational secrets unknown to the rest of the world, Nun said, 'Yes.'

The Sea Lord seemed to be casting about in his mind for technical questions to ask, but the King intervened smoothly: 'I am sure the Sea Lord would be delighted to ask you down to Mallia to talk about navigation. The rest of us are but landlubbers.' The Sea Lord bowed and sat down with relief, and so did Nun. The King then addressed the Chaldean.

'You spoke of matters of grave import to the realm, Chaldean. If they are merely mathematics, you must excuse me. I have a bad head for figures, but I am sure my councillors would be deeply interested.'

The face of the Chaldean became even graver. 'Your Most High Majesty,' he said, 'is pleased to be modest about his understanding of the mystery of mathematics, but he will know that we servants of the heavenly bodies, we astronomers, must speak of divers things. As astronomers we may speak of astro-navigation: as astrologers we may have to foretell the disasters of nations. In Chaldea I and my fellow magi read strange signs in the House of the Bull. These signs led me westward to the isle of Thira. There the signs and portents spoke more strongly, and as a man, I weep for it. I learned in Thira what I sought to learn; I confirmed it in the stars over Crete. For myself, all I need do is return to my country. But what I have learnt concerns Your Majesty, your country, and your people, and the peoples who dwell on the edges of the sea. If Your Majesty wishes to know, bid your servant speak: but do not blame your servant if the tidings are too heavy to be borne.'

Once again something inside Nun's breast chilled and turned over, as he wondered what the Chaldean had learnt. But as he looked round the room he was amazed to see that the councillors, instead of looking grave, were exchanging little smiles as if they had heard a good performance by a singer and were expecting more. There was even a gentle murmur of applause, and he heard the fastidiously dressed gentleman sitting next to him say in a low voice to his neighbour: 'Always good value, these Eastern sages.'

The King's face was expressionless as he answered the Chaldean. 'Tell us. It is most kind of you to think of the future of our country.'

The sage stood like a rock, fixed his eyes on the King, and spoke on. 'O Great King, I have seen the peoples who live on the shores of the sea. I have seen towns and ports and palaces on mainland and island, but nowhere have I seen such flourishing commerce, such royal magnificence as on this your island of Crete.'

'It is kind of you to say so,' said the King. 'But this anyone can see. Tell me what you *fore*see!'

'I am not accustomed to doubt, O King,' continued the sage. 'But the stars bid me tell things that I do not wish to believe, and still hesitate to speak of. Is not the Bull the sign of your royal house?'

'That is well known,' said the King.

'And is not the Earth-Mother the object of your worship?'

'Of course, who else?'

'These then are the signs. I see the House of the Bull standing in all its magnificence and glory. Then, lo, I see a portent emerging from the body of the Earth-Mother. I see a blinding light flashing from the dark of the underworld, then darkness that covers the face of the sun at noonday. I see a stirring of the body of Earth so that all things standing on it crumble and fall, from the lowliest hut of the peasant to the loftiest palaces of kings. I see much trepidation upon the waters that the sea shall raise itself like the hills and invade the land: all that dwell by the shore shall be swept into the sea and only the high mountains shall be spared. Then I see stillness and the dropping of a rain of bitter ashes.'

There was silence, and as the King stared darkly at the Chaldean, the sage gazed steadily back, while the councillors did not know where to look.

'When will this happen?' said the King at last.

'Before the sun leaves the House of the Bull,' was the Chaldean's reply.

The King looked away, and let his gaze travel round the faces of his courtiers before returning to the Chaldean. The King spoke one word.

'Unless?'

The Chaldean, too, paused before he spoke: 'My Lord, I do not understand.'

'Come, come!' said the King, his voice growing petulant. 'You understand as well as I do. This is your trade. There is always an "unless" to these prophecies. Such catastrophes can be bought off with sacrifices, with building of temples, with placating of gods we never heard of before, and with paying large sums to priests. What is it worth to you?'

'I seek no profit, Most High Majesty.'

'Then perhaps you are well enough paid already. Are you not sent from the Eastern Empire to put fear into the hearts of my people so that your King may come with ships and armies and meet no resistance?'

'Indeed, Lord, this is nothing to my King.'

'Nothing! My palace will crumble, you said. Is that nothing?' The King now spoke angrily. 'You see these stones, these beams and pillars! You prophesy that they will fall into dust, and you say it is nothing! Who sent you here?'

'I came of my own accord, Great Majesty. I seek only to learn the truth about the future, and to tell it to those who will listen. I know only that these things will happen, to you and to other peoples who dwell by the sea. Would that they could be prevented! – but the best you can do is to avoid the most terrible consequences –'

'Enough!' cried King Minos of Crete, anger filling his face with blood. He turned to his councillors. 'Remove this mountebank! He amuses me no longer! Colonel of the guards, see to it!'

The Chaldean bowed very gravely and backed towards the door. A councillor rose and signalled to the guards, bowed to the King, and left the room too. Nun realized there was only one thing for him to do, and he rose to his feet also, bowed with no great decorum, and joined the Chaldean. He would rather be with him than alone among that crowd of courtiers, whatever their fate was to be. Then they were being hurried through the antechamber full of staring and tittering courtiers, flanked by soldiers and accompanied by the colonel of the guards.

Only the Chaldean seemed to have kept his composure. 'I am sorry that His Majesty should take offence in this manner, but I have done what I had to do. Sir,' he said to the officer, 'all I now ask is leave for myself and my young friend to depart from this place –'

'Depart!' expostulated the colonel. 'Most unlikely, I assure you. You realize His Majesty received you as a guest and an ambassador. You put on an exhibition of what I can only call extremely bad taste, and you think His Majesty will let you depart! I can tell you, my only doubt is to what category of custody I am supposed to consign you!'

'Must be difficult for you, sir,' Nun could not help saying, though he was feeling sick and indignant inside. 'Why not just call us former friends of the King?'

The colonel halted in the middle of the corridor and eyed Nun stonily. 'And what am I to do with *you*, young man? His Majesty gave me no instructions about you. Where are you accommodated?'

'With the Young Foreign Visitors,' said Nun. 'But the chamberlain said it was a mistake.'

The colonel looked him up and down. 'I think His Majesty will wish to perpetuate the mistake,' he snapped. 'You'll see your young friend in the arena, Chaldean. With the bull!'

And they were marched off down separate corridors into the depths of the palace.

6

The Return of Zayin

Zayin the soldier in the camp of the Scythians –
The secrets of horsemanship – Information of impending
attack by the Mitannians

Zayin looked down at the figures milling around on the valley floor, and up at the figures outlined like a frieze against the sky. The sun was climbing towards its noonday height, and his head swam from the heat among the rocks. All he could think was that he had found his fabulous centaurs, the man-horses. Or rather, they had found him, for as he watched he could see signals being exchanged between those above and those below. Then a flight of arrows shattered themselves among the rocks where he and the sergeant were hiding.

'You see, sir! They can shoot, too, these monsters,' gasped the sergeant as they ducked for cover again.

But Zayin's eyes, in the shade of a rock, were now more clearly focused on the figures in the valley. He felt his voice must show his disappointment as he replied: 'Not monsters, Sergeant. Just as I said. Horse-men, not man-horses.' For he had seen far below, a party of ordinary two-legged men detach themselves from their four-legged mounts and approach the base of the cliff.

'We might as well go down and meet them, Sergeant,' he said, standing up and raising his hands in surrender. 'We're caught – but at least they're human.'

The figures below shouted something in a tongue unknown to him and gestured to them to go down. As he neared them, Zayin could see that they were not very skilful mountaineers. They seemed to wear tubes of cloth on their legs, there was a lot of fur about their hats and clothes, their hair and moustaches were wild, and their skin rather yellow than brown. They glared at him as he reached them on the slope, took away his sword, and gestured to him to keep moving downwards. He descended with care, not wanting to arrive at the bottom again in a shower of stones.

Even when he reached the valley floor and approached his mounted captors, he still felt an absurd disappointment that his monsters were not monsters after all. Yet these men who seemed to be more at home on the back of a horse than on the ground were almost as strange. The cart had come before the horse in Zayin's experience. He was used to the idea of yoking an animal, ox or ass, to a heavy vehicle. And peasants sometimes even sat on overloaded asses. But these shaggy men sat on these fierce restless animals with nothing but a sheepskin rug between them, and a simple rein and bit to control them. The oxdrover or the peasant had a goad or stick to make the beast move: these riders seemed to have the greatest difficulty in making their mounts stand still. They tossed and chafed, stamped and scraped with their hooves, backed, sidled, and pranced without ceasing while the riders spoke to them with what sounded like low-pitched oaths.

The leader of the horsemen, or so he seemed from the size and fierceness of his moustache and his horse, had been glaring at Zayin with piercing black eyes, and now hurled towards him a string of words that meant nothing. Zayin stood erect and stared back. There was a short conversation between the leader and other warriors, then those that were on foot remounted the horses which the others had been holding for them. And from the rear of the group a mounted man led a spare horse towards Zayin and made emphatic gestures at him. They could only mean one thing. He was to get up on it.

Well, if it was a thing a soldier could do, he would do it. At close quarters the brute seemed a lot bigger. Its back was higher than his shoulder. Zayin looked for a handhold: there seemed to be plenty of hair at the base of its neck, and he had seen the other men grasp this and vault on to their mounts. He made a spring, but the horse shied sideways and he lost his grasp and fell forwards on the ground. A roar of laughter went up from the rough warriors. Zayin felt his face turning red, but he picked himself up and approached the horse once more, determined at least to get on top of it. He grasped the mane again with his left hand, and with his other hand the strap which went round the animal's back and belly, and heaved himself up and forward, kicking with his legs. But the animal kicked with its legs too, its hind-quarters went up, and he felt himself sliding head-first over its back and on to the ground again the other side.

The peak of laughter from the audience was even more delighted this time, but it only made Zayin the more determined to succeed. There seemed to be more to getting on a horse than appeared at first sight, but a soldier and a general was not to be discouraged by difficulties.

He walked up to the horse again and spoke to it, more to give himself confidence than in the hope that the animal would understand. Indeed, he felt a little foolish addressing a dumb beast, but was comforted by the thought that the men could understand just as little.

'Listen, beast!' said Zayin firmly. 'I am Zayin of Gebal, soldier and leader of soldiers. Mountains have I scaled, deserts and rivers have I crossed, foes I have overcome in battle. Do you think that you, a mere horse, can thwart me?'

The horse rolled its eyes. Zayin crouched, took a run, leapt and twisted, and for a minute felt himself on the horse's back with a leg each side. The next instant Zayin saw the horse's head and neck rearing up in the air like the prow of a ship in a great storm, and he found himself sliding backwards down over its tail and he landed heavily on the ground again.

This time he was quite severely shaken, and the horsemen, weak with laughter, were themselves nearly falling from their mounts.

Zayin paused to get his breath back. The horse calmed down a little and began casually to eat grass, while Zayin looked at it with respect. He stood up and approached it, remembering all of a sudden pigeons which his little sister kept, and how she fed them with corn. Feeling in the bag at his belt, he found a forgotten crust of bread.

'Oh, horse,' said Zayin in a respectful tone. 'You have humbled Zayin the warrior three times in three different ways. I see that you are a beast of great agility and cunning. But Zayin comes in peace. Will you accept peace from me?' He held out the crust of bread, the horse took it and munched, standing quite still while Zayin sprang gently from the ground and twisted himself on to its back. He was up! He was a centaur. Four horse-legs connected him with the ground, which seemed a long way down now, while he surveyed the countryside from a commanding height.

The other horsemen burst into cheers of applause, and Zayin looking round saw that the wounded sergeant had been helped on to another pack horse. Then they were moving.

It was surprisingly comfortable at first, moving at a walk over the soft turf. But then something happened and he felt himself being shaken up and down like a rattle. He was jolted forward, jolted backwards, jolted to this side and that. One thought stuck in his mind – only a barbarian would ever think of travelling on top of a horse! But then again the pace changed, as the cavalcade broke from a trot to a canter. Now there seemed to be no reason why he should stay with the horse at all. He clung desperately to its mane as it sprung along, leaving the ground at each stride. But when he looked round at the other riders he saw that they were sitting comfortably and easily, their bodies swaying with the movement of the horses. They seemed to be a part of their horses, rather than passengers sitting on them. They might be detachable, these Horse-Men, but when they were together they nevertheless became another species – Men-Horses. But it did not seem to Zayin at that moment that he himself would ever become one.

As their ride went on and on Zayin became less and less sure that the men part of this partnership *were* ordinary men like him. To watch them was a pleasure: to imitate them was torture. This was a thing that he did not so much think with his head, as feel with the whole of his body. His back was wrenched with the unaccustomed movement, his legs ached with gripping the horse's sides and his arms ached with clutching the mane; and no longer was there any comfort in sitting. His thoughts were jolted and jumbled, and he was hardly capable of wondering where he was going or what was going to happen to him. When some of the party set up wild yells and went galloping ahead of the rest, crouched over their horses' necks, he only hoped that he was not expected to do the same himself.

Then he saw ahead of them, at the mouth of the valley, some kind of camp or settlement. He could make out huts, the smoke of cooking-fires, many horses hobbled or tethered, men, dogs, and even, as they drew nearer, women and children.

The whole party galloped up to the camp with a flourish, coming to a halt by a group of huts. The other riders leapt from their horses and Zayin did his best to look as if he, too, were not merely falling off. Only then, as the strange tribe gathered round, old men, young men, women, children, and dogs, did it come home to him that he was a helpless captive among an outlandish people, with whom he did not even have a word in common. He felt very weary, hungry, and defeated, but he tried to put on a bold front.

'I am Zayin, commander of the army of Gebal,' he said. 'I demand to see your ruler.' But his words meant nothing to them. They just stared and laughed a little. The leader of his captors came up to him and felt his muscles approvingly. Either they're going to eat me or make me their slave, thought Zayin. Yet he hardly cared which.

There was a big cooking-pot bubbling over a fire of branches near his captor's hut, but it seemed that Zayin was to feed out of it rather than be put into it. For after the leader and the warriors had been fed, followed by the women and children, and the dogs had been given the bones, Zayin was allowed to scrape it out. There was quite a lot of stew in the bottom, and it tasted good to the hungry Zayin. He wondered whether these people ate horses too.

When he had eaten the women made signs to him that he was to scour the pot out. For a moment Zayin boiled with indignation. He had never washed a pot in his life. That he should finish his quest for monsters by working as a scullion in a camp of barbarians! It was all so casual. He felt he could have stood imprisonment, chains, even torture – these were the common fortunes of war and defeat. Great kings made captive generals wait on them at table at their ceremonial banquets, loaded with golden chains. But there was no ceremony here: these barbarians, once they were off their horses, were a squat and squalid lot of bandy-legged little men. Their homes were made of skins and canvas on poles, and the only things fine about them were the carpets they sat on. And they did not even pay him the compliment of putting him in chains: they just let him sit around the camp with the stray dogs. What was to stop him running away? He was sure he could outrun any of these short-legged savages. But then he looked at the dogs: *any* fugitive would soon be pulled down by them, and every tent seemed to have a horse hitched to it. The camp was in the middle of the plain at the mouth of the valley. If he ran, there would always be someone to leap on a horse and hunt him down. The only thing that was swifter than one of these horses was another horse. Zayin wished he knew the secret of riding them.

In the days that followed Zayin learnt to make himself useful around the camp. He carried fuel for the fires, was taught by the women how to scour out a pot properly with water and ashes and hay, chopped meat for the stews, and churned butter in a leather bag. But life was simple and there was not much domestic work to do, so that more and more he was allowed to give a hand with the real business of the tribe – the care and training of the horses.

He began by cutting and carrying green fodder for the tethered horses. These animals, trained and accustomed to being ridden, were hobbled and allowed to graze for themselves. But sometimes the men rode out into the valley, unarmed and carrying ropes with nooses. They went among the grazing herds, singled out the nearly full-grown foals and brought them back, wild-eyed, shying, and bucking, in tow on the ends of their ropes. They were tethered among some older, quieter horses and fed by hand. This became Zayin's job. Skilful horse-breakers began training them, making them circle at the end of a rope, accustoming them to being handled and mounted, teaching them the meaning of the controls of rein and bronze bit. Zayin watched every stage of the training with fascination. The hardest lesson, it seemed, for these wild horses, was learning when to stop. It was in their nature to fix their eyes on the horizon and gallop for it; they needed little urging to go forward. But how, Zayin wondered, could a man, mounted on a horse's back, bring it to a halt? He had been on his brother's ship, and to stop it drifting with wind and tide they had thrown out a stone anchor on a rope – but there was no anchor you could use on a horse. There had to be an understanding between horse and rider about starting and stopping, and some horses never seemed to learn.

There was one horse in particular which Zayin began to notice. It came in with a lot of young horses from the valley, but it seemed to be bigger and older than the others. Perhaps it was one that had been missed at the time when it was young enough to train. While the other youngsters were shy and suspicious of everything – of the rope with which they were led, the halter and the tether, even the bundles of fodder Zayin offered them, which they would sniff at for a long time before touching – this one seemed remarkably quiet during its first introduction to the camp. It stood quietly, fed well, and even circled obediently at the end of a long rein. Then the day came for a horse-breaker to mount it.

It was the turn of a young boy, and it seemed that the older trainers looked at each other and winked and smiled as he approached the horse. But there was no bucking and plunging as the lad got up on its back, and sat there, cocksure and proud, with another man still holding the horse's head. The man let go, giving the horse's rump a smack with his hand as it passed. The horse threw its head up and forwards, seemed to bunch its muscles, and shot out of the camp like an arrow from a bow. The boy tugged at the reins, but nothing that he could do seemed to make any difference; and as they receded rapidly into the distance the other trainers slapped each other's shoulders and supported each other as they staggered around, weak with laughter at their successful horse-play. This was early in the morning: it was nearly dark when the lad arrived back in the camp, furious and scowling, on foot and without the horse.

As the days passed, Zayin was allowed to mount and ride one or other of the older work-horses when the foraging parties went out farther from the camp. The tribesmen were

not at all fond of such work as cutting grass and were glad to
have their slave do it for them: but, on the other hand, they
did not like to see a grown man walking on his feet, even if
he were a slave. The great moment came when Zayin was
given a pair of old trousers so that he could sit a horse in
comfort. He felt ridiculous on the ground with his twin stalks
under him, but once mounted it made all the difference. He
learned to handle the reins, and his muscles became accustomed to the various paces of the horse so that it was no
longer agony to keep up with the working-parties.

One day he was washing a horse on the outskirts of the
camp. Horses did not often get washed, and men never, but
this was a white horse – though with the summer dust you
might well call it grey – which belonged to the chieftain. It
had got well caked with mud fording a river. So Zayin had
been given a bucket of water and told to get on with it.

It was a nervous, well-fed animal, but it seemed to enjoy
its ablutions, and Zayin had got used to quietening his charges
by talking to them. It also gave him an opportunity to speak
his own language, which he was afraid of forgetting, after
they had sent his fellow-prisoner, the sergeant, to another
camp. He had come to realize that though a horse might
really understand two or three words, beyond that it was not
particular about the language in which it was addressed.

'Stand still, then, can't you!' Zayin scolded. 'A nice wash
you're getting, you dumb bottom-half of a centaur, you! All
right, it's those young men galloping round there that's
upsetting you! Easy now, easy!' Not far off a group of young
warriors were galloping around a sack stuffed with straw
and shooting at it with bows and arrows. Two of them,
intent upon the target, nearly collided with each other, but at
the last moment the horses swerved and avoided each other.

'Now there's where man plus horse scores over a mere
centaur. Two pairs of eyes are better than one, and horse-
sense is useful as far as it goes.'

The warriors were now attacking the leather bag with lances, riding full tilt and crouching in their saddles. 'What can a mere footslogger do about *that*?' Zayin continued to the horse. He sighed. 'D'you think they'll ever let me become a mounted soldier?'

Then Zayin laughed. 'Get over, you brute!' he said curtly to the animal. 'You don't realize the honour being done to you. You're being washed by General Zayin of Gebal, no less. And General Zayin's wondering if they're going to let him play soldiers. You know what? General Zayin's going to command an *army* of horse soldiers one day. D'you hear that?' And he slapped the animal a little too heartily on the hind-quarters, and it began to dance around the picket to which it was tethered, and Zayin the groom had to speak honeyed words to calm it down again.

The young men finished their military exercise and walked their steeds off to the horse-lines, and Zayin got on with his job in peace. But not for long. Soon the horse began to prick its ears again and snort, and suddenly it gave forth a strident neigh like a war-trumpet.

'What's got into you now?' Zayin wondered, looking around. 'Aha, visitors!' For on the horizon to the East was a cloud of dust advancing towards the camp, and now he could detect the drumming of hoof-beats which the horse had heard before him. As far as Zayin knew there were no parties away from the camp at that time, so they must be strangers. His military instinct told him to give the alarm or call out the guard, but he shrugged and carried on with his work. He was only a groom, after all.

The dust cloud got nearer and the hoof-beats louder, and the barking of watchdogs and neighing of other horses soon roused the camp. When the party galloped up with the usual flourish of whoops and yells, Zayin could see that they were tribesmen similar to his own captors. But the leader, a young man with more than the usual amount of gold ornaments about him, seemed to be a person of some consequence, for the chieftain of the camp himself was hurriedly called from his tent to meet him. The young man flung himself from his horse and the two chiefs embraced each other with extravagant gestures. A carpet was brought out and laid before the tent, women were sent for food and drink, and the two men and their companions settled down for what looked like a formal conference.

'This might be interesting,' murmured Zayin to the horse, and proceeded to lead it back to the chieftain's tent, without, however, showing any outward interest in what was happening. He busied himself with tethering and settling the horse in its usual place by the tent, but kept his ears open for any words he could pick up. His knowledge of the tribal language was still very slight, but it was more than the tribesmen thought.

The conversation consisted for some time of formal greetings. Then Zayin could detect a change of tone as they got down to business.

'A hundred horses for Nineveh!' That phrase came over clearly enough. Zayin had gathered already that much of the wealth of the tribe came from supplying schooled horses to the capital of the East. But a hundred at a time was a big order from such a small tribe. Even the chieftain showed his astonishment. There followed an impassioned speech from the young man, of which Zayin understood nothing except some threatening gestures and a lot of pointing, directed towards the West. And then he was sure that he heard the words 'Ugarit' and 'Gebal'. Gebal! What could these wild men know of his home city? What business could they have with the coast there, and with Ugarit, the next city to the North. Why were they recruiting horses by the hundred? Whatever was afoot, it boded no good for Zayin's people. It could only mean invasion, perhaps a great movement of armies westwards to the sea. At last, Zayin thought, he had come across the military information which the King had sent him to find – but what use could he make of it, a captive and a slave?

He heard then the chieftain of the tribe speak the words 'Man of Gebal', and saw that he was pointing Zayin out to the guest. The other said something. 'He does not understand our language,' the chieftain answered. So Zayin continued to polish the bit of the bridle he was holding, and pretended not to have noticed anything. But it confirmed that he was not mistaken: it was certainly Gebal that the warriors were talking about.

The conference on the carpet seemed to come to a climax when the young envoy reached into a leather wallet he carried at his waist and took out a small, square clay brick, which he handed with a flourish to the older man. Then there was a great deal of laughter as it was handed from one to another of the shaggy men sitting there: it was obvious that it was a written message of some sort that of course not one of them could read. The last man to be handed it showed the general contempt which they felt for it by tossing it over his shoulder into the dust.

Later that evening Zayin, doing his rounds with a crude wooden bucket and shovel to clear up after the horses, picked up the brick. He looked at the neat rows of characters impressed into the clay, each one like an arrangement of little nails, sharp at one end and with a head at the other. It meant nothing to him either, yet something made him put it into his pouch.

The days after that were full of activity. Horses were being judged and selected for the draft to Nineveh, the schooling of the half-trained horses was intensified, and more and more were brought in from the plain to replace them. Now

Zayin's mind was filled with one thing only: the possibility of escape. But his chances seemed no better than before. He had to work harder, the camp was in a wakeful bustle all day and most of the night, and even the watchdogs seemed to be more alert.

Then one day the big bay horse that had run away with the boy came back. A rounding-up party had gone out as usual, and returned with the bay trotting tamely on the end of a rope. It was clear enough to Zayin that the drift of the ensuing argument was: 'Why bring that animal back to camp again? We can't do anything with it, anyhow.'

Then Zayin noticed that among the rounding-up party was the lad on whom the trick had been played, and he guessed that he wanted to have a second chance at breaking-in the animal.

That evening as Zayin was carrying fodder to the tethered animals, the young horse-breaker came up to him and said something abrupt to him.

'I don't understand a word, my boy,' said Zayin in his own language. 'All I know is that it's my job to feed these horses.' He threw down a measure of fodder in front of the bay, but the young man again spoke sharply to him, and gestured as if he was to take the fodder away again. Zayin looked at him. 'I see, my young cock,' he said slowly. 'You can't ride this beast when it's well fed, so you want me to starve it for you.' And he laughed mockingly.

The young man struck Zayin across the face with his whip, kicked the pile of fodder away from the horse, and stormed off. Zayin stood there, clenching his fists. He longed to fall upon the young man and beat him into the dust, even if it were the last thing he did. But at that moment a very different idea flashed across his mind. He stood for a long time while plans formed in his head.

After dark he saw to it that the bay was well fed and

watered, and he spoke to it quietly: 'We captives must help each other, eh?' That night he went to sleep on his pile of old sheepskins in the rough shelter where the fodder was stacked, but by his side was a leather bag full of cheese, dried meat, and odd scraps of food he had been able to steal from the women's quarters.

He woke at dawn and lay there awhile, thinking over his plan. It all seemed so simple, even too simple. What was there to prevent his riding away before the camp was roused? But there would be no savour in that.

He deliberately carried out his duties as usual – or rather he made it look as if he were doing so. He went among the horses apparently checking their tethers; but in fact he was loosening picket-pegs and easing knots so that the slightest pull would free them. He collected together all the bridles and reins he could find and hung them along a line ready for use; but he took care that they were all cunningly threaded, one through the other. He was even able to cut half-way through the bowstrings of some bows that were hung outside ready for use. Then, going from horse to horse of those that were hitched outside the tents, ready to be mounted at a night alarm, he made sure that each one was unobtrusively attached to a cooking-pot or sleeping mat, or even to one of the now friendly watchdogs. The only horse that remained properly bridled and ready to mount was the big bay. The men of the camp watched him approvingly as he went busily about his jobs.

He waited until the men started coming from their tents, and the horse-breakers were making their way to the horse-lines. Then he untethered the big bay and led it into the middle of the exercise ground. The men seemed surprised and they looked at each other and asked who was foolish enough to want to waste time with this bolter. The young man was crosser than ever: he was not ready to make a fool of himself yet again. But Zayin smiled cheerfully at them and said politely and clearly, using the few words he knew in their tongue:

'Me – ride – this horse.'

And pausing just long enough to see understanding dawning on their faces, followed by various expressions of astonishment and fury, he leapt on to the back of the bay.

The horse threw its head up, bunched all its muscles, and bolted. It was the one thing it had learnt to do with a man on its back. Zayin made no attempt to stop it. He concentrated on staying on, yet he could not resist turning his head to see what was happening in the camp. As he had intended confusion at once broke loose. Men rushed for the horses tethered by the tents, mounted and discovered too late that they were galloping off with a cooking-pot behind them, or a sleeping-mat flapping wildly through the air, or an excited dog making rings round the horse on the end of a line. Others rushed for the bridles, and cursed as they fought to unravel one vast irreducible tangle. Bows were snatched up for the bowstrings to snap in the archers' face. Green horses reared in alarm at the horse-lines, pulled up their picket-pegs, or slipped their head-ropes, and milled around adding to the confusion. Zayin was only sorry he could not stay and watch the fun.

He had seen the bay gallop, and he was satisfied that there was no other horse in the camp that could catch it, even without the handicaps he had prepared for them. All he had to do now was to cling on, and use what influence he had to guide the horse's flight in a generally south-westward direction. He found the first to be easier than he expected: the horse seemed to speed smoothly through the air like an arrow, its feet hardly touching the ground. And by pulling on the left rein only and leaning his weight to the left he was able to persuade the bolting animal on to a curving course which led, he hoped, where he wanted to go. As for the horse, it did not seem to care where it went as long as it bolted.

Zayin guessed that it had had more than one experience of running away with a man, who had been only too pleased to let it go, and walk back. What the foolish animal did not realize was that this time it had a passenger who wanted to run away just as much as it did.

Zayin had been prepared for a rough ride, but he was amazed at the comfort of going at a flat gallop. He whooped and sang to himself and to the horse, which pricked up its ears, laid them back again determinedly, and hurtled on over the plain. He looked back and saw figures far behind him in pursuit. He whooped and flourished his whip, but did not need to use it. He looked ahead, saw the dry gully of a stream and had no time to wonder what the horse would do before they were sailing through the air. He lurched as the horse landed, but stayed on and his mount continued at renewed speed. When he had recovered his seat he looked round again. There was no sign of the pursuit. Already they must have called it off. Apart from revenge for the trick played on them, what were they losing after all? A troublesome slave and an uncontrollable horse. He did not think they would go to great lengths to recapture him. He was on his own. Except for the horse.

The next part of his escape Zayin had not been able to plan. Presumably even this animal could not go on for ever, but when it would stop and what it would do then he had no idea. In the meantime he was happy to go on and on, adding up the leagues between himself and the camp. The surprising thing was that the horse was not even showing signs of fatigue. It seemed to have only one pace – flat out. Two paces, perhaps, thought Zayin – flat out and stop. So look out for the stop, he told himself, it might be sudden.

That thought probably saved Zayin. He was determined

not to part company with his mount. He did not waste time
trying to control it, but concentrated on staying on. And so
when the stop did come suddenly, he was prepared for it.
The animal all at once put out its forelegs and slid on its
hocks to a halt. Zayin lurched forward on to its neck, but
clung on. The horse stood there, breathing in great gasps,
turned its head, and looked at him rather foolishly.

'Yes, my friend, I'm still here,' said Zayin.

The horse stood there, gradually getting its breath back,
but not moving a limb for what seemed a long, long time.

'Take your time, boy,' said Zayin, 'I've nothing else to do
either.' He sat there, waiting for the horse's next move, still
prepared for something sudden. He had seen all that horses
could do when they were untrained – buck-jumping and
rearing and twisting. But this horse seemed to have no such
tricks.

And all of a sudden they were off again. From a dead stop
the horse seemed to spring into full gallop, but Zayin kept his
seat and the horse kept the pace at which he had started in
the morning. Zayin had no idea of how long they had been
travelling, but he felt as if they had already covered half the
weary march between Gebal and the Valley of the Horses.
All the same, he doubted if any animal could keep up this
pace all the way to Gebal. For now Zayin was determined to
bring the animal back home – or rather that it should bring
him back. But he was beginning to be afraid that it might run
itself to death before they ever got there.

They were still travelling along flat, level ground, but the
plain seemed to be closing in again to form a river valley, and
there seemed to be mountains ahead. Zayin began to worry
what would happen if they met rough country, rocks and
gorges perhaps. This animal was no sure-footed mountain
goat. And he nearly paid the penalty for not concentrating,
for the horse once again came to a sudden slithering stop.

Zayin lurched forward again, slid over the animal's neck, and this time slipped to the ground. But he landed on his feet and stood there, firmly holding the reins.

'Well,' said Zayin to the horse. 'We have travelled far, you and I, thanks mainly to you! And I am free, but you, I fear, are not. We shall keep together, and we shall go the way *I* wish. Come, let's drink on it!' And he led the horse towards the river, the animal following docilely.

Nearby a shallow stream rippled over a stony bed, surrounded by trees and rocks. They both drank thirstily; then Zayin carefully hobbled the horse, putting a short length of hide rope between its forelegs so that it could take short steps among the rich herbage of the river-bank, but could not run away. Lastly he sat down under an overhanging rock, took some food from his bag, and ate.

By the sun, the time was well on into the afternoon. Although he did not know where he was, he felt he had travelled far enough for that day. He lay on his back and watched the branches against the blue sky. A flock of birds flew overhead, very high. Pigeons! He thought of the birds his little sister fed, and wondered if they flew as far afield as this. Then in the hot afternoon he fell asleep.

When he awoke he took the bow which he had brought with him from the camp, and wandered around the river-banks looking for something to shoot. But there were only some small birds, and he was not going to waste his few arrows on such difficult targets. Instead, he found some wild berries, refreshed himself with them, and took a little more food from his bag as an evening meal. How he envied the horse for being able to find fresh food growing in any place where herbage grew. It was a better soldier than he, living off the land as it did. Then, making himself comfortable under a rock for the night, he shut his eyes and went to sleep again. But in the cold of the night, and without any covering, he did not rest very well.

Next morning he washed and breakfasted and went to catch the horse, which he did without much difficulty. The horse, at least, looked refreshed and full of energy again. Zayin bridled it, took off the hobbles, and stood holding it in doubt. For a moment he wished that he had stolen an animal that was better trained for his journey. Would this mad creature set off at a blind gallop again as soon as he was on its back, and possibly break a limb among the rocks or hurl them both over a chasm? Would it even head back to the open plains from which they had come the day before? Ahead, the valley became narrower, and the way more and more broken. Zayin decided to lead the animal through the valley. A horse with no medium paces was all very well for a dramatic breakaway, but it was not to be trusted over rough country. Yet he wondered if he was not being faint-hearted.

They made some progress in this way during the forenoon, along the banks of the river. As usual, the horse behaved itself perfectly when led, but Zayin felt vexed and frustrated at having to walk. So when they came to a meadow entirely surrounded by steep rocky slopes, with no horizon to run for, he decided that this might be the place for a little schooling. Zayin led the horse to the middle of the grassy space and got on its back. Its head went up, and it looked around, snorting and quivering. Then, seeing no outlet, the bay simply stood still and tried to graze. When Zayin struck it smartly with his whip it started jerking backwards. A simple forward walk or trot was what this horse found impossible. Zayin dismounted, cursing, and once more led the animal on foot.

So for two or three days they travelled along the valley through which the river descended from the high inland plain. Every day Zayin asked himself why he burdened his existence with this animal. All it did was carry his food-bag, and that was nearly empty, though he rationed himself strictly. The horse, of course, gorging itself on lush grass every night, grew fatter. But still, it was some kind of company on the march.

Then on the third day they came to a place where the valley bottom suddenly broadened out again, and when they skirted round a low hill there was nothing but flat land between them and the horizon. A dead straight, deep blue horizon – the sea!

Zayin and the horse both lifted up their heads and sniffed the air – Zayin because he was back on the coast after all these weeks, the horse because it was free of the hemming-in mountains. Zayin suspected that it might never have seen the sea.

Zayin smiled. 'Horse,' he said, 'I shall call you Horizon, because that is what you always aim at. Horizon, here we come!'

He leapt on Horizon's back, the horse threw up his head, looked at the far distance, and bunching his muscles shot off like an arrow from a bow, with Zayin clinging with his legs and waving his arms and hallooing. Down the last grassy foothills of the mountains they galloped, across the coastal flatland, bursting through clumps of reeds and sending flights of duck flapping madly into the air, between dunes of white sand, and on to the firm level beach. And then Horizon, feeling nothing but space around him, put on a burst of even greater speed and headed for the flat calm sea. There was barely a ripple on the surface, and to Horizon it must have seemed merely a vast blue plain with no obstacles to his headlong progress.

The salt water splashed up in showers that drenched them both all over. The horse's movements, for the first time, became hesitant and doubtful, and then they were moving slowly forward, breast-high in the warm water.

'Well, Horizon, my friend,' laughed Zayin. 'What are we stopping for? Are you letting a little water damp your spirits?

There's nothing between us and the Isle of Cyprus, so they say. Except water!'

But the plains-bred horse was baffled and bewildered, and completely out of his element. For the first time ever, he felt that the rider was master of the situation, and obeyed the control of the reins. Zayin turned his head south, for somewhere there lay Gebal, but he kept the horse in the breast-deep water, and Horizon, cured at last of his longing for far distances, proceeded calmly along at a gentle walk. Zayin even found that, between land and water, he could urge his steed to a trot and canter, and ease him back to a walk again. So he kept him at it, and they continued southward at a fair rate of progress, and Horizon's education progressed at the same time.

That afternoon Zayin saw houses ahead on the coast, and he reined the horse to a halt. Where were they? It could not be Gebal yet, and if it was not it must be another of the coastal cities, Ugarit perhaps, where they had no love for the Giblites. Somehow he must get round it. Inland lay mountain country which he did not know, and he could not rely on the horse in the mountains. He would have to try to slip by along the shore. On thing he was sure of, that once Horizon took to his heels no man could catch him and it would have to be a swift arrow that would overtake him.

The town ahead seemed to be of a considerable size, but there was no port and the boats were drawn up on the beach. But as he drew near he saw that he was unlucky, for the shore was crowded with people. What should he do? Turn back? If he left the sea there was no knowing what the horse might do – bolt in the wrong direction perhaps. The animal was getting excited now and less controllable: seeing the crowds perhaps made it think they were a herd of its own kind. Zayin edged it farther into the water and tried to turn back, but it would not turn. It forged ahead, half swimming from time to time. They were getting dangerously near the crowd on the beach, but Zayin could do nothing. He was near enough to see heads turned in his direction. They had been seen, and the horse was still going on. And the deep water was the one place where Horizon's speed could not save them.

Then Zayin saw the crowd stirring as if swept by the wind. All the faces were turned towards him – except for some that were already turned in flight. He heard cries of alarm, and the shrieks of women. Many of the people on the shore were now running headlong towards the town; others, too old or too overcome by the panic, were grovelling in the sand. A white bull, probably a sacrificial animal, had broken loose and was cantering around among the fleeing people. What had caused this rout?

Then it occurred to him to think what he must look like, emerging from the waves like an unknown monster. He was a sea-god, visiting the scene of sacrifice! He waved cheerfully to the few who were left on the beach and had the courage to raise their heads. 'Sorry I can't stop, my pious worshippers!' he called. 'My thanks for the sacrifice!'

So Zayin rode past Ugarit in the sea, and added another legend to its annals.

That evening he frightened a family of fisherfolk from their hut, and helped himself and the horse to bread and corn.

From there onwards, the coast became more rocky, and on the following days he had to take to the land. But every day his confidence as a horseman grew, and every day Horizon became more accustomed to pacing carefully along stony tracks, trotting along level stretches with Zayin on his back, and stopping and turning obediently at dangerous points. The mountains were always on one side and the sea on the other, and Zayin kept the horse's head firmly turned towards the South.

And then one hot afternoon, as Zayin lay resting in a grove near the sea, a flock of pigeons settled around him, and one pure white bird alighted on his knee. Zayin gently took it in his hand. 'I know you, little bird,' he said. 'You come from my sister.' And he took a ring from his little finger and tied it to the bird's leg, and watched it as it took off again and flew away with its companions to the South.

7
The Bull-Dancers of Knossos

Nun, the sailor, on the island of Crete – The bull-ceremony – The Queen from Tyre, and the myth of Europa and the Bull – Information of impending attack on Gebal by the Cretan navy

It was the Day of the Bulls at Knossos. The court and the common people were gathered around the arena, the courtiers appearing indifferent and bored, the people expectantly awaiting the opening procession.

First came the bearers of jars, great coloured vessels of mingled wine and water. This they sprinkled over the dancing floor, the wine to placate the Earth-Goddess, the water to stop the dust flying in the eyes and noses of the spectators.

Then came the soldiers, slim of waist, broad of shoulder, helmeted, and carrying their painted shields of bull's hide, shaped like figures of eight.

Then came pipers and drummers and trumpeters.

Then came the bearers of the golden double-bladed axes, glinting in the sun, not weapons but symbols of ancient power.

Then came the priestesses, gaily skirted, bare-breasted, dancing as they came, making with their arms the sign of the bull's horns, and in their midst the chief priestess, holding in each hand a snake, dweller in the earth, symbol of the Earth – Goddess of fertility.

Then came the young acrobats, the bull-dancers, in their groups, fair-haired, dark-haired, long-nosed, snub-nosed, all young and proud, each one confident of defying death at the horns of the bull.

Among them was Nun. He alone felt apart from the pageantry. What am I doing here, citizen of Gebal, sea-captain, cedar-salesman, he was thinking; what have these fripperies to do with me?

To the music of the pipes and drums the procession wound round the arena. As each section passed the royal box they turned and saluted King Minos and his Queen with upraised arms, sign of the Bull. Then they took their own seats.

Nun found himself beside the tall young man of the North. In the ring was the first team of performers. 'What team is that?' Nun asked his neighbour. 'Where do they come from?'

The other shrugged. 'They say Ateni, Atenai, Athenis – something like that. I never heard of it. Some little town.'

The team marched to the centre of the arena and then took their places in extended formation. They had danced the bull-dance before and their drill was perfect.

A trumpet sounded, a door opened, and a bull ran out into the arena and stood snorting and stamping and glaring around him.

For the first figure of the dance the bull was lured into the centre of the ring of dancers and stood there, uncertain which one to attack. The dancers stood around, calling to the bull in solemn mockery, making the sign of the two uplifted arms or the two uplifted fingers, provoking him, eager for the honour of being the first to be attacked. The bull fixed his eyes on one of them and charged. This was the test – the dancer who provoked the charge had to stand his ground. Then at the last moment the dancer next to him ran across and deflected the charge to himself. Then, when the bull seemed to be gaining on the second dancer, a third would interpose and the bull would follow him. The music still played, and Nun found it difficult to believe that the bull was not deliberately joining in a formal dance, setting to a different partner in turn and threading an intricate measure in and out of the ring of men. But the sweat on the bodies of the men and of the beast was proof of the strain and exertion of what was going on in the ring. The bull had no rest as each of the team led him a dance: he was at full gallop all the time and Nun saw that he must be getting tired. But there were many occasions when his pointed horns missed brown bodies by less than inches, and the dancers' faces sometimes showed how narrow were the escapes. At last the bull came to a stop, the dancers re-formed the ring around him and held his attention until a second team came up behind them and took their places.

'Girls now!' grunted the fair young man, and Nun realized that the next team consisted of maidens, with flowing, bright-coloured scarves over their shoulders. They stood solemnly round the bull and greeted him gracefully. The bull stood a little bewildered, breathing heavily. Tired by the galloping first figure of the dance, he was lured into a formal ballet, a gavotte. He trotted after the whirling scarves appearing docile, but Nun looking intently could see that the sweeps and hooks of his horns were as vicious as ever, and that the serious-faced girls were all the time very carefully watching their distance. As a climax, two girls held out a wreath of flowers between them. The bull charged, and at the end of the charge he was standing rather foolishly, wearing the wreath round his great neck. But Nun's heart missed a beat as he saw that one of his horns had carried away the scarf from one girl's shoulders.

The dancing girls retired, and in the ring with the bull there was now a team of three, two young men and a girl, all of them very slim and wiry and light on their feet. They stood before the bull and provoked him with hand-springs, cart-wheels, and somersaults. The bull, tired by his dances, stood still, baffled by the spinning bodies, but looking as furious and regal as ever. While the bull was watching the girl and one of the men, the other ran to the side, ran lightly towards the bull's flank, sprang, and with his hands on the bull's spine flipped over in a neat hand-spring on to the other side. The animal whipped round indignantly and hooked with his horns, but the acrobat was out of range. The crowd clapped and cheered.

Next, the two men held the bull's attention while the girl ran to the side and performed a hand-spring over the bull's back. Then she executed a whirling one-handed cart-wheel in front of the bull while the two young men approached from opposite sides and flipped over simultaneously.

The crowd cheered, and then was silent, expectant, as if they knew what was coming next. Now all three acrobats stood some distance in front of the bull, one of the men in the middle. The man advanced at an easy run straight towards the horns of the bull. What was this? Everyone had been avoiding the bull's horns – was this one sacrificing himself by throwing himself on them? Nun looked open-mouthed at the fair young man. 'What – ?' he gasped.

The Northman grinned back. 'Man charge bull!' he laughed.

The acrobat seemed to hurl himself on to the lowered horns of the bull. Nun shut his eyes so as not to see the sharp horns goring the man's body. There was a shout from the crowd and enthusiastic applause. Nun forced himself to open his eyes. There was the acrobat, very much alive, on his feet behind the bull and facing away from the bull's tail, while the animal looked even more baffled and enraged. How had he got there? What had happened?

The team of three was again standing in front of the bull.

The girl this time was in the middle and seemed to be preparing to take her turn. She was thin and boyish with hard
muscles, and very much resembled the two young men:
indeed, they might have been sister and brothers. The men
were watching the bull carefully, and by calling and clapping
their hands, were trying to lure him towards them. The
acrobat runs to the bull, or the bull runs to the acrobat, it's
the same thing, Nun reasoned, watching closely. The team
provoked the bull to attack at a gentle canter; Nun's heart
stood still as the girl stood her ground and reached for the
lowered horns; her body arched and her legs went up; the
upward thrust of the bull's powerful neck lifted her into the
air; heels over head she flipped over, came down both feet
together on the bull's back and hopped off behind its tail on
almost exactly the same spot she had taken off. The spectators
applauded – fellow-acrobats warmly, knowing how difficult
the feat was, the court languidly, politely approving the
elegant spectacle.

Nun was almost tempted to think the whole thing was easy,
if a mere girl could do it so gracefully. But the second man's
attempt at the same trick came near to disaster. The bull was
moving at almost a gallop when acrobat and animal met, and
at the last moment it hooked sideways instead of upwards.
The man twisted awkwardly and fell beside the neck of the
bull, who whipped round and made to gore him. Immediately
the other two ran in; the girl slapped the bull's muzzle to
distract it, the brother hung on to its horns until the one who
had fallen was able to spring to his feet. Nun applauded the
courageous rescue, but most of the other teams were silent
and, looking at the court, Nun could see frowns of displeasure
at the clumsy performance. The performer was badly shaken,
but clearly determined to try again to retrieve his reputation.
He ran before the bull, provoked it to a furious charge, and
then started running towards it at full speed. When they met

their combined velocity was so great it was difficult to see what happened; the man gave a great leap right over the bull's lowered horns, landed with his hands on the bull's back, and leap-frogged to the ground behind it. Even the court applauded enthusiastically. The honour of the team was saved, and they and the bull were allowed to retire from the ring.

Nun sat back in his seat and relaxed, with the feeling that the Minoan Bull-dance was a more pleasant spectacle than he had feared. But just then a haughty young Guard ensign came up. 'You next. Northmen and the Giblite!' he said, and Nun's heart plummeted again to his sandals.

Ag sprawled in his seat and looked at the officer. 'You wish we should dance with the bull? We not pretty girls, nor circus men. What we do?'

The officer sneered down at him. 'You don't think the Earth-Mother will be satisfied without some blood, do you? And the court wants to know what colour yours is. Is it white? Are you afraid?'

Ag showed no emotion. 'No, we not afraid of your he-cows. Nor your Godmother neither.' The officer eyed him, wondering whether this was deliberate blasphemy; but deciding the man was a northern barbarian oaf who knew no better he merely snapped: 'In the ring all of you! You too, Giblite! The court didn't think much of your performance last night. Now's your chance to please them – so long as you don't actually run away.'

Nun stood up shakily. If he had to go in the ring with a bull, there was some comfort in being with these huge, red, unconcerned men. But he could not see them skipping lightly aside from a charge, or turning nimble somersaults. They were too ponderous and slow-moving.

'What are we going to do?' he asked Ag as they walked towards the entrance to the ring, trying to make his voice sound unconcerned.

'Not to worry! We have plan. You not run, though. They kill, if you run,' said Ag, indicating the guards. Nun wished he knew what the other rules were, and what the plan was they had prepared. Perhaps they had hidden arms – but at the ringside the guards searched them to make sure they had not. If there was to be blood, the Cretans wanted to make sure it was not the bull's.

The Northmen lumbered casually into the ring, saluted the crowd perfunctorily, and gathered in an untidy group to exchange last-minute instructions. But as it was all in the outlandish murmuring northern tongue it was still no comfort to Nun. As they stood talking, the trumpet sounded, the door opened, and another bull entered the arena. It seemed to be twice as big as the last one, and Nun recognized the great beast they had overtaken in the cage the day before. The Northmen went on talking, until Nun nudged them and pointed out the animal standing switching its tail at the other end of the ring.

'Oh, yes,' grunted Ag. 'Come. Cattle-market begins.' They all moved off at a shambling pace towards the bull, who stood pawing and snorting and shaking his horns at them. The bull lowered his horns and took a few steps forward as if thinking of charging. Still the men took no notice but advanced towards it at a walk. 'Heigha! Gerrup!' called the big red-bearded Ug, flapping a large hand. The bull stopped uncertainly. Ug walked up to it, slapped it playfully on the nose, and it turned tail and ran away from them round the edge of the ring. When the bull stopped on the other side of the ring, the men stopped where they were and shrugged their shoulders. There was a stunned silence at first from the crowd, then catcalls and cries of disapproval. The men ignored them and stood talking as if they were discussing the price of beef, as indeed they may have been.

But Nun saw that a soldier at the ringside was jabbing at

the hind-quarters of the bull with a long lance, trying to stir up its cowed fighting spirit. The bull whirled round, but seeing nobody because the soldier hid behind the parapet, faced the team again, and the soldier gave it another nasty jab that sent it charging angrily towards them.

'Look out!' cried Nun. Must not run, but no harm in getting out of the way. He skipped aside from the path of the charge, but facing the bull all the time, hoping that he looked poised and defiant. The others looked round. They had not bothered to notice the way the soldier had goaded the bull, and this unprovoked charge did not seem to fit in with their plan. They scattered clumsily, and to his horror Nun saw that Ag had stumbled and fallen over his big feet right in the bull's path. The bull was passing Nun and he was the only one who could save Ag. Nun the sailor knew little about animals, but he knew a lifeline when he saw one. He made a desperate grab at the bull's tail as it whisked past, hung on, and dug his heels into the sand of the arena. The braking effect was sufficient to allow Ag to get to his feet and out of the way, but Nun now did not dare let go. There he was, being towed round the arena in a cloud of dust at the tail of the cavorting bull – and he realized that his team-mates were merely standing around cheering encouragement to the bull and holding their sides with laughter.

So long as the bull's horns were pointing away from him Nun felt safe – though far from comfortable. But suddenly the bull came to a halt and started bucking round in a circle, trying to dislodge him with its horns. Nun held on desperately, but a last flying kick made him lose his grip, he was hurled to the ground and the bull was upon him.

But the other men were upon the bull. Four of them tackled the bull at once, grabbing a leg apiece. Ag and Eg each clung on to a horn. Ig got astride the neck. Heads down and arms locked round each other, the rest got their shoulders against the bull's flank and heaved, and the great beast went over like a house falling down. All that could be seen under the mass of brawny bodies was its muzzle and one despairing eye.

There was a great stillness around the arena. Then the royal trumpeter sounded the call for the end of an event. The Northmen got up and dusted themselves down. The bull scrambled to its feet and made sheepishly for the open gate. Never had a Cretan bull been so humiliated.

There was uproar in the stands. As far as Nun could make out, standing in the middle of the arena feeling foolish and exposed, both court and commons were split. Some were delighted by the exhibition of clowning and sympathized with the tall blond strangers: others were howling for blood. Some of the courtiers, the younger, sophisticated set, were pleased with the originality of the performance and were applauding, but the more serious councillors were plainly horrified and angered by this act of sacrilege. People started throwing fruit, and the Northerners good-humouredly fielded it and chucked it back. Nun looked at the section of the stand reserved for the priests: there was no doubt their reaction was one of black fury. Much of the solemnity of the rites had been destroyed. Among the priests Nun could see the Chaldean, sitting silent and impassive. Nun could not tell what he was thinking.

They were hurried out of the arena under guard and the games went on. The prize bull was not reintroduced, and Nun supposed that its nerve had been too shattered by the experience. There were some rather botched performances by second-rate bulls and teams, enough blood was spilt to satisfy the spectators, and presumably the Earth-Goddess, but Nun was too apprehensive about what would happen at the end of the games to take much in.

Sure enough, as soon as the final flourish of trumpets had sounded Nun felt a tap on his shoulder. It was what he had been expecting, but he jumped violently. It was the officer of the guard.

'You're wanted,' said the officer.

'You want us?' asked Ag unconcernedly.

'Not you, cattle-herds,' said the guard contemptuously. 'Just the Giblite.'

'What you want him for?' demanded Ag.

'Maybe they give him prize for pulling bull's tail,' said Ug.

'We come with you,' said Ag protectively.

'No, no,' Nun protested. He didn't want to cause any more trouble. 'I'll be all right. I'll see you later.'

'But maybe we not see you,' said Ag. 'We go back North. Come with us, no?'

But Nun also had business to attend to. So they said affectionate farewells in the palace corridor, in case they never met again, with a special hug for Nun from Ag for saving him from the bull. Then Nun followed the Cretan guard.

'Where am I wanted?' Nun asked as he was again marched along the labyrinth of corridors.

'Royal chambers,' was the curt reply, and the escort would say no more.

As they passed through apartments which, by their magnificence, seemed to be ante-chambers to the royal quarters, they were stopped by another officer of the guard.

'Is that the Giblite you have there?' asked the second officer.

'Yes.'

'I've orders to take him to the Sea Lord.'

'And I've orders to take him to the Queen.'

The Queen! What could she want with him, Nun wondered.

'But I have the Sea Lord's special authority,' said the second guard, and produced a seal ring.

The first guard looked a little confused, and spoke to Nun. 'Giblite, haven't you the Queen's seal?'

Nun looked blank for a moment, and then thought of the cylinder that had got him into the throne room the night before. He felt in his bag and took it out. 'Do you mean this?' he asked.

'Yes,' said his escort. 'The Queen's own seal, the lion and bull. That's worth more than the Sea Lord's,' he said, turning to the second guard. 'Let me pass, please. You can have this man when we've finished with him.' And he led Nun on.

The chamber that Nun was at last shown into was even more beautifully painted than the King's throne room. There were patterns of great rosettes all over the beams and uprights, and a great panel of swimming dolphins, little fish, and sea-plants. But the most beautiful thing in the room was the woman sitting among a few attendants, her great dark eyes on Nun as he came in. He realized that she must be the Queen – and yet something about her reminded him of the girls he knew in Gebal.

'Is this the foreigner who pulled our sacred bull's tail?' came the cool voice of the Queen. 'Let him approach so that I can see him.'

Nun and his escort went up to the Queen's chair, and Nun knelt before her. It seemed the natural thing to do, and he felt none of the awkwardness he had felt when he had met the King. And she was speaking his language as if it was native to her.

'Are you aware, Giblite, that you have offended my Lord the King and shocked our holy priests and priestesses?' said the Queen in a level voice, with a strange expression in her eyes.

'We must have disgusted you with our rude performance, Your Majesty,' said Nun. 'I am sorry for that. But I'm only a simple sailor. I held on to the first thing that came to hand.'

The Queen turned her head, so that Nun could not see her

expression, and spoke to her attendants. 'Retire!' she ordered them. 'As priestess, I must speak to this man alone.' The attendants and the guard hesitated a little, then, after an angry flash from the Queen's black eyes, moved to the other end of the chamber, looking more than a little shocked and disapproving.

The Queen turned her face back to Nun, and this time her eyes were twinkling with laughter.

'I want to thank you, Giblite. I have not enjoyed the bull games so much for years.' Once again Nun felt taken aback, and this seemed to amuse the Queen even more. 'You are surprised,' she went on, 'to hear me speak your language perhaps? I was not born a Cretan, but a princess of Tyre, your neighbour state. Oh! I know that Tyrians and Giblites are not always friends at home, but I like to speak to sailors from that coast. I was tempted to come here by stories of the Bull King – there is even a foolish belief that I swam here on the back of a bull. But I am frivolous, I suppose, and still cannot take our games as seriously as my dear husband would wish. It was good of you and your friends to make me laugh.'

'It might not have been so funny for me if it hadn't been for the Northerners,' said Nun. 'Will they be allowed to go now?'

'Do not worry about your friends,' replied the Queen. 'They are barbarians, clowns. What can you expect from people with yellow hair and red faces? They will be permitted to leave. But I am concerned about you, Giblite.'

'Your Majesty is most kind,' said Nun, the anxiety returning within him.

'What I am going to tell you is a secret of state,' the Queen continued. 'I am only letting you know of it because you have no possibility of escaping and telling your people. The King my husband has plans to harry the coastal cities with his ships. Gebal and Sidon will be attacked: Tyre is, of course, in league with us. You know how strong our navy is. Nothing can withstand them. They want you as a navigator. If you refuse, they will certainly not let you go, but you will be put to death for sacrilege. They say you know strange secrets of navigation, but that means nothing to me. I merely wish to save you because you are of my race – and because you made me laugh. Here, take this! It is my royal commission, sealed with the seal of the lion and bull, that seal of which there are only two copies. One I sent as a token to Babylon for the Chaldean astrologer, and one I keep myself.'

The Queen handed to Nun a clay tablet, covered with the incomprehensible long-legged script, with the lion and bull across the bottom. He stood, holding it, and the only words that came to his lips were 'I cannot accept. If Gebal is to be attacked, my place is at home.'

The Queen looked at him with compassion. 'I tell you, Giblite, if you work for us and have my backing there is an honourable future for you. Nothing can save you otherwise.'

And at that moment there was a disturbance at the entrance to the chamber, and in strode the distinguished white-haired councillor whom the King had addressed as Sea Lord.

The Queen rose to her feet. 'Sea Lord,' she said icily, 'this intrusion is very sudden!'

'A thousand pardons, Your Majesty,' said the Sea Lord smoothly. 'It did not enter my head that you could be in – ah, private audience with this person.' He looked coldly at Nun. 'As you know, he is urgently invited to a – er – a conference on nautical affairs at Mallia. That is, of course, if he deigns to accept hospitality at my humble country mansion.'

Nun bowed, not to be outdone in politeness now that he knew how little it was worth. 'Your Sea Lordship is most kind,' he said. 'I have already heard of your delightful residence at Mallia.'

'That's settled then. An honourable escort awaits you and

your – ah – mathematician friend. Infinite apologies again, Your Majesty, for the intrusion. But it was His Majesty's express wish.'

The Queen nodded to the Sea Lord, but said nothing. She held out her hand to Nun. He knelt and kissed it.

'Farewell, Your Majesty,' he said. 'And thank you.' But he could not see the expression in the Queen's eyes.

Nun and the Sea Lord left the chamber, and outside they met an escort of soldiers with the Chaldean among them. They were taken from the palace to where a painted chariot waited to drive them to Mallia. Nun and the Chaldean travelled together in the same chariot, but his companion was very silent. Hardly a word passed between them, even when they came to a high part of the coast road and they both suddenly saw directly to the North over the blue sea, just above the horizon, a harmless-looking cone with a faint wisp of smoke coming from the top. It was Thira, the island of menace.

But nothing could be more peaceful than Mallia. After driving across a fertile coastal strip, they emerged from olive orchards to see a palace of golden stone standing in a semicircle of soft, rounded hills. At the seaside was a small harbour where a few ships lay. Everything was on a much smaller scale than at Knossos, and instead of the bustle and magnificence of the King's palace, here all was luxury and calm. They were shown into airy apartments hung with fine linen, but they did not know whether they were prisoners or guests, and when the Sea Lord sent for them after dinner he himself seemed uncertain how to treat them.

'I understand that Her Majesty the Queen sent for you in the first place, Chaldean, and that you, Giblite, came over with a cargo of logs. That is correct?' And without waiting for a reply he continued, 'Good. Then let's begin with the facts. Now we in Crete, of course, always welcome traders from abroad, and Her Majesty's particularly interested to see jugglers and magicians from the East. But we have in Crete certain standards, you know. We like to think of ourselves as civilized, and it's not asking much for visitors to our shores to pay a little regard to the decencies and so forth. So it's my embarrassing duty to make you realize that your respective public performances at Knossos made a very bad impression, a very bad impression indeed. Let's take the incident with the bull first. You foreign visitors are not expected to be able to play the game as we Cretans do, of course. But we do expect you to remember that it's an honour for you to take part in our bull-festival. I admit it was a mistake to invite those northern barbarians – they're just not civilized like us, and people with skins that colour never will be. But you Giblites aren't savages. I should have thought the honour of repre-senting your city in front of King Minos would have been enough to make you take the bull by the horns, and so on, instead of pull – instead of acting as you did.'

The recollection of the bull's tail being pulled seemed to give the elegant gentleman pain. 'You don't look like a coward. Well, there it is, a very good bull with its nerve gone – it will never fight again – and the priests foretelling all sorts of trouble with the harvest.'

The lord turned in his chair and faced the Chaldean. 'And that brings me to your performance, Chaldean. I won't say your prophecy wasn't very well delivered, perfectly correct in its form. And it would have been quite in order to foretell a little famine or so, some disaster threatening the common people. But to accept the hospitality of His Majesty King Minos, to stand in his palace and tell him to his face that it's going to fall down – well, I mean it's beyond the bounds of decent behaviour. I think His Majesty took it very well. He's graciously given orders that you should be well treated at present. And he is paying you the compliment, both of you, which I for one – with all respect to His Majesty – believe to be thoroughly undeserved, of taking the rest of your story seriously, and asking me to find out about it. So now you know what you're here for.'

Nun had rather lost the thread of that last sentence, and permitted himself a glance at the Chaldean. But his friend's face was expressionless.

The Sea Lord continued his monologue. 'You know very well what I mean. You claimed that in an ordinary laden cargo vessel you made the passage from the port of Gebal to Crete in two days. It was quite obvious to anyone who knows anything about the sea that this was the normal sort of exaggeration you Orientals go in for. My flag officers' – he glanced at the languid young men sitting around – 'have advised me that the minimum time for that passage is four days, even with the most favourable winds. You talked some nonsense about sailing at night and being directed by the stars. His Majesty seemed to think it might be a practice the Cretan Navy could adopt – though wisely he's left it to me, and while I'm responsible there's no danger of our ships being allowed to blunder around in the dark.' He laughed, and the flag officers copied him. 'And unfortunately for your claim it's been refuted by your own crew. I had some trouble rounding them up and bringing them and your vessel to Mallia for examination. But they saved me a lot of trouble. They all agreed that it had in fact taken you four days to get from Gebal to Amnisos. So there it is. I don't suppose, in the face of that, you will want to press your fantastic claims about a new-fangled method of navigation.'

The Sea Lord was silent and sat with a bored look on his face. Nun looked over at the Chaldean, who met his gaze, and it seemed that they were sharing the same thoughts. The members of the crew had, of course, told the truth. They had arrived at Amnisos four days after leaving Gebal, having spent two nights at sea and two in the islands. And after that self-satisfied harangue, neither of them felt inclined to convince the Cretan of the facts of star-navigation even if he would have listened.

One of the flag officers broke the silence, addressing Nun in a sneering voice. 'Well, Captain? You have heard his Lordship's question. How long did you take from Gebal to Amnisos?'

'Four days,' said Nun.

The officer raised his eyebrows and turned to the Chaldean. 'Is this the truth?'

'The voyage took four days,' said the Chaldean.

There was a silence. The wind had been taken out of the questioners' sails so suddenly that they were at a loss for what to do next. A weather-beaten, middle-aged man who had the looks of a real seaman broke the silence.

'If I may put a question, my Lord –' he said tentatively.

'Oh, certainly, yes,' murmured his Lordship.

The man turned to Nun. 'Captain,' he began, 'I'll admit that even four days from Gebal to Crete in a craft of your type was a pretty smart bit of sailing. Perhaps you'd tell us the facts now, how you planned the voyage, the course you steered on, and so on.'

'Why? Are you thinking of taking the same trip?' asked Nun pleasantly. They would like to know, so they can plan their campaign against the mainland, Nun thought. What the Queen said was true.

'Taking the same trip?' repeated the other. 'No, no, not at all, why should I? Just for general interest, though,' and he tried to make his smile look pleasant.

'Oh, quite,' said Nun. 'You just want the facts.' He'd give the facts, he thought. 'Well, first of all there was Balaat-Gebal –'

'Where's that,' interrupted the other.

'Where?' exclaimed Nun, pretending to be deeply pained. 'I am speaking of our revered Mother-Goddess. It was a matter of beseeching her aid, and requesting favourable winds, which I must say She was gracious enough to grant us most of the way, though, indeed, I have been often neglectful of Her rites and observances –'

'Yes, of course, very pious and proper,' put in the Sea Lord. 'These things have their place. But we were thinking of more material –'

'Oh, sir!' continued Nun. 'Don't imagine we neglected the material offerings. Our priests are not as neglectful as that. They were kind enough to accept a gold figurine, a Cretan one indeed. I had got it here on a previous voyage, and good value I paid for it too. You see, it doesn't pay to skimp these things. And look what a lovely east wind we –'

'Yes, yes, yes,' the weather-beaten seaman interrupted again. 'I'm sure you did the right thing. But what about stores, and rigging, and so on. As one seaman to another, you know, I'm interested in these things.'

'Ah, there's one thing I should mention. This anchor. A good big one it was. The priests of Reshef suggested it would be a good thing to dedicate to their God, for a safe passage you know. So we lugged it up and put it among the obelisks there. And very efficacious too, not an enemy did we meet all the way. All friends . . .' He looked at the faces around him, all more or less bored at his pious chatter, with perhaps a hint of suspicion that he was pulling their legs.

The Sea Lord's voice sounded again. 'Kindly tell us, Captain, exactly *how* you directed your ship from Gebal to Crete. And it might be better if you just related the facts of your voyage.' Now his voice carried a threat.

'Oh, the *fact*, my Lord,' said Nun without thinking, 'is that we started by following the Little Dog –'

There were angry exclamations from more than one voice at this: 'Following a little dog! The man's an idiot! He's mocking us!'

'I *mean*, my Lord,' Nun went on hastily, seeing that he had gone too far by telling the truth, 'I beg your pardon, one of our sea-going terms. I mean I just pointed the ship towards Crete and kept going –'

But the Sea Lord was on his feet. 'I think we have heard enough,' he said to the gathering, without even troubling to look at Nun. 'I'm satisfied that the fellow is wandering in his wits and whatever he knows can be of little value to us. If anyone else wishes to get sense out of him tomorrow, let him try whatever method he chooses. This meeting is adjourned. Meanwhile the prisoners are to be confined to the North Tower.'

The Sea Lord made a dignified exit, the meeting broke up, and Nun and the Chaldean were marched off to confinement.

Their accommodation as prisoners was not so fine as when they had been guests of the palace. But it was by no means a prison. It was a loft in a tall watch-tower, reached by a kind of ladder, which the Chaldean climbed with some difficulty. The soldiers stayed in the room at the bottom of the ladder, satisfied that there was no other way out.

The first thing Nun did was to go to the window overlooking the sea, but the drop to the ground was too great to think of letting himself fall, and the building was of smooth stone, impossible to climb. There were two low beds in the room. The Chaldean sat down on one and Nun on the other, and they looked at each other.

'We must escape,' said Nun quietly.

'My dear young friend,' protested the Chaldean. 'You may think of these things. I am too old. I must stay here and await –'

'Await what?'

'Await the destruction that will certainly overtake this palace.'

'There is no doubt, then, about this happening?' asked Nun.

'For me there is no longer any doubt. No place by the sea like this can possibly survive.'

'The more reason for us to escape,' said Nun, briskly, getting to his feet and going to the window again. He looked up and down the coast. There was a quarter-moon shining on the still waters of the bay beyond the harbour – and Nun caught his breath. But it was not the natural beauty of the scene that made him do so, it was something he had noticed. There was a little island a very short distance offshore, with a building or two on it. And moored there, and clearly outlined against the path of the moonlight, was a ship. There was no mistaking its lines. It was his own ship.

'Look, Chaldean!' he exclaimed, only just remembering to keep his voice down. 'It's our ship!'

The Chaldean did not trouble to look. 'Indeed, the Sea Lord told us he had brought the ship here, and her crew. But it must make you happy to see her,' he said sympathetically.

'I had forgotten. I wonder where the men are?' said Nun, and he started pacing restlessly about the chamber. How to escape from the tower? A rope, that was all he needed. The room was bare of hangings and there were only rotten pallets on the beds, nothing he could tear up to make a rope. He looked at his garments and those of the Chaldean, and thought of the long drop outside and shook his head.

He sat down despondently on the bed – and no sooner had he sat than he sprang up as if he had been bitten, and before the astonished eyes of the Chaldean flung the pallet off the low bed. He could hardly restrain an exclamation of triumph. The bed was a rough affair of wood, but the mattress was supported by a network of good strong cord, woven from side to side and from head to foot, fathoms and fathoms of it. What had been woven could be unwoven.

In feverish but systematic haste he set to work, undoing the lashings, unthreading the warp and the woof of it, cursing beneath his breath at the tangles in the kinked cord. For the more he undid the longer was the part he had to pull through each time. The Chaldean watched him remotely, not offering to help. But he wandered over to the trapdoor at the top of the ladder. And when there were only a few lengthwise strands left to undo, Nun heard his voice saying very loudly, 'Welcome soldier! It is kind of you to visit us in our comfortable quarters.'

Wildly Nun gathered up the loose cord, flung the mattress back on the bed, and by lying uncomfortably across the framework managed desperately to keep the mattress from falling through on to the floor.

'My companion is asleep,' said the Chaldean calmly, as the head and shoulders of a soldier appeared through the trapdoor. 'Ah, you have brought food. You are most kind. Set it down. Please do not trouble to serve us.'

The soldier dumped a jug of water and a plate of bread on to the floor, took a look at Nun's contorted body on the bed, grunted and retired down the ladder. And not a moment too soon, for one side of the mattress immediately flopped through the gap in the support and Nun nearly fell through with it.

Nun let out a sigh of relief, and then had to smother his laughter at this absurd episode. The Chaldean carried the food back to his bed and began to eat the bread. Nun realized he, too, was hungry, but he could not stop the work he was doing. He took mouthfuls of bread from the Chaldean and chewed them as he went on. Soon he had finished unstringing his own bed.

'I'm sorry, sir,' he said urgently but quietly to his companion, 'yours now.'

'My dear friend,' said the old man mildly. 'You are

welcome to all I have. But let me say now, in case you have thoughts of my descending like a spider on a thread from this tower, that I have no intention of doing any such thing. It is many years since I played such boyish games, and even as a child I was far from adventurous.'

'Don't worry, sir,' said Nun. 'Leave everything to me. It's not a difficult bit of seamanship, if the gear will stand it. I'll have you down there as safely as off-loading a basket of eggs.'

'But –' protested the old man.

'Why should you stay here to share the fate of Crete?' asked Nun urgently. 'You have done what you can to save these people. Why should you perish with them? Besides, how can I escape without you as my navigator?'

His companion moved, still protesting, to the floor, and Nun set to work on the other bed. He worked more quickly as he got the hang of it, and soon had four or five tidy coils of cord.

'Now for testing,' he said. 'Don't worry, sir, a seaman leaves nothing to chance, even if the world is coming to an end.'

The rafters of the room were not too far off the floor, and he was able to pass each length of cord over them and try his weight on every fathom of it. Doubled, it took the strain well. Single, he was not so sure of it. He looked at the Chaldean's heavy, bony frame. He could hardly trust that to a single strand. But was there enough to reach the ground doubled? The only way to be sure was to try. He carefully knotted the lengths together and lowered the doubled line out of the window, having made as sure as possible that no one was likely to be passing below. It reached, but only just. He hauled it in again, then tested each knot separately by hanging from the rafters.

He was satisfied with his rope, but then it struck him that

if it only just reached from the window to the ground, there would not be enough to pass round the Chaldean and for him to hang on to at the top. He must think again. He looked at the Chaldean's flowing cloak.

'Sorry, sir,' he said. 'Your cloak, please.' Meekly the Chaldean took it off and handed it to him. He considered it for a while, and at last devised a kind of sling that could go under his companion's armpits and which he could wriggle out of when he reached the ground.

The beds, now deprived of their stringing, could still be useful. He stood one against the wall by the window, and the other on its side upon the first. This provided a solid bar across the window frame which could not possibly slip through it. He passed the cord several times round the bar, so that he could lower the weight of the Chaldean slowly to the ground by easing the rope out round the bar.

'We're ready, sir,' he said to the old man. Without a word, the Chaldean let himself be secured into this sling. Nun showed him how to climb through the window and lower himself from the bar until the rope took his weight. Then, muttering what was presumably a prayer to his gods, he took his hands from the bar and Nun paid out the rope as slowly and smoothly as he could, and watched the courageous old man descending, as he had said he would never do, like a spider on its thread to the ground.

Nun sweated quietly as the friction of the rope round the bar caused a groan like the rigging of a ship in a storm, and the knots threatened to snag and jam – and then he felt his heart stop as the dead end of the rope came into his hand. The strain of the Chaldean's body was still on the rope, which meant that his feet were not on the ground, and there was no more to pay out! He hung on blindly to the end of the rope, while beneath him the Chaldean seemed to be floundering like a fish on the end of the line, trying to free himself,

Nun supposed. Then the rope snapped slack, and Nun leant his head against the bar and felt he would cry like a child, as he realized it had broken!

He took several deep breaths and controlled himself. Then he forced himself to look down into the obscurity below. The Chaldean was not lying in a broken heap below the window, as he had feared, but had moved away a little and was standing against the wall. Nun could see his white face looking up. Then he let his eyes follow the rope dangling down the wall. His heart settled to a normal beat again as he saw that there was still quite a length of rope, perhaps two-thirds of it, intact. There was nothing else for it, he must slide down what was left of the rope, and drop the rest of the way.

It was Nun's turn to pray to his gods as he secured the end of the rope to the bar and swung off on to it. It is not easy to slide down a thin doubled cord with knots in it. He braked himself with his legs and feet as best he could, then he was dangling only by his handhold, and then there was nothing he could do but let go. The drop was shorter than he had thought it was going to be, and he landed hard but safely on his feet.

The Chaldean came up to him muttering something about 'Too old for this kind of thing'. But he seemed to be unhurt, and Nun took him by the arm and hurried him off towards the shore, and the ship.

They made their way in silence along a sandy track that led through cultivated ground behind the harbour, and came at last to the beach. The landscape was so peaceful under the setting moon, the air was so balmy with the scent of growing things, and the sea was so calm with its tiny wavelets falling softly on the sand, that Nun found it difficult to believe that he was still in great danger; he had to remind himself that he had not the slightest idea of how to get out of his predicament.

They walked along the beach until they were opposite the island. Nun judged it to be within easy swimming distance from the shore, though after misjudging the length of the rope he did not have too much confidence in himself. It was certainly near enough for him to be able to hear voices drifting over the water. Somebody on the island was singing – and then Nun clutched his companion's arm and stood listening. He knew the song, a doleful sailor's love-song from Gebal – and what was more, he knew the singer. There was surely only one man in the world who sang that song with always the same mistakes, and he knew just which member of his crew it was. So the crew, or at least some of it, were on the island too.

Nun took off his upper garment and handed it to the Chaldean in silence. His companion became agitated, put his mouth to Nun's ear and whispered, 'I cannot swim!' as if fearful of being forced into some other impossible activity.

'Stay here!' breathed Nun. 'Don't move. I'll come back for you.' And he slipped as quietly as he could into the warm clear water.

Gently he launched himself into deeper water and began to swim towards the island, trying not to break the surface with his arms. If the crew and the ship were on the island, there must be guards to keep them there, though they might have little reason to be vigilant in this peaceful spot. He made for the ship, which seemed silent and deserted, and after a while he was in its shadows and his movements were less conspicuous among the cluck of waves that surrounded the hull.

There was a rope hanging over the side, and Nun grasped it, hung on for a while listening hard, and then pulled himself painfully and carefully out of the water and into the ship.

For a time he was content to rest upon the planking, as if he had come home at last. But what to do next? He listened to the voices on the island. A regular sing-song was now shattering the peace of the night, and as far as Nun could make out there were Cretan songs as well as the songs of Gebal. Apparently the guards were joining in. This might be to his advantage, he thought. Then he froze as he saw a figure outlined against the stars, coming along the wooden jetty towards the ship.

The man carelessly put his foot on the bulwark of the ship, causing the whole vessel to roll, and jumped aboard. He started rummaging about among the stores stowed in the forepeak, cursing as he blundered against the timbers in the dark. The curses were from Gebal too. Nun took a chance and let out a low hiss to attract his attention. The man straightened up, and said in a normal voice, 'Who's there?' and Nun recognized the tones of the boatswain.

'Shh!' hissed Nun. 'It's I, Nun, the captain.'

The boatswain came over to him and peered at him in the dark.

'That really you, sir? What are you doing here?'

'We're escaping, boatswain. Is all the crew here?'

'Yes,' came the reply. 'All present, sir. They're treating us well enough, as you can hear. Having a good time. They call us their guests, but I reckon we're prisoners just the same.'

'You're right, boatswain. How many guards?'

'Fewer than we are, anyway. But they've taken away our weapons, and they're fully armed.'

'Could you rush them?' suggested Nun.

The boatswain considered. 'I daresay we could, with things as they are. All very matey tonight. Why don't you join the party, sir? Guards wouldn't notice another Giblite among the rest of us.'

'Very well. But find me some clothing. It will look pretty odd if I appear naked.'

When the boatswain had found Nun a sailor's tunic, they went back together along the jetty and casually joined the party of Giblites and Cretan guards who were sitting around on the rocks by the light of one or two torches. No one took any notice of them in the gloom. It was not a very hilarious party, rather a means of whiling away the tedium of the hot night, it seemed. The Giblites had embarked upon one of their interminable, repetitive chorus songs – and Nun seized his opportunity. He joined a little group of sailors, and confident that whatever words might be sung would mean nothing to the Cretans, joined in the chorus loud and clear, but with his own words:

> *'I am your captain, I am Nun,*
> *We must escape from Crete.*
> *When this song ends, rush the guards!*
> *Bind and gag them, keep them quiet!*
> *Then to the ship without a sound,*
> *And off we'll go to sea!'*

The sailors looked startled, and nearly stopped singing, but Nun kept the rhythm going with hand-claps. When he saw by their nods that they were understanding, he moved on to another group, and repeated the chorus to them. The words caught on, and he could see the men grinning and joining in the joke. As the song continued the original words of the chorus, were abandoned, and one by one the sailors joined in together with:

> *'When this song ends, rush the guards!*
> *Bind and gag them, keep them quiet,*
> *Then to the ship without a sound,*
> *And we'll away to sea!'*

It was not poetry, but it was certainly popular. Clearly none of the guards understood the language: and to Nun's delight he heard some of the Cretans trying to join in the song parrot-wise, little knowing what they were inciting the prisoners to do.

The, presumably, sad old story of the girl that had loved a sailor drew to its end. The sailors rose to their feet as the final chorus was reached. Then with a united shout on the words '*We'll away to* SEA!' each Giblite jumped on the nearest Cretan soldier. The guards, too astonished to do anything, had their heads muffled in cloaks and their limbs secured with good sailors' knots before they knew what was happening.

'Keep singing, boys!' said Nun. If anyone was listening from the shore a sudden silence might raise suspicion. Keeping the regular chorus going as they made for the ship, the sailors unshipped the oars, cast off the moorings, and pushed off from the jetty. When the ship's head was pointed north to the open sea, Nun gave the order, 'Heave away!' and the vessel leaped forward.

Then suddenly – 'Avast! Hold water! Back her down!' Nun cried, to the bewilderment of the crew. 'Ye gods! We've forgotten the pilot!'

They backed the ship over the short stretch of water to the shore. As they got as near as Nun dared, he could see the Chaldean standing patiently on the beach, holding Nun's clothes. 'Come on, sir,' he called across the water, 'you'll have to get a little wet.'

Without hesitating the Chaldean walked into the dead calm water until it was up to his shoulders and he was under the quarter of the ship. Then Nun and the boatswain quickly reached over and hoisted him aboard.

Once again Nun gave the order to row, and the ship moved away from the land. Soon, as they moved farther out, they began to meet rougher water and could feel the breeze from which the mountains had hitherto protected them. Putting the steering-oar over Nun turned the ship's head to the East.

'Which stars for the eastern passage, Chaldean?' he sang out.

8
The Mine in the Desert

Aleph, the scribe, continues his journey – The Dead Sea –
The Egyptian copper-mines in the Sinai peninsula –
Information of attack on Gebal by the Egyptians –
The first inscription in the new alphabet – Pigeon post

When Aleph returned with Ish to Jericho, after their patrol in
the mountains, they found everything in a state of turmoil.
The column was already re-forming, getting ready to resume
its march south. Though the soldiers of the patrol, and Aleph,
and Ish, were weary, the commander of the column told
them to prepare to leave at once and barely listened to their
report on the hill tribes. Ish was roughly ordered to get his
things packed, and Aleph was beaten for being late to fall in
with the prisoners. The easy-going discipline of the previous
part of the journey had vanished, and there was nothing but
bad temper, cursing, and grousing. What had happened?

Soon they were on their way again, marching due South.
Aleph was surprised when an hour's march over the plain
brought them to the shore of another sea. It was more than a
lake, for though both sides were easily visible its ends could
not be seen in the hot haze that hung over it. There was
something strange about its waters, a leaden colour even in
the sunlight, and a sluggish motion to its waves, but the sight
of it was refreshing as they journeyed along at the foot of the
mountains on its eastern shore. The air was oppressive, the

sun beat down and there was no vegetation at all, yet Aleph felt happier to be between the mountains and the sea again; and he promised himself the pleasure of a bathe when they halted in the evening.

The sun was going down behind purple mountains on the far shore when they halted and prepared camp. Aleph approached the sergeant in charge of the prisoners.

'May I bathe?' he asked.

The sergeant exchanged a curious glance with some of the other soldiers. 'Feel like a nice swim, lad?' he grinned.

'I can't swim,' Aleph said, 'but I'd like to cool down after the march.'

'Better have a proper swim, hadn't he?' the sergeant said to the soldiers, and they laughed.

'But I can't swim,' repeated Aleph. 'I'll just paddle in a shallow place.'

The sergeant turned cross. 'You prisoners come to me and bother me with requests to go paddling like children! We'll give him paddle, won't we, men? All right, you four, see that this prisoner has his swim like a man. See that he dives in where it's good and deep.'

The four soldiers got up grinning and took hold of Aleph. 'No, no!' he protested. 'I don't want to swim, I can't swim. I don't know how.'

They dragged him to a rock overhanging deep water. 'Don't push me in! I can't dive! I'll drown!' cried Aleph.

When he struggled in panic they found a rope and tied his hands and legs and carried him bound to the water. 'How can I swim if you tie me up?' moaned Aleph. Why had they suddenly decided to drown him? 'You'll get into trouble if you drown a valuable prisoner,' he panted. 'They need me in Egypt, I'm a scribe.'

The soldiers roared with laughter, swung him three times, and launched him into the water. His last hour had come, and he prepared himself to sink into chill depths and never breathe air again.

But what was this – mouth and nose full of the tastes of an apothecary's pots? Eyes smarting with salt? A warm sticky liquid that bore him up and left him floating ridiculously on the surface, while his arms and legs stuck up in the air, and to his ears came the shouts of laughter from the soldiers on the shore?

They left him in the Dead Sea until he drifted like a log to the shore. It was Ish who helped him out and untied him; he was none the worse except that he felt ridiculous and longed for a wash in fresh water to get rid of the salt from his body and clothes. But it was to be a long time before he would be able to do that.

Ish, as they sat talking that night in the camp, told him the reason for the sullenness of the troops and the despondency of the prisoners. The news had got round that they were not going to Egypt at all. There was a shortage of workers in the copper and turquoise mines of Sinai, and so the destination of both guards and prisoners had been changed.

Aleph was silent. Was he not even to see the palaces and temples of Egypt, after all this journeying?

'What is Sinai like?' he asked.

'I know a little about it,' Ish replied. 'A God-forsaken wilderness of barren mountains, they say. Only a Pharaoh could condemn people to live there, and only copper and turquoise come out of it.'

It was a dreary march from then on. They came to hate this sea of dead chemical liquid, where no fish jumped, no birds hovered or dived, but when they left it there was even less relief for the eyes among the burning rocks. They climbed up again to plateau country, where the air was drier and more tolerable, then to a few oases and cultivated settlements, and at last to a port on what Ish said was an arm of the Red

Sea. This was a real sea, apparently linked with the great ocean that surrounded the world.

Ish had sought out Aleph among the prisoners the day after they arrived, and found him looking longingly at the waves.

'If I got on a ship here, could I sail back to Gebal, do you think?' Aleph asked him.

'It is best not to torment yourself with such thoughts,' said Ish. 'Besides, I think that would be impossible.'

'All the same,' said Aleph, 'it looks the same as the sea at Gebal. It is some comfort.'

'I am glad,' said Ish, 'for fear I have little comfort for you. You must go your way to Sinai. And I —'

'You are not leaving us?' said Aleph anxiously.

'I am to take a ship to Egypt,' said Ish.

Aleph hung his head. 'It is a good thing for you. I am happy for it,' he said at last.

'Perhaps we shall meet again,' said Ish encouragingly. 'In Egypt, perhaps even in Gebal some day. And maybe some good will even come of your being in Sinai.'

They said their farewells, but Aleph felt they would not see each other again.

Aleph was never to remember much about the southward march to Sinai. He was not living, yet not dead; he had no friend, no hopes, and hardly any recollections. Existence was merely a matter of putting one foot before the other in the shimmering heat of the rocky desert, and collapsing into exhausted sleep at the end of each day. The one thing that reminded him that he was a person, with a life of his own, was the companionship of the incongruous bird in its cage, miraculously thriving despite all the rigours of the march. The effort to keep it alive was perhaps the only thing that kept him going. Perhaps it would have been kinder to have let it go before, but Beth's words ran through his head as if they were a solemn vow he had taken. 'Let him go when you get to where you are going.' And while he still had to put one foot in front of another, he had not yet got there.

He was hardly aware of arriving at their destination, a valley like a great open oven among the baking mountains. Scorched slaves toiled in galleries digging out the copper ore and carrying it away in baskets on their heads; others suffered worse torments at the refinery, where the heat of the smelting furnaces was added to the fantastic heat of the sun. He looked dazedly at the infernal scene. Could anyone live long in such a place? Or had he perhaps died already and been sent to a region of eternal punishment?

Yet when he was led to his place of work he found that he was asked to do something even more impossible. He was being asked to work with his brain, although he felt that it had long ago oozed out in sweat through his scalp.

He was received by the chief of the clerks, a dried-up chip of a man. He asked Aleph if he could count and tally in the Egyptian manner and assigned him to the stockpiles of smelted copper from the refineries. The penalty for any deficiency or mistake was to be sentenced to stoking the furnaces. 'They only last a few months there,' said the chief clerk. 'That's why we're short of tally clerks at present.' It was some time before Aleph's slow brain worked out what he meant.

His name had to be registered on a big scroll of papyrus. When he said he came from Gebal, the chief clerk gave him a sharp look from his black gimlet eyes. 'You've got yourselves to thank for this extra work, then, you Canaanites,' he said.

Aleph stood dumb and uncomprehending. The chief clerk went on speaking, not that he cared to enlighten this wretched Giblite, but in this outpost of exile he liked to keep his brain going by talking politics. 'All the news comes here, you know, and none goes out. So there's no harm in me telling you.

Tyre, Sidon, Gebal – these places have always belonged to Egypt. But since the revolution you've all wanted to be independent. Especially rude and defiant your King was, they say. That's why Pharaoh wants weapons to arm an expeditionary force. They're going to march up the coast and put things to rights. Going to raze Gebal to the ground and put your lot to the sword, I'm told. And we've got to sweat to make the copper.'

Slowly Aleph began to understand what the chief clerk was saying. It was not enough that he should suffer here but everything he did would be helping to make weapons that might be used against his own family.

'Get on with it, then!' snapped the clerk. 'Don't stand there! You can start at once!'

Aleph turned away, but the chief clerk called after him, 'What's this about a bird you've got? See that it's turned in at the temple, we're always short of sacrificial animals here.'

Aleph walked slowly out of the building to where he had left the pigeon in the cage, and looked at it without feeling. This was the end of his journey, sure enough. This was where he was going to. All he had to do was to open the door of the cage and let the bird go. That it would make his captors angry did not matter; he was glad to be capable of this small gesture, even though it would do him little good. Yet it was difficult to believe the bird would find its way back over all those weary marches to Gebal. Gebal? It existed in another world, and it was in another age that he had said good-bye so casually to his sister, that he had looked down upon the city from the height, that he had looked over the mountain range for the first time, and even felt a childish excitement at the prospect of seeing Egypt. And if her white pigeon were to arrive at the loft, what could it tell Beth of her brother's sufferings? Nothing. And if it could, would that make her happier? Perhaps it was too late anyhow, and

Pharaoh's armies had taken Gebal by surprise and put it to the sword.

He picked up the bird-cage and walked in a stupor to the sweltering warehouse where he was to work. In a corner was a rough table, papyrus rolls, pens, and ink. Other clerks were stacking ingots of copper in piles and morosely tallying them on the strips of papyrus. He looked at the thin papery strips, the pens, and the ink; then at the bird. What about the sign-game he had played with his sister? How much of it, he wondered, did she remember?

Perhaps it was not too late to get a message through to Gebal – a message that would tell his sister what had become of him. At the same time it might warn the King of Gebal of the danger that threatened the city. But it was unheard of, to send a message through the air a distance of many weeks' marches. Fearful doubt told him it was preposterous, but he *had* to believe it was possible. It was possible, and that was enough to make him forget the oppressive heat and the hopelessness of his situation.

He must take no risks with his plan, nor arouse any suspicions. He put the bird-cage inconspicuously in a corner and set immediately to work with the other clerks, piling ingots, checking and tallying them, packing them in panniers ready to be sent off by ass-train to the armourers in Egypt. It was exhausting work, physically and mentally, yet he kept a corner of his brain alive and apart, and through it paraded the signs that meant nothing in the world to anyone but him and his sister – the twenty-two letters. Could he remember them himself? He said their names over:

'Aleph – the ox
beth   – the house
gimel – the stick
daleth – the door

    the little man who said Ha!
    waw   – the peg
    zayin   – the weapon
(and where was he, Zayin, his elder brother?)
    keth   – the hurdle
    teth   – the ball of twine
    yod   – the hand
    kaph   – the palm branch
    lam   – the rod
    mem   – the water
    nun   – the sea serpent
(and the sailor, voyaging confidently over the seas)
    samekh – the fish
    ain   – the eye
    pe   – the mouth
    quoph   – the monkey
    resh   – the head
(and he thought of his father, head of the family)
    shin   – the teeth
    taw   – the mark they put on the felled timber
and ssad   – the grasshopper'

He recited the list over and over like a magic spell, and it
gave him a marvellous confidence. And yet the words were
not magic. There was no mystery to them: if you remembered
them correctly, they were as sure as counting; it could not go
wrong. Just put the first sounds together, and you could
make any word in the language.

Of course it wasn't real writing, Aleph still told himself.
But he no longer cared what the priests or the gods might
think. They could not condemn him to any worse punishment
than that he was suffering now; bodily here in Sinai and in
his imagination whenever he thought of the Egyptian armies
descending upon Gebal.

When the long day's work came to an end and the exhausted workers trailed off to their quarters, Aleph pretended he had a spoilt papyrus to recopy, and stayed behind in the shed with the pens and the ink to write what he had to write. The light was fading, and in addition he was exhausted, but he forced his brain to remain clear and his hand to write neatly and clearly in tiny characters. He knew he must do it that night, for he was sure tomorrow they would take the bird from him. The guards looked curiously at the new slave working overtime, but the last thing that entered their heads was that he was writing a message of vital importance to his sister.

Aleph finished writing and hid the tiny missive safely in his dress. The sun was setting. He could not set the poor bird free unfed and in the dark. He took it to the sleeping quarters, where he presumed there would be food and water for the prisoners; indeed, by the time he got there he found barely enough even for a pigeon. He was desperately anxious lest they should take the bird from him that night. One of the soldiers threatened to do so, but Aleph managed to make it appear that the man was trying to make off with a sacrificial fowl for his own purposes, and the soldiers were just sufficiently respectful to the clerks, slaves though they were, for Aleph to have his way.

In the squalid, stifling sleeping quarters, Aleph spent a restless night during which sheer exhaustion battled with anxiety for his plan, and with desperate dreams in which he was flying over mountains or falling helplessly into deep gulfs.

He was awake before dawn, and in the dim light he managed to wrap the message round one of the pigeon's legs and tie it with a thread pulled from his garment. As the sun rose, and the rest of the workers were roused, Aleph announced that he was taking the bird to be sacrificed.

The temple was near the clerks' quarters. As he approached the priest standing outside he called out: 'I have here a dove for the sacrifice.' And at the same time he opened the cage door and held the bird aloft in his hand. 'See, a snow-white dove!' he cried.

Then, in front of all the guards and priests he pretended to stumble. As he did so he let the bird go. The pigeon was so astonished that it fluttered to the ground. Aleph ran at it shouting and flapping, as if to catch it, and now the bird took fright and fluttered up, up into the air. The priest cursed him for a fool, the soldiers laughed at him, and he stood there and watched the white bird, bright in the rays of the early sun, circling higher and higher into the blue sky.

'Go with the gods to Gebal!' said Aleph quietly. The sun was rising on his right hand, but the pigeon continued to circle above him, until Aleph's heart sank: how foolish it was to expect it to know in which direction its distant home lay. Then suddenly the bird straightened out on a course that lay directly in front of him. Gradually Aleph watched the pigeon dwindle out of sight, to the northward.

Only then did the thought come to him that, even if his message did get through, he would never know. Yet as he returned to the work of the sweltering copper-mine, and day after day passed in relentless routine, a spark of hope kept him alive: the hope that the pigeon might survive the dangers of the desert, and arrive in the pigeon loft in Gebal to tell Beth that he had not forgotten his family; and a fainter hope that Beth might find and understand the message he had carefully composed in their private sign language, that it might even somehow help Gebal in its danger. And deeper still within him was a faith so faint that he did not yet acknowledge it to himself that his twenty-two letters might be neither a sin against the gods nor a childish game but something for which he, Aleph, might be remembered.

There were days when these hopes were all that saved him from feeling that his spirit was being sucked from his body by the pitiless heat as water evaporates from a jar. And there were days when he felt clearer-headed and more able to think – and this was worse, for he would tell himself that all his hopes depended upon a bird, already perhaps no more than a few feathers blowing in the desert wind, a frail monument to be remembered by!

At the back of his mind during all this time, there must have been forming the idea of leaving for himself a more lasting monument. Yet what opportunity did he have? There were no holidays in this inferno, and no rest hours while the sun was in the sky. Every hour of work was organized according to the ruthlessly efficient Egyptian production system. At night the silence of exhaustion fell on the valley and a few soldiers kept guard and saw that the slaves did not move from their sleeping quarters.

When his opportunity came at last, he did not immediately recognize it. The small temple used by the overseers and soldiers needed a new inscription. Aleph, it was discovered, was not only a clerk but also an apprentice monumental mason; since there was none other on the staff of the mine he was taken from his tallying job and told to copy out an inscription in hieroglyphs on to the rock face near the temple. The Egyptian symbols had now come to stand for everything that Aleph hated, and at first he considered pretending that he was incapable of the job. But at least it would be a change from counting copper ingots, so, taking the engraving tools and the hammer and constructing for himself a rough scaf-folding to stand on, he set to work.

The work took days, and when the Egyptians saw that he was keeping at it conscientiously they left him to it. But something was forming in his mind as he chipped away: another inscription, in different letters.

In the middle of a forenoon, he finished the hieroglyphic inscription, with its usual fulsome praise of Pharaoh and its dedications to the Egyptian gods. Then, moving his scaffolding to another smooth rock face, and with his heart thumping, he began to work, cutting his own signs into the rock and spelling out words as he went along. He carved out a dedication to his own goddess, Balaat-Gebal. Then he climbed down and stood back to admire his work. He could not feel very proud of it. It looked crude, formless, almost barbaric compared with the stylish neatness of the Egyptian writing. But it was his own!

It was at this moment that the priests of the temple came to inspect his progress. When they saw what he had done they were aghast. Was he mad to deface the approaches to the temple with this illiterate scrawl? Why had he not been supervised? Take the slave away! Give him fatigue punishment! Let him learn his place!

Aleph did not mind. His letters, and the name of the goddess of Gebal, were cut truly and deeply into the rock of Sinai. They would stand as a memorial to him for many years to come.

They stand there today.

But even today there is no one who can explain the working of the brain of a white pigeon that was carried in a wicker cage all the way from Gebal to Jericho and Sinai, and suddenly released over the desert.

For weeks now this bird had been carried southward at the slow human pace of the march, over mountains, through valleys, by the shores of seas and across deserts. Absurd to say that its small round eye had registered the details of the landscape and that its tiny brain had remembered them for the return journey. Every day the sun had wheeled overhead at right angles to the line of march. Had this perhaps been automatically recorded on some mechanism of orientation in the bird's brain? Or had it been all the while conscious of invisible forces, magnetic fields stretching from pole to pole of the globe, which its human masters had never even thought of? Or did it possess some extra sense of whose existence we still know nothing which enabled it to find its way over the surface of the earth?

The eyesight of the white pigeon was good, yet when it suddenly took off into the blue, alarmed by the clumsy behaviour of the human who had set it free, its bird's-eye view showed it nothing but barren, unfamiliar mountains and featureless desert, with the hazy western arm of the Red Sea to the south-west. If it had memories of tree-clad mountains and fertile coasts, nothing the pigeon could now see recalled them. It circled upwards from the inhospitable landscape, gained height, continued to circle – and then – ?

And then all we can say is that the watchers on the ground saw it suddenly straighten out on a course north-north-east, and head directly for the pigeon loft in Gebal, some four hundred miles away as the pigeon flies.

For several hours, with nothing in the dry brown landscape below to tempt it down, the pigeon settled to a steady course. The keen eye of a desert hawk, perched on a stone in the middle of the flat wilderness, spotted it high in the southern sky, and took off to intercept. The pigeon was high, and moving at speed; the hawk was hard put to it to overtake its victim and gain superior height for the strike.

Suddenly the pigeon sensed the hawk above and behind it. But where to hide from its enemy in this emptiness of sky and sand? The hawk stooped out of the sun, the pigeon saw it coming and jinked wildly, the hawk missed, plummeted hundreds of feet below with the momentum of its stoop, recovered itself, and climbed again to the attack.

The pigeon was now diving very fast towards the ground.

The hawk had little time to steady for its next stoop, and when it did so it had to check to avoid dashing itself against the rocks. The pigeon jinked again, dodged among boulders, close to the ground, and disappeared into a tiny cave among the eroded rocks. Aloft the hawk flapped frustratedly, but once out of sight the prey was soon out of mind, and the hawk took off again for the South.

The pigeon stayed in hiding until its feverishly beating heart settled a little, then it rose once more into the air, circling until the course established itself in its brain, and flew on northwards. A tiny oasis, a mere spot of green in the desert below with a promise of water tempted it down a few hours later. It drank, but there was little in the way of food for a pigeon accustomed to the fertile fields of Gebal, and it was not long before the bird was on the wing again. But as the sun sank slowly in the west, its gleam was reflected by a sea horizon. To the east there were hills and mountains, and below was greenness and cultivated fields. The bird planed down and landed near a stream, drank, flapped over to a field of vetches, ate greedily, flew to a tree, and found a roost for the night.

If it had not been for the boy with the herd of goats, the Giblite pigeon might have stayed in that fertile plain instead of returning home, and this story might not have been written. Indeed, it may be that no stories would have been written in this manner, for the bird carried with him a secret that was then unique in the world.

The little goatherd came on the scene next morning, while the pigeon was sitting on a branch idly surveying the cultivated crops all round him. The boy was armed with a leather sling, and fitting a smooth round stone into it, he whirled the sling round, and let the stone fly at the bird on the bough. The stone crashed noisily through the leaves, but missed its mark. The pigeon took off in alarm and rocketed into the sky. Then, as it circled doubtfully in the clear morning air, the mysterious mechanism came into action again, the longing for home made itself felt, and it settled once more on to its north-north-easterly course.

This day, as the bird flew, it could see to the East a hot misty depression filled with a dead salt sea, then a muddy river wriggling along the bottom of a deep valley, then a sparkling blue lake, then a snow-streaked mountain. But these features of the landscape meant little to the bird's brain, though it was the country through which, in the cage, it had made the painful march south. The little clusters of sunbaked brick or stone, that were the towns, meant even less. And who knows what the bird made of the dust clouds raised by columns of men, whose weapons and armour glinted in the sun – Pharaoh's armies marching north?

Still on its dead-straight course, the bird found itself between mountain and sea over a coastal strip that grew narrower, and also more familiar. Late that day it came to a limestone rock standing in the sea, through which the waves had begun to carve an archway. It was swarming with pigeons, its own wild cousins. But it did not stay to pass the time of evening. Every feature now was well known. Two more blue bays to cross in the light of the sunset, and there was Gebal, lit by the last rays of the sun.

9
The Day of
the Offering

A festival in Gebal – The tomb of the King –
Return of Zayin with the secret of horsemanship –
Return of Nun with the secret of navigation –
Return of the pigeon with the alphabetical message

It was the Day of the Offering, the day when Abishram, King of Gebal, was to count his people and learn how rich his kingdom was in worldly goods. And for Beth it was her last day at home, the day when she was to begin her duties as a Temple Maiden, in the Temple of Balaat-Gebal.

There was a stir in the streets of the town from earliest dawn. Peasants were arriving from the countryside with donkeys bearing well-filled panniers, flocks and herds were being driven through the town gates, porters were carrying up bales of merchandise from the harbour, and every craftsman wanted to be first in the queue to deposit his offering and avoid the long wait in the heat of the day.

Only in the house of Resh, it seemed, was there no last-minute bustle to prepare a gift. And yet Resh himself was nervous, irritable, pacing up and down in the house and refusing to touch his morning meal. Beth herself felt strangely calm, full of expectation though she was, but she was worried to see her father so unhappy.

'Father,' she said tentatively, 'your gift – it is ready, isn't it?'

'My offering?' Resh snapped. 'Of course it's ready. I trust His Majesty will be well aware of what my services are worth to him.'

'Are you thinking of Zayin and Nun and Aleph, Father?' Beth asked.

'Of course I am,' said her father. 'What else would I be thinking of on a day like this? It is a day when a man needs his sons.'

'Perhaps we shall have news of them today,' said Beth comfortingly. 'Who knows, perhaps today Nun's ship will come in, and the army will return, and – and Aleph will come down the mountains, and they will all bring rich offerings for the King. Wouldn't that be wonderful, Father?'

'Wonderful indeed!' muttered Resh. 'I am too old to believe in wonders.'

Beth felt it was a little unfair that her father should be brooding in this way over her absent brothers, while apparently forgetting what an important day it was for her too.

'Father,' she said again meekly, 'when should I go to the Temple?'

'You?' said her father, apparently surprised. 'Ah, child, I was forgetting. I am also losing a daughter today.' The thought did not seem to make him any happier.

'I shall not be far away, Father,' she said. For herself, she was looking forward to living in the Temple quarters, though she was still a little vague about what her duties would be. 'But should I go this morning?' she asked.

'Oh, any time today, child,' her father answered. Beth became impatient.

'Please, Father,' she said. 'Take me to the palace and the Temple now. We can see the first ceremonies, and find out what I should do.' And it would be better for him, she thought, than standing around at home. He must have felt the same, for he agreed, and they went together to where the offerings were already being made.

It was more like a market than a ceremony. As the priests and clerks checked and tallied, peasants were unloading sacks of corn or dried lentils – nothing perishable, Resh said, was accepted on the Offering Day – fishermen laid down piles of sun-dried fish, owners of olive orchards delivered great jars of oil. Potters were queueing up with samples of their best decorated pots, weavers of flax and wool were standing with lengths of useful cloth in their arms. There were even wild mountaineers, bringing pots of honey, and Resh explained that, although they might have avoided the offering if they wished, they would be considered as slaves if they were unable to produce as a gift something that could be weighed or measured. The merchants and traders, of course, made the best show. They paraded, family by family, offering bales of purple cloth from Tyre, copper vessels from Cyprus, spices from Southern Arabia, gems from Egypt and gold from the far corners of the earth. There was one rather ragged sailor who had recently returned from a coasting trip to the North. All he had was a long skewer-like poignard of a strange hard metal: most of its shaft was blackish, tinged with red rust, but its tip was sharpened and polished to a silvery point. The simple sailor did not know the name of the metal, and the clerks were doubtful of its utility, but they accepted it contemptuously and put it among the bronze tools and weapons.

There was a stir among the watching crowds in the public places, and suddenly they saw people making for parts of the town overlooking the sea. Resh explained that the shipwrights were making a communal offering of a new vessel for His Majesty's Navy. It was too big, of course, to be brought to the Temple, so it was to be rowed in review round the point. It came into sight, gaily decked, with a band of musicians on board. The music floated across the waters, but the occasion was spoiled by a quarrel that broke out among the representatives of the shipwrights on the shore. Resh said that there was a group of men, mere labourers who had felled the trees and carried the timber, who were trying to get a share of credit for the finished job of the master shipwrights. But they were told that they would no more get credit than the galley slaves who rowed the ship, or the musicians, and were sent packing. Beth wondered if this was fair, but her father merely said that a craftsman was a craftsman.

As the morning went on the piles of produce and stacks of manufactured goods grew in the royal courtyard; clerks were kept busy tallying the quantity of each sort; slaves laboured to carry it all to the warehouses. The herds of sheep and goats and cattle began to be troublesome. Animals, Resh explained, were accepted from the herdsmen on Offering Day: they were needed for the sacrifices in the Temple, but it was a nuisance to keep so many of them near the palace. They had to be farmed out again to landowners to be looked after – and some envious people said that these were better off after Offering Day than before.

Beth had been excited by the crowds of people thronging in to the town and by the market-day feeling in the air, but after a time she began to tire. There was so much merchandise, so many animals. 'When are you making your offering, Father?' she asked. 'And when – ?'

'The masons' offering will be a special one, like the shipwrights',' said Resh. 'There will be a ceremony.'

'And when will you take me to the priestesses?'

'Don't be impatient, child,' said her father testily. 'You don't want to make it look as if I'm offering a daughter because I've nothing better to give, do you?'

Beth felt shamed and angry. 'Am I nothing better than a cow or a sack of corn, Father?' she exclaimed.

'I did not mean that, my daughter,' Resh said in a milder

tone. 'Come, perhaps I could take you now to the inner court, and ask the priestess what you should do.'

They passed through an entry guarded by sentries, who recognized Resh, and Beth saw that they were in the courtyard in which she had confronted the King. There stood the mysterious square object, and there stood the tall obelisk, both swathed in cloth. Beth felt her courage ebbing at the sight, but her father escorted her through to the Temple, where they found one of the priestesses. Beth was still awed by the surroundings, but the conversation was very matter-of-fact. She was told which of her belongings she should bring, and that she would have to present two white doves as a sacrifice.

'That is easy,' said Resh. 'Beth, remember to bring two pigeons from your flock.'

But at that moment the courtyard began to fill with people, priests, scribes, and notables of the sort whom Beth had seen in the procession when she had been there, illegally, before. Her feelings of terrible guilt returned, but the priestess quite kindly said that she could wait in a colonnade at the back, with the other novices who would be watching the ceremony.

A hush came over the assembly, as the King entered at the far end of the court, and took his seat on a throne placed there for him. Then the High Priest mounted the steps, bowed before the King, and spoke.

'Most High and Sacred Majesty,' began the High Priest. 'May you live for ever, and may the abundance of your kingdom never grow less! On this auspicious day your devoted people have brought the good things of this world to lay at your feet. They have offered them in the sight of the gods to bear witness to the prosperity of Your Majesty and of your kingdom. Nowhere in the world is there found a prince more favoured with richness of belongings: your fields produce corn and beasts, your enterprising merchants bring to your shores rich materials purchased on very favourable terms. Your Majesty's servants care only for your welfare, day by day, and it is their joyful duty to do so. But we, your priests, think of Your Majesty's glory, not for today and the next day only but for all eternity. The goods that are brought to Your Majesty today will last while they are needed, but the corn will be eaten, pots will be broken, robes of fine tissue will wear out, beasts will die or must be killed. What Your Majesty's devoted priests have to offer, however, are things that will not be consumed or outworn. They are such that generations yet unborn will look upon them and say "Great is Abishram, King of Gebal!" They are such as will enshrine the name and person of the High and Mighty King Abishram for all eternity!'

The folds of cloth were pulled away from the obelisk, and the inscription, now neatly finished and painted in gorgeous colours, was revealed. At the same time the cloth was removed from the great square object, and a vast and magnificent burial sarcophagus, a huge stone coffin, was revealed with its massive lid propped open to show the rich lining of the inside.

A murmur of appreciation rose from the crowd, the King spoke a few words of thanks, and the ceremony seemed to be over. Then Beth noticed her father making his way through the throng to the High Priest and plucking in an agitated manner at his sleeve. But the High Priest seemed to be ignoring him and brushing him aside, for the King was now condescending to examine at closer quarters the great stone box in which he was to spend eternity. Resh turned away and retired to the back of the assembly. There seemed to be something so strange in the way he was standing that Beth slipped away from her colonnade and went to his side. Her father was weeping.

'What is it, Father dear?' Beth asked, taking his hand.

Her father spoke, but he seemed to be talking to himself.

'The ingratitude of priests! Yet what should I, a poor master mason, expect in the way of gratitude or recognition? I, a man with no sons at my side! What have I to do with the King's gift? I only saw the stones cut from the quarried blocks, hewed, hollowed, fitted, and smoothed. Why should I be proud? There are many men who could do that – none in Gebal, but perhaps in Egypt, in Babylon. But, Beth, my daughter' – and here he took Beth by the arm and pointed to the great sarcophagus – 'do you not see! See how the cover of the coffin, in white stone, fits on to the body of black basalt. What king in the world has a coffin in two colours? And this *I* thought of, this was my idea entirely!' He choked with indignation. 'And see the High Priest, how he shows it to His Majesty as if it were his own creation! Not a word of credit to the masons for their work! Oh no, it is the priests' gift. And I, I have nothing to offer of my own, and I have no sons to bring gifts for me, and what is to become of me I do not know. I am finished, and my sons are all dead!'

Beth did what she could to comfort him as they walked sadly home, but there was little she could say. He had expressed what she had been trying to ignore, that her three brothers who had been away for such a long time might never return, that they might already be dead. And she must leave her father in the empty house and go to the Temple.

When they got home she remembered the two white birds which she must bring as an offering to the Temple. It made her no happier to think that two of her little flock must be sacrificed, but in this sad hour it was only one more thing to regret. Then it struck her: she *used* to have two white pigeons, but now there was only one.

The birds had not yet returned from their day's foraging. Beth climbed up on to the city wall above the house, from where she often used to call the flock down out of the sky. She could not see her flock against the mountains, where every tree showed clearly in the level rays of the setting sun. She shaded her eyes and looked along the sea horizon, into the low sun's glare. A lonely sail stood up against the glow of the sky, but there were no birds. But there, yes! – from the North, where the headlands receded into the blue distance, a little flock was approaching.

The birds circled round between the town and the mountains, and with the sun behind her Beth could see plainly – yes, there were two white birds, so – but no, she was not looking for a flock with two white birds! It was strange how she still forgot. The flock swept round and made for where she stood, and she thought she could recognize some of the other birds of her flock. There were certainly two white ones among them now, and that morning there had been only one. Well, no . . . That morning she had been too busy thinking of the day's events to look at her pigeons. Now she was surrounded by a flutter of wings, and they were alighting around her. She held out her hands to the white birds and called to them. 'Lady Snow, come, come to me! And is it – can it be your husband, White Snow returned? Come, don't be shy!' And now the two white birds were perching on her hands, and as she looked at them her heart leapt and she saw that to the leg of one was tied a golden ring, and to the other a tiny scroll. And at once she said to the one in her left hand, 'You have come from Zayin, for that is his ring, and he cannot be far away.' And to the bird in her right hand she said, 'And you have come from Aleph, and what that strange scroll you have brought can mean I cannot imagine, but perhaps it will tell me what has happened to my brother.' And as she stood on the city wall, something made her raise her eyes to the lone sail she had seen, and something told her that at this happy time it must be Nun's ship homing on the wings of the wind over the sea.

*

Zayin, mounted on the horse Horizon, was riding through an olive grove in the northern approach to Gebal: Zayin now very much at home on horseback, riding easily and gracefully, keeping a light touch on the reins, murmuring words of encouragement to the horse as they jogged along. It was the end of a long day, the end of a long ride of many days. Horse and man had got used to each other and were confident together: there is nothing like the companionship of a long journey to get rid of suspicion and mistrust.

Now, as they neared strange habitations and passed astonished peasants and donkeys on the track, the horse only pricked up its ears a little, pranced a little sideways sometimes but quietened down at a word from the rider. But when at long last they came among the crowded streets of the port and the town, it was different. Heads appeared from doorways, children fled, or followed, staring. Zayin, feeling for the first time the lofty superiority of the man on the horse over men whose feet are merely on the ground, waved graciously. And the citizens muttered, 'Can that be General Zayin riding that great beast in that strange manner?' The horse showed the whites of its eyes and snorted, but Zayin urged it firmly onward, through the streets and towards the palace.

The guards at the entrance to the palace were weary and ill-tempered after controlling the crowds that had been flocking to the offering all day; they cursed the latecomers who were still pressing round the gates. As Zayin clattered up the steep street they must have thought the hoof-beats were those of yet another ass laden with parched corn. But when they looked round and saw Zayin mounted on the magnificent horse they were struck dumb with astonishment.

Zayin was about to swear at them for their unsoldierly reactions, when it suddenly came to him that he must present a strange picture in his trousers and cloak of skins, with ragged hair and beard. Indeed, after their first shock of surprise the soldiers levelled their spears at him and barred the way. But he called out: 'Do you not know your general when you see him? It is I, Zayin. Let me pass!' And at the well-remembered sound of his voice the soldiers stood aside and stiffened to attention.

In the palace yard, everyone from the King to the lowest tally clerk had been feeling the exhaustion that comes at the end of a day of empty ceremony. Heads turned at the sound of the horse's hooves, and a sudden tense silence fell. The next minute, the King, the priests, and the people were gaping at the man and the horse, and the crowd were falling back to give him passage. And Zayin was equally overcome with amazement at the unexpected sight of the King and his whole court: after all he was only a ragged fugitive, returning without his army and empty-handed. Except for the horse, of course – and the animal, sensing the tension in the air as horses do, began to prance and fidget nervously.

It was the High Priest who broke the silence, for it was his ceremony of the offering that was being interrupted, and he spoke the words with which all who came to the offering were addressed.

'Who are you that come to present offering to the Most High and Mighty King of Gebal, and what offering do you bring?'

Zayin's mind moved slowly, but at last he understood. 'Ye Gods!' he exclaimed to himself. 'I have arrived on a Day of Offering!' and aloud he cursed his horse, that was backing and sidling and tossing its head.

Zayin collected himself, did his best to control his horse, and spoke: 'Zayin, son of Resh, General of the Army of Gebal, salutes and does homage to His Most High Majesty (Stand still you brute – it's the King!) I bring this horse as humble tribute.' But the last words were spoken in the wrong direction, for the horse had spun round and they were facing the palace gates.

The tension broke, with a gasp of astonishment from the crowd as they recognized the figure on the strange animal as their general; but Zayin could also hear laughter at his odd arrival. And then through the entrance gates appeared his father, Resh, who was returning to the palace in the last hope of retrieving his reputation from the priests. Resh stared, as everyone else had stared, but he recognized his son, and holding out both arms – and ignoring the increasing alarm of the horse – he ran to embrace him.

But the headlong approach of Resh was too much for the horse, and Zayin's concentration was too much distracted for him to control it. He fell from the back of the rearing animal almost on top of his father, while the horse, panic-stricken, at last bolted through the palace gates, scattering the guards and peasants from its path.

The courtyard was in an uproar of exclamations and laughter, and the High Priest had to call for silence repeatedly before he could make himself heard. He was furious at the unseemly interruption to his ceremonial, and jealous that the return of Zayin might steal the glory of his Offering Day.

'General Zayin, His Majesty bids you welcome on your return from the wars on this auspicious day,' boomed the High Priest. 'What rich tribute, what plunder and captives does your victorious army bring to lay before His Most High Majesty?' The priest's eyes were on the ragged, lonely figure of the General, and it was clear that he suspected the truth, that there was no victorious army, neither plunder nor captives.

Zayin walked up to the steps on which the throne and the High Priest were standing, made a formal obeisance to the King, drew himself up, and spoke.

'Most High Majesty!' he began. 'The animal which I have brought you is but one, and I dedicate it to Your Majesty's service.' If it hasn't already galloped back to the Valley of Horses, he thought to himself. 'But more than that it represents military power such as we have not dreamed of before, a principle –'

'General Zayin must be aware,' interrupted the High Priest smoothly, 'that the Day of Offering is not a time when credit is given for principles – nor dreams. We cannot count or weigh them. As for the uncouth and unmanageable beast which you presented in such an unusual manner – I do not see it either,' and he craned his head round in an exaggerated pantomime of looking for the horse.

'If the palace attendants cannot hang on to a good horse when they see one, so much the worse for them,' Zayin rejoined, losing his temper. 'It will come to hand in time, no doubt. In any case, I have more important things than gifts. I have news, much of it bad, I admit. I have military intelligence which vitally –'

'The General must also be aware,' once more interrupted the priest, 'that today is no day for inauspicious news or business matters. Have you *nothing*, Zayin son of Resh,' – and the priest's voice grew ominous – 'to offer to the King?'

'High Priest!' retorted Zayin angrily. 'I return from many weary weeks of campaigning and dangers. I'm neither a potter, nor a peasant, nor a priest! As you suspect, I am empty-handed and there is nothing in my wallet.' He put his hand in the leather bag at his waist, and his fingers encountered something hard. Then he remembered. 'Except this – perhaps you can weigh and measure it!' He took out the tablet covered in the nail-shaped marks which he had saved from the dust of the northern camp. Restraining himself from flinging it at the High Priest's head, he tossed it contemptuously to a scribe in attendance. 'Accept it as my offering – you may even be able to read it!'

As he strode angrily out of the palace gates, Zayin, the

soldier, met Nun, the sailor. The two brothers halted and stared at each other, then they embraced, and stood back laughing.

'Well, General,' said Nun. 'What strange customs have you been adopting in Gebal since I've been away? A beard? And skins round your legs like a roll of canvas! What have you been doing here?'

'Here?' echoed Zayin. 'Ah, you sailors always think time stands still while you're at sea. Others travel too, you know. I've seen stranger things by land – but this is no time for exchanging yarns. You've come at the very moment to save the family fortunes, Nun my boy. I've no doubt you've swindled the Cretans out of a rich cargo. Take it to the King – it's Offering Day!'

'So they told me down at the port,' said Nun thoughtfully. 'But all I've brought back is a leaky ship. I have news though, Zayin. Not good news but of vital importance –'

Zayin laughed shortly, but Nun continued –

'And, Zayin, I have learned a skill that will set our sailors before those of all other nations. The stars, brother! How to steer by them! All thanks to my friend from Chaldea. This is he,' and he gestured to the figure of the sage, standing near by in the shadows. 'Your Reverence, this is my brother Zayin.'

Zayin bowed to the Chaldean. 'I wish you luck if you are going to the King with your news and your star-lore,' he said to Nun. 'A few painted pots from Crete would be more acceptable on Offering Day, I feel. And as for your reverend friend,' – he lowered his voice – 'I think we have more than enough priests here already. Be careful!'

Nun looked at Zayin with raised eyebrows. 'But have you brought no offerings, brother?' he asked.

'Mine seems to have given me the slip,' replied Zayin. 'You haven't seen a horse, have you?'

'A horse? We were nearly attacked by something as we came from the port. I thought it was a wild Cretan bull. Where are you going, Zayin?'

But Zayin had made off without another word towards the port. Nun shrugged his shoulders and led the Chaldean towards the palace.

Resh, for the second time shuffling abjectly away from the place of offering in deep despair, was overcome at the appearance of his other son. He tottered to embrace him in transports of relief.

'Ah, Nun, Nun, saviour of your family,' he wept. 'I knew you would return in time, and here you are. My old heart beats with hope again. Tell me, tell me, what have you brought to offer to the King?'

'Father,' said Nun, 'I rejoice to see you. All will be well, I am sure. I have things that the King must know, that may save us all from destruction; and I have strange secrets. But for offerings, I have nothing but a leaky ship –' and while his father began wringing his hands again in another rush of doubt and despair, Nun strode towards the High Priest and the throne.

The keen eye of the High Priest had not missed the exchange between father and son, though he could not have overheard their words. 'Who are you,' came the voice of the High Priest, 'that come to present offering to the Most High and Mighty King of Gebal, and what offering do you bring?'

Nun spoke up calmly and clearly: 'Nun, son of Resh, sea-captain, salutes and does homage to His Most High Majesty. Your Reverence knows well that on many voyages I have brought back goods from distant lands to enrich His Majesty's kingdom. This time I am fortunate to have escaped with an empty ship from the enemies of Gebal. But I have knowledge and news to impart to His Majesty that are of more weight than any gift of precious things –'

'Son of Resh,' interrupted the High Priest in a cold voice, 'you must know that on Offering Day knowledge is not a thing we can measure, neither can we weigh news. We must record that you, too, come empty-handed to the offering.'

'High Priest,' said Nun impatiently, 'my hands may be empty, but my head is not! Can you or your scribes steer a ship by the stars?'

This time the High Priest's reply was a burst of cold laughter, which was faithfully copied by the other priests and scribes. The High Priest's voice came more coldly than ever.

'If you have been meddling with heavenly knowledge, the concern of holy priests, it is no wonder that you return with an empty ship from a disastrous voyage, Captain – they tell me ships are best steered by a steering-oar!' Again the priests and scribes snickered. 'Your brother, by impiously bestriding an animal, lost himself an army. Have you nothing more tangible than news and knowledge, of which anyone can boast, to lay at the feet of His Majesty on Offering Day?'

A thought occurred to Nun, and feeling inside his tunic, he took out the clay tablet with the long-legged script and the seal of lions that he had been given by the Queen of Crete. He handed it calmly to the nearest scribe.

'Only this. It may speak for itself, if your scholars can read it,' he said evenly.

The High Priest gave it a contemptuous glance, and then turned to the distracted Resh. 'Resh, father of Zayin and Nun, are two handfuls of clay all that your family has to offer? Have you no other sons?'

Resh sank to his knees and twisted his hands. 'Your Reverence,' he replied in a choked voice, 'I have only one other son, and he is weak in the head, and no one knows where he is!'

There was a hush while the High Priest gazed with triumphant scorn at the abject Resh, and drew breath to speak. But the silence was broken by a small, feminine voice.

'I know where he is. He is three weeks' march away from here.'

And all eyes turned to Beth, standing on the steps of the Temple, holding a white bird.

'Beth! Beth!' came the strangled voice of Resh, who was beating his head with his hands as he knelt. 'What are *you* doing here again, girl?'

'You forget, Father,' said Beth, 'I am no longer a mere girl, I am a maiden of the Temple and have a right to be here. And since His Reverence wishes to know, I can tell him. My brother Aleph is many days' journey away, in the land of Sinai, and sends his homage to the King.'

'How can you know this, Beth?' asked Nun.

'This little bird has just told me,' said Beth seriously. 'And it, too, has news of great concern to His Majesty.'

Once again came the cold laughter of the High Priest. 'So this bird, too, has news, like the other members of your strange family. I am surprised that it does not also have mysterious lore or knowledge in its possession, which will be to the benefit of the whole nation!'

And the priests and scribes laughed again – but Beth's eyes suddenly widened, as if a great thought had come to her, and she said simply, 'Indeed, perhaps he has.' But the High Priest did not notice.

'Temple maiden,' said the High Priest coldly, 'His Majesty is weary of evasions and excuses. You may offer that bird for sacrifice as a token offering on behalf of your family. It is little enough, but it is better than nothing. Is that your intention?'

'No, Your Reverence,' replied Beth. 'The bird goes free. He deserves it.' And she tossed the white pigeon into the air and it fluttered off.

At this act of defiance, the High Priest was incapable of speech. Then there was heard a voice that seemed to be weary and strong, gentle and cruel at the same time, the voice of the King himself. He had sat all day on his throne, a silent witness of the ceremonials of the Day of Offering, but up to that moment he had stayed aloof from the proceedings and left the talking to his mouthpiece, the High Priest.

'High Priest,' spoke Abishram, King of Gebal, 'let it be known that, deeply as we are touched by offerings such as dried fish and pots of honey, we feel that there may be a time on Offering Day for less ponderable tributes. Horses that carry soldiers on their backs, ships that follow stars, birds that bear messages which girls can understand – these things weary us less than numbering bolts of cloth and flocks of goats. Let the Chief Mason and his sons and his daughter be received in private audience after the ceremony of offering is over, and let that be a time for hearing news and weighing knowledge.'

The High Priest bowed low, but his face showed that he knew he was defeated in his desire to humiliate Resh and his family. Resh bowed low too. His face showed merely that he could not yet believe his good fortune.

There had scarcely been time to find Zayin, to help him dress and prepare himself for the audience, and to decide among themselves how and in what order they were to speak, before the family of Resh were assembled in the pillared council chamber of the palace. The sun had set, and in the hall, now lit with oil-lamps, only the high priests and a few councillors were in attendance upon the King.

Zayin was the first to speak. He told of his northward march with the army, of his quest for the monsters, and of how his army had been scattered in the encounter with what they conceived to be six-limbed creatures, part man, part horse. 'Most High and Gracious Majesty,' he continued, 'your servant fell into the hands of these monsters, and behold, they are not monsters at all – not man-horses, but horse-men. Nevertheless, I have a mystery to relate of them, a mystery which, as their slave and captive, I was able to study and master for myself. It is this. These people, Your Majesty, have learned so to tame and train a certain breed of horse that it is, indeed, an extension of a man's body and limbs, and no longer a mere draught beast to pull a chariot. Such a horse will carry a man on his back at the walk, trot, or gallop, will obey his slightest indication to start or stop, will charge the enemy, wheel and sidestep, leap over obstacles impossible to chariots, run up and down steep slopes – in fact, go almost anywhere a trained soldier can go on the battlefield, with much greater speed and agility. On long marches, the soldier can sit on the horse and not tire himself. In battle, the soldier is free to use his sword or lance, and has the advantage of the horse's height over his foe. These northern tribesmen can even shoot arrows most accurately and effectively from horseback.

'Your Majesty, may we not one day have an army of mounted soldiers to defend your kingdom? I, Zayin, have acquired the secrets of breeding, training, and controlling horses. I place them, and myself, humbly at Your Majesty's disposal.'

Zayin's voice, which had been ringing with enthusiasm for his theme, now dropped and became more urgent. 'But, Your Majesty, another thing I learned in the North which is of more immediate concern to Your Majesty and your kingdom, and this I could not possibly have learned unless I had been a captive. It is, I fear, not good news. The nations of the North-East are planning war, and mean to invade the coast as far south as Gebal. This I heard from their own mouths. There is little time to be lost in preparing our defences, and I beseech Your Majesty's authority to raise more forces in readiness.'

Zayin ceased, and there was silence. Then the High Priest spoke: 'Gracious Majesty, our General returns alone from the North with a strange tale indeed. Might we not ask some evidence in support of what he says?'

'Did I not bring a written tablet from the enemy's camp which I gave to one of the scribes?' demanded Zayin. 'Where is it?'

A scribe standing at the back of the priestly party came forward holding the tablet and handed it to the High Priest.

'Well?' Zayin demanded. 'Is it or is it not evidence of what I say?' And the King turned to the High Priest and raised his eyebrows as if waiting for him to read.

The High Priest hesitated, then turned to the other priests and scribes and there was a murmured discussion over the tablet. When he spoke, there was embarrassment in his voice. 'Most Gracious Majesty, this is a most corrupt and unscholarly piece of writing. It will take – ah – a little time to interpret.'

'Let it be done, High Priest,' said the King coldly, 'and meanwhile let us hear the second son of Resh.'

Nun then stepped forward. He had been turning over in his mind for a long time how he should relate his story, for it was no simple narrative of exploration, battle, captivity, and escape as Zayin had told. He sometimes doubted whether he had ever spent that strange night on the island of Thira, or whether he had dreamt it. And what should he say about the prophecies of doom spoken by the Chaldean? He resolved to give his account as soberly as he could, leaving nothing out, however strange it might sound.

'Most High and Gracious Majesty, I set sail from the port of Gebal with a cargo of cedar-wood, bound for Crete. But at the request of the court I took as passenger a sage of Chaldea. This man from beyond the eastern desert guided me by the stars over the western sea, so that we sailed by day and night without a sight of land. But before landing in Crete we sailed north to the islands, and there we found the burning mountain that stands in the sea, and on it we were entertained by men who told us of the race of Giants that are imprisoned in the burning mountain, and indeed the whole island shook beneath our feet and we were very glad to leave the next day. We then proceeded to Amnisos, discharged the cargo, and at the insistence of my passenger I went with him to the court of King Minos at Knossos. Here we were received in audience by the King, but the Chaldean, when called upon to speak, prophesied doom and destruction upon Knossos, much to the King's displeasure. I was therefore delivered as a sacrifice to the fighting bulls, from which I was only saved by strange northern men with red faces and yellow hair. Fortunately, I was taken to the Queen, who as you know came as a bride from this coast, and she, believing me to be a prisoner, revealed the intention of King Minos to send his fleets to attack your kingdom. I managed to escape from the prison with the Chaldean and we put to sea in the darkness. And though we were delayed by contrary winds we returned to Gebal, guided again every night by the Chaldean's strange star-lore. And all I have brought back, Great King, is this new knowledge whereby a ship may be steered with more confidence on a starry night than it can by the light of the sun itself. But, Your Majesty, what infinite opportunity for exploration and trade may this knowledge offer us! What endless voyages may your adventurers make without hugging hostile shores! To what ends of the earth may the name of Gebal now be carried! I dedicate this learning to Your Majesty and your merchant seamen.' He paused, wondering whether he had made his tale too brief for comprehension, then he remembered something. 'And as for the intelligence about the plans of King Minos, your scribes will by now have interpreted the tablet I received from the Queen of Crete herself, giving details of their preparation for war.'

There was more murmuring among the priests and scribes,

the tablet with the long-legged script was produced, and the King waited for the High Priest to speak. Again there was embarrassment in the High Priest's voice as he said, 'Your Majesty, this writing is of course known to us. But it is merely an unsanctified code of signs, used for book-keeping purposes by lay clerks. However, if Your Majesty considers that it may contain matter of importance, we shall, of course, be able to have it interpreted in a few days.'

'Let it be done, High Priest, let it be done,' came the voice of the King, even colder than before. 'And now where is this daughter of Resh, maiden of our Temple?'

Beth came forward nervously, clutching a corner of her robe, but when she spoke her voice was steady. 'Most High and Gracious Majesty, I have never in my life been away from Gebal and its mountain. But my brother Aleph went away many weeks ago, and took one of my pigeons. Today I found that it had returned, with a message on papyrus round its leg. I can't ask the High Priest to read it because he would not understand – I mean it's written in the signs my brother and I invented, as a game. But look, Your Majesty, even you could read it in a few minutes if I showed you. Only twenty-two letters!'

Not noticing the outraged expressions on the faces of the priests and scribes, Beth had impulsively approached the throne with the little scrap of paper that had come so many miles on the pigeon's leg.

'Look!' she said. 'Here's a letter Aleph, that's my brother's name. And here's a Beth, that's for me.' But then she hesitated. 'Oh, Your Majesty,' she faltered, 'I'm afraid you are not going to like this. I had forgotten what it spelt. It says the Egyptians are advancing up the coast to attack Gebal.'

10
The Dog River

*How the Dog River got its name – Gebal withstands
the Egyptian army from the South, but the Mitannians
break through in the North*

'I used to think it was an easy thing to be a king,' Beth told
herself as she sat quietly in a corner of the council chamber.
'But, poor man, what a difficult problem he has to solve!'

King Abishram of Gebal was no longer the remote, haughty
monarch he appeared in peace-time ceremonies. He was
striding up and down the council chamber with a frown on
his face. He was even twisting his fine beard. The council of
war had gone on all night, opened by Zayin's fiery proposal
that they must attack and destroy all their enemies. Sub-
sequently, many councillors had put other points and suggested alternative plans. Now the King was trying to reach
a decision.

'General Zayin, what was it you were saying in your simple
soldierly way at the beginning of the meeting?'

'I merely said we should meet our enemies with force.
But I see now –'

'You were right, General Zayin. Make immediate dispositions to resist attacks from north or south. And you,
Captain Nun, must help to do the same by sea. The council is
ended.'

The council members bowed and withdrew, relieved that

the long session was over and decisions had been made. But the King stayed, twisting his beard, oppressed by the weight of his responsibilities.

A little south of Gebal is a point where the steep mountains come nearest to the seashore. There is no coastal strip, only a narrow ledge between the cliffs and the water. And at this point, a river flows down a deep gorge into the sea. It is a gently flowing river, and its banks are covered with trees and orchards. Zayin chose this spot to defend the southern approaches. He was satisfied that no better place existed for a small army to resist a large one. The Egyptian troops would have to pass in almost single file along the narrow ledge, and a few determined men could block their passage indefinitely. Besides, it was a pleasant and suitable camp, with plenty of fresh water, and supplies of food could be brought from the interior along the river valley. He was wondering now if it was not *too* pleasant.

The trouble was that the troops did not believe in the emergency. They had marched out full of fight and defiance, singing their battle-songs and shouting their war-cries. Then they had reached the river and camped. The first night they had slept under the stars with their weapons by their sides. By the next night little shelters had sprung up, thatched with leaves. As the days passed, and no enemy came in sight, a village of little huts had grown up, in which the men had made themselves comfortable.

Zayin, as Commander-in-Chief, could not stay in camp all the time. He had got his horse again – the only horse in the Army of Gebal – and he was able to ride between the southern and northern defences and inspect their state of readiness. One day he had arrived unexpectedly at the camp on the river and found that whole families had come out to keep the soldiers company – women, children, sheep, goats, and dogs.

He soon sent the women and children packing, but he kept the sheep and goats to provide fresh meat and milk, and the dogs to look after them. Another time he had arrived late in the evening to find all the troops that were off duty gathered round fires singing at the tops of their voices and dancing to the sound of drums and other instruments. There was nearly a mutiny when he strode into the circle of firelight and told them to stop. They had listened with sullen faces when he asked them what was the point of lying in ambush if an enemy could hear the noise they made ten miles away. He was sorry he had to shut them up: he was all for a bit of song and dance himself and it was difficult to keep the troops cheerful during a long wait like this; but the defence of the country must come first.

The days and weeks passed, and still the patrols in the North brought no reports of the Mitanni, Nun's guardships that cruised offshore saw no signs of the Cretan Navy, and no Egyptian advance guard appeared up the coast road from the South. Back in Gebal even their friends had begun to laugh at Zayin and Nun and Beth, asking them what had become of their 'intelligence' and their prophecies. The troops themselves were incredulous. Many of them were conscripts, rather than professional soldiers, and they thought of their neglected farms and trades as they waited around doing nothing. Yet they still had enough respect for their General to put up a show of efficiency even when he turned up unexpectedly – in fact, Zayin suspected that they kept a better look-out for his visits than for the enemy. To find out what the state of morale was really like, he decided to make his inspections dressed as an ordinary soldier.

It was night at the southern river. The main camp slept, guarded by sentries who stood in pairs, talking quietly to each other. At some distance from the camp was the farthest outpost, on the ledge between the mountain and the sea, where two look-outs were supposed to watch the track from the South by night and day.

The two look-outs, two ordinary soldiers whose names were Ain and Shin, had in fact found themselves comfortable seats in a niche of the rock from which they could see nothing but the light of the setting moon glittering on the sea. They had kept watch together like this for many nights, they knew each other well, and they did not have much left to talk about.

'One thing,' Ain was saying, 'soon as that moon goes down we won't be able to see a thing. Be too dark. Might as well have a sleep.'

'Makes no difference,' said Shin. 'Dark or not dark, there's nothing to see. You know it and I know it. Might as well sleep, anyway.'

'You're right. Not a living creature on this coast for a hundred miles – except that old dog barking out there. We're wasting our time. You know it and I know it. Dare say even the General knows it. Keep your eyes skinned for the Egyptians, he says. Egyptians! What would they be doing here?'

'Remember my old grandad saying he seen Egyptians up the coast.'

'In the olden days, maybe he did. There was a real Pharaoh those days. You know what? They say there's a woman rules Egypt nowadays. Reckon we don't have to worry about the Egyptians.'

'Don't know though. Women! They can cause more trouble than anything. Wouldn't trust a she-Pharaoh farther'n I could see her.' There was a pause while he looked at the setting moon. 'Wouldn't mind holding hands with a girl and watching that old moon though.'

'Girls! Don't talk to me about girls. You know, we wouldn't be here if it wasn't for a bint.'

'What you mean, wouldn't be here?'

'Haven't you heard? It's all over the camp. There's this young woman, see, and she's a witch. Some say she's the General's sister, or something. She got animals and birds that talk to her, and they told her the Egyptians was coming up the coast to attack us. Why else do you think we're here?'

'A witch, eh? Maybe she knows something then. We had an old woman in our village – she was a witch. Cured our old cow though, that she did. She knew what she was doing all right.'

'Well, I reckon this one don't. Else why are we sitting here night after night, and nothing happening?'

Shin suddenly stiffened: 'Shh! Someone coming!'

'Can't hear nothing,' said Ain. "Cept that old dog, barking down the shore there. You're imagining Egyptians, with all this talk.'

'Not that way, from the camp, you donkey. It may be the sergeant.' Shin got up and looked towards the camp.

'It'd be the first time the sergeant's been up this time of the morning for long enough. May be our relief though. Early for once – instead of two hours late!'

The moonlight showed a solitary figure with the spear and helmet of a common soldier approaching beneath the cliffs. Shin whistled, but the newcomer made no sound until he had come up to the niche where the men rested.

'What's the matter with you, then?' asked Shin. 'Too hot to sleep in the camp?'

'You two seem to have made yourselves comfortable enough here,' said the newcomer.

'Yes, it's a cosy little kip, see! And nobody can't creep up from the camp without us seeing them,' said Shin.

But Ain was looking hard at the newcomer in the moonlight. 'You're new, aren't you? Who sent you up? There's supposed to be two reliefs.'

'Not time to change the watch yet,' said the third man shortly. 'I've come to strengthen the guard. Special instructions.'

'What's on, then?' asked Ain. 'General's inspection or something?'

'Don't worry about the General,' said the newcomer. 'I can promise you if you haven't seen him yet you won't see him for a long while. Anything to report?'

'Anything to report!' mocked Shin. 'Hark at him! You *are* new, aren't you. Where have you been — staff headquarters?'

'We don't say as how we haven't slain a few score Egyptian charioteers in the silent watches of the night, like,' said Ain. 'But nothing really to report, apart from that. Things are pretty quiet.'

'And if it wasn't for a fool of a dog barking at a jackal down the coast there, keeping us awake, we'd have had a nice long sleep.'

'Had a look down the coast recently?' asked the newcomer.

'Now look here!' said Ain. 'You may be new to this unit, but you'd better get used to things as they are. Down the coast there, there may be ghosts and demons and evil spirits for all we know, but there ain't a flesh-and-blood human being, let alone an Egyptian soldier, for a hundred miles. I know it, and my mate Shin knows it, and the sergeant knows it, and all the other silly soldiers as have been sitting on this rock for weeks knows it. And the General himself knows it. Only because of this here witch with the talking birds he don't dare tell the King. All we got to do is make ourselves comfortable, and see that no brass-helmeted officer don't creep up on us unawares, and after a few more weeks sitting on this here rock looking at nothing we'll all go home and see to the harvest, if there is one. So don't you come along at this hour of the night and start making things difficult. All right, son?'

Zayin – for the newcomer was no less a person than the General himself – said nothing. He had visited the post to find out for himself just what the soldiers on guard were thinking and doing. He did not want to arouse suspicion by insisting on greater attention to duty. The worst of it was that he was beginning to have the same sort of doubts about the reality of the invasion. He had seen for himself in the North the preparations for a campaign, and yet no enemy had appeared from the North. His brother Nun was a hard-headed sailor, even if he were a little crazy on the subject of stars, and no doubt he had good evidence of the Cretan threat – yet still no hostile warships had appeared over the horizon. As to the Egyptians' intentions – all they had to go on was Beth's mumbo-jumbo with the bird and this infantile secret writing which only she and Aleph were supposed to understand. For some reason it had impressed the King, but as grounds for mobilizing an army it was beginning to look a little shaky.

He took a seat in the niche of the rocks and looked at the sea. The moonlight made a path right up to where the moon was about to sink behind the horizon. Little waves broke gently on the rocky shore below them. It was all very peaceful – except when the yapping of the dog disturbed the silence again. It was getting shriller, and more and more excited.

'What's got into that wretched animal, then?' asked Shin. 'Why can't it sleep at this hour of the night, and give us a bit of peace?'

'Cornered a jackal, like you said,' murmured Ain.

'Yes, but come to think of it what's a jackal doing down on the shore?'

'All right, then, it's a fish he's got cornered, what's it matter?'

Zayin hardly heard the conversation about the dog. He was thinking about his family, about the King, about the High Priest, who he knew would be happy to ruin him and all his relations; he was wondering what would happen in the future if all the talk of war proved unjustified. They would all look fools, and it might, indeed, mean ruin.

'Some folks say dogs can see spirits,' Shin was saying nervously.

'Why don't you go and see for yourself what the brute's barking at, then?' said Ain irritably. 'And give it a kick and tell it to shut up while you're about it.'

'You come with me, then.'

'What, both of us go! Who keeps a look-out towards the camp, then?'

Zayin could not help smiling to himself. 'I'll do that,' he said. 'I'll make sure the General doesn't catch us unawares. I'd recognize him if I saw him.'

Ain sighed wearily and got to his feet. 'Anything for a little peace and quiet,' he said. 'Though it's a wonder the General lets those noisy beasts stay around.'

Zayin was left with his thoughts as the two soldiers went off round the cliff face. If peace-time conditions returned, where did he stand in Gebal, with his father and brothers? A General who had lost an army, a Captain who had lost a cargo, a scribe who had run away, and the father of a family who had nothing to offer on Offering Day. He was so wrapped up in his bitter thoughts that he hardly noticed the two soldiers returning. They were moving quickly, but with surprisingly little noise; near to, Zayin could hear them breathing hard and thickly, and even in the moonlight their faces looked unusually pale.

'What is it, then,' he asked. 'Bad spirits?'

'Gods of Gebal!' gasped Ain. 'It's the Egyptians! What'll we do?'

Zayin sprang to his feet. 'Egyptians!' he exclaimed. 'You saw them? You mean you two have been sitting here and the enemy's almost upon us!'

But he found that the spear of Ain was levelled at his own throat. 'Don't give us none of that!' Ain was grating, still panting for breath. 'You was sitting here, too, whoever you are. It's Egyptians all right – plain as anything in the moonlight. Now what are we going to do – that's what I want to know?'

He's right, thought Zayin. He knocked the spear down with his hand. 'Come on then, man, tell us what you've seen,' he said in a voice of authority. 'How many of 'em? Advance guard? Main guard? Are they advancing or halted? How far off are they? Don't stand there, man, speak!'

The soldiers seemed to recognize the authority in his voice. They stood to attention and gasped out their report.

'Scouts – a handful of 'em – coming along the cliff ledge!'

'Another lot rounding the far point – saw their helmets in the moonlight.'

'Scouts'll be here any minute.'

'Just the old dog on the ledge – barking and growling at 'em – hold 'em up for a bit – before they do him in.'

'That dog will get a medal, or a monument!' muttered Zayin. 'Right, who can run fastest?'

'Shin, he's younger,' said Ain.

'Move then! No noise mind! Straight to the camp-commandant. Tell him to stand the troops to according to orders. No drums or trumpets! What are you waiting for then? Want to stay here and die?'

'No, but –'

'Well, man, what is it?'

'Whose orders shall I say?'

Zayin pulled a ring from his finger. 'Take this! Tell him General Zayin sent the orders – and that the General and one

private soldier are engaging the enemy until he brings reinforcements.'

Zayin heard another gasp from the soldier, this time of
astonishment, and then the man moved swiftly off towards
the camp. Zayin turned to his companion.

'Well, man, what are your duties when you sight the
enemy?'

'I – I can't remember, sir.'

'I'll tell you then. This niche may make itself useful after
all. The scouts will have to come round this point of rock one
after the other. By the favour of the Gods, we know they're
coming, and they don't know we're here – they didn't see
you, did they?'

'No, sir, we took care of that.'

'Right. They must not see us. Keep close until they're past
– then they must die without a sound. If their army's got any
march discipline, the advance guard won't come on until the
scouts signal all clear. That will hold them up for a bit. If
not, we two will have to hold up the whole advance guard.
Understand?'

'Yes, sir,' said Ain grimly. 'I understand.'

The General and the private soldier drew back into the
darkness of the rock. Zayin unsheathed his sword, Ain held
his spear at the ready. They listened to the frantic barking of
the dog. Then it stopped suddenly. The two men exchanged
looks in the obscurity, as soldiers do on the battlefield when
a casualty occurs. There was now no sound but the washing
of the sea.

They waited. After an age, there was the clang of a shield
against rock. They waited. The steady sound of footsteps on
the stony track came to their ears, and then muttered words.
Both men held their breath. One after the other, two figures
appeared, outlined against the stars and the sea. One each!
The Egyptians stood there, looking onwards up the coast,

their backs to the crevice that concealed Ain and Zayin. Zayin nudged Ain with his elbow, they moved together. Sword and spear found their marks, and the Egyptians fell without a cry. One sprawled on the track; the other pitched forward on to the rocks below, and his shield first clanged on the rocks, then splashed into the sea.

Silence returned. Zayin and Ain waited, as the enemy troops round the corner must have been waiting for the scouts who would never come back. The moon dipped below the horizon, but already a grey light was filtering over the black mass of the mountain wall. The night was nearly at an end. If the enemy was to attack in force, it would be at dawn. Zayin took off his helmet and handed it to the soldier, and clambered up to peep over the shoulder of rock. He must see what was happening. It was very shadowy under the cliff; shapes, that he knew must be rocks, seemed to move as he stared at them. Then a small sound caught his ear, and his eyes focused on a party of men advancing cautiously along the cliff ledge. He could not make out their number but it would be more than one each next time. He went back to his companion and held a whispered conference. Then they withdrew together, not this time into the niche in the rocks, but up a bank of loose rock and shale to the side of the track, at the top of which they flattened themselves against the cliff face.

The sounds of the approaching party became clearer, though they were moving with more caution than the first two scouts. They are wondering what happened to the scouts, thought Zayin; their nerves are on edge, they know something's wrong. Zayin kept a hand on Ain's arm as they watched the men round the corner, all the time looking carefully about them. Zayin had been right, a silent short-range attack would not have worked this time. One, two, three, four, five, and then a sixth was outlined against the phosphorescence of the sea, and the party stood, exchanging low whispers as they surveyed the next bay and the cliffs ahead.

Then Zayin moved, and so did Ain. Clashing their weapons and shields, kicking loose rocks ahead of them, whooping and hollering until the echoes aroused from the cliffs made them sound like a charging battalion. They hurtled down the slope. Two of the startled enemy stepped back into thin air and fell into the sea below without being touched. Zayin and Ain engaged a man apiece, shield to shield. Zayin gave his adversary a stab in the side, and by sheer weight bore him backwards off the ledge; immediately he noticed that another had turned aside and stumbled over the first scout's body; this one he killed too, before the man could recover his feet. Then Zayin turned to Ain who was struggling with another Egyptian, and between them they soon disposed of him. They paused, breathing heavily, and looked around for more.

'There were six,' said Zayin.

'The other man must have run away,' panted Ain. 'He will tell them we're here,' he added anxiously.

'Never mind,' said Zayin thoughtfully, 'the time for secrecy and surprise is over. He will go back and tell the main guard that the pass is held by a strong force. There will be a breathing space before they attack again.'

Ain nodded, and then suddenly held his breath and listened. 'Then what's that?' he demanded. To their ears came the tramp of deliberate marching feet, the sound of many soldiers and at no great distance. Zayin held his breath too, while his heart missed a beat. Surely they could not be pressing on the attack so soon! Then he heard a gasp of relief from Ain, who was pointing back up the coast. 'They're ours, sir,' he said thankfully, and now in spite of the distortion of sound among the cliffs, Zayin realized that the marching feet were those of his own army approaching from the camp.

As the sky brightened over the ridge of the mountains, the

Giblite army was drawn up for battle at the coastal pass that would be known for ever afterwards as the Dog River, in honour of the unknown animal that had saved a nation. The plan of battle could hardly be simpler. The battle-front consisted of twelve men, for there was only room for twelve men to stand side by side on the part of the ledge they were defending. But then, too, there was room for only twelve Egyptians from the whole of Pharaoh's host to attack. The rest of the Giblite army stood to along the banks of the river. Just as the water of the river flowed continually to replenish the sea, so the columns were able to keep moving down its banks, to replace the twelve fighters in the forefront of the battle.

Zayin mounted a rock where he could be seen by as much of his strung-out army as possible. Standing beside him, Ain displayed the helmets and armour of the three available Egyptian victims. At that early hour and in that grey light, Zayin did not feel like giving an impassioned oration. At dawn, a few words are enough.

'You've been wondering what you're here for,' he cried, his voice echoing along the gorge. 'Now you know. Your General and one of your comrades have already disposed of seven men between them. The rest will soon be here – and even if the odds are seven to two, what have we to fear? Our enemies are at the end of a long march in strange country. We are defending our homes and families. Stand firm – we have more to fight for than the enemy. I'm only sorry you can't all fight at once. Be patient though – I'll see that you all have your turns.'

They waited impatiently for the expected attack. The advance guard of Egyptians came round the corner of the cliff in a determined rush, met no resistance, and then saw the motionless line of armed men blocking the base of the cliff farther along the ledge. On Zayin's orders, his men remained quite silent. The Egyptians marched to within a javelin's throw of the Giblites, and a herald stepped forward and spoke:

'In the name of Pharaoh, let us pass! We will do you no harm if you lay down your arms and go home.'

An echo from the face of the cliffs threw back his last words: 'Go home!' Zayin himself was awed, and knew that no other reply was needed. The Egyptians, seeing the towering cliffs and the silent soldiers of this unknown north-ern country, faltered. But it seemed that their orders had been to attack and test the defences. They formed up on as broad a front as they could manage, twelve abreast on the rocky ledge, set their spears at the ready and their shields before them, and in silence, too, advanced at a steady pace to the attack.

Seldom has a battle been joined in such cold blood. Though each army had put its most hardened soldiers into the front rank, there seemed to be a moment when both sides hesitated to break the silence of dawn with the clash of arms. Then shields met shields, sword parried spear, and the first grunts, curses, and cries of anguish awoke the echoes of the gorge. There could only be one outcome of this first engagement. Men fell on both sides, but every empty space in the Giblite ranks was quickly filled. The Egyptians had no means of telling how great were the defences, but they soon discovered that this was no mere handful of men masquerading as an army. At a word of command, the advance guard disengaged itself and retreated back along the ledge more quickly than they had advanced, but still with disciplined deliberation. A hail of javelins now helped them on their way. Leaving their wounded on the ledge, they fell back round the point to regroup and report to the main guard.

There were exclamations of jubilation among the Giblite troops, but Zayin quelled them. 'The battle's not over yet – it's not even begun! Well done though, they've had a taste of our mettle!'

Another wait followed. The wounded in the front rank were replaced by fresh soldiers — many of the former protesting that they had hardly had a chance yet. But Zayin knew the next attack would be more determined.

When at last it came, it was obvious that the Egyptian commander had decided upon the maximum show of force. A broad column of marching men appeared round the corner and advanced in a compact mass along the ledge, uttering rhythmic war-chants and filling the air with the sound of their advance. It seemed that the mere pressure of bodies from behind must make them irresistible and that nothing human could stand in their way. But Zayin called above the noise, 'Stand firm, Giblites. They can still only fight twelve at a time!'

Then he saw what must be done. Instead of presenting a square block across the path of the advancing army, he re-formed his troops so that they stood diagonally across the ledge. The head of the column met the ranks of the defenders. The Giblites kept formation and hacked savagely at the leaders of the column. There was now no attempt at silence and coolness; men were grappling at close quarters and sheer weight opposed sheer weight. But the leaders of the column were stumbling upon heaps of dead and wounded, and were being crowded by their fellows behind them. Unable to go on or disengage themselves, and swollen by more files of soldiers urged on from behind, the column began to swell until it was a tight-packed mass of struggling men, unable to use their weapons. The wedge-shaped barrier of Giblites, combined with the pressure from the rear, forced the men at the head of the column outwards from the cliff until they began to drop off the ledge into the sea by dozens, howling and cursing. Zayin himself, perched above the seething mass, felt sickened. This was no heroic battle — it was like sheep attacked in the fold by wolves. But it was war. He gave a signal to the parties of mountaineers half-way up the cliff above the ledge, and they began to loosen rocks and boulders so that they fell on the heads of the enemy below, some of them starting small landslides. The panic on the ledge became a rout. Soldiers near the front turned round and started using their weapons on their own troops, shouting to the officers in the rear to stop sending more men round the point. Men were dropping off all along the ledge, some dislodged by the falling rocks, some pushed off by their friends. The flow round the point ceased, then began to ebb backwards. When the pressure was released, the battle at the head of the column became freer and more furious for a while, until the leaders became aware of the retreat behind them. Then they turned and fled, followed by more showers of javelins. The triumphant Giblites were about to pursue them, but Zayin shouted to them to keep their ranks. There was no advantage to be gained from chasing along the coast towards the main army.

What now? So far it was a victory for the Giblites. So few of them had been able to get at grips with the enemy that their casualties had been very low, while the ledge was strewn with dead and dying Egyptians, and many more bodies washed around in the sea below. And yet it was unlikely that the Egyptian general would let it go at that. The glory of Pharaoh was at stake. It was impossible that one small city-state could defy the might of Egypt for ever.

Zayin relieved the defenders again, though there were still men among the first contingent who had been within a few yards of the battle and had not struck a blow – and at the other end of the army, in the gorge of the river, soldiers were still asking when the fight would begin. But from his high point above the pass, Zayin was better able to understand what was happening. What would he do, he wondered, if he were attacking.

'If I were the Egyptian general,' he said to himself, 'I would know that my reserves were as the sands of the seashore compared with the handful of grit that is the Giblite army. I would consider that, given an equal chance, one swordsman is more or less equal to another. I would tell myself that as long as my troops are willing to fight and are given room to manoeuvre, I can wear down any opposition in time. All the same, they've had a shock and a defeat and they won't feel much like going back on that ledge again.'

The unknown Egyptian general down the coast must indeed have been thinking on those lines. When the next attack came, half-way through the morning, it was made by picked fighters from Upper Egypt who advanced in open order, section by section, and fought fiercely and well, giving the Giblites little rest and causing many casualties. But still the ranks were closed by fresh troops from the river, and there was time to carry the wounded and dead to the rear. Each Egyptian attack was met by apparently the same wall of armed men, while the number of Egyptian dead and wounded could be seen by each wave of attackers. One wave was composed of nearly naked black Nubians; another one, in the dead of the afternoon, was of wild men from the desert with fuzzy hair and long lances; but the Giblites, now sweating in the direct rays of the sun, fought on grimly like men caught in a machine. There was nothing else they could do but fight man to man and keep closing up the ranks – until there were no men left to close them.

That was the last attack of the day. The Giblites remained in formation until the sun went down into the sea; then Zayin made his dispositions for the night. He ensured that the outpost was well manned – he hardly needed to tell them to keep a good look-out tonight – and that enough troops were in armed readiness at the pass in case of a night attack. Only then did he realize that he was himself dropping with fatigue and hunger; he could not remember when he had last eaten or slept. He crammed some food into his mouth, stretched out on some dried leaves in a hut, and fell into a deep sleep.

He thought it was a bad dream, that someone kept shaking him by the shoulder saying, 'A message from the King. You are to fall back on Gebal.' Then he opened his eyes. Someone was indeed shaking him. He leapt to his feet and reached for his sword. 'What is it?' he exclaimed 'Are they attacking? Strange! – I dreamt there was a message from the King, saying, "Fall back on Gebal."'

The messenger hesitated, standing there holding a flaming torch, and still breathing heavily after his long run. Then he said, 'That was the message, sir.'

'But the Egyptians are here. This is the only place where we can defend Gebal. His Majesty knows that.'

'I am to say that there will be no city to defend, if you do not return within the walls. The enemy from the North are nearly upon us.'

Zayin sat down again, feeling sick and defeated. He might be winning a battle here, but they were losing a war waged on two fronts.

It was nearly dawn. When the army had formed column again and marched off towards the city, most of the soldiers thought the battle was won and they were returning victorious. They left a handful of men to make a show of defence, but Zayin knew that the Egyptians would soon find out the truth, and would be advancing on the city. He felt in his heart that it was the end of everything.

11

The Darkening
of the Sun

*The earthquake under the
sea – The Chaldean
announces that the day of
destruction has come – The
escape of the people of Gebal
– The catastrophic eruption
of Thira takes place – The return of Aleph – A prophecy of
the greatness of the Phoenician people*

The King of Gebal was sitting in a small room of the palace,
overlooking the sea and the whole line of coast from north to
south. He was talking to a prisoner who stood in chains,
flanked by two palace guards.

'General Zayin knows me,' the man was saying. 'I was his
staff-sergeant in the expeditionary force he led up north. We
were captured together, then I lost sight of him. They say he
escaped. Me, I was taken to Carchemish, and then to
Nineveh. And all the time I was prisoner they were preparing
for war. Or maybe they're always like that, the Mitanni.
Keen soldiers all right, even if it is all chariots. So when the
time came to invade the coast here, they wanted me as a
guide, knowing I was a Giblite. What could I do, Your
Majesty? I thought maybe I could lose them somewhere,
mislead them like. Anyway, I was with the leading unit.

Chariots it was, mainly. Ugh! No way for a soldier to travel – give me two feet any time –'

'So you guided the enemy to our land?' interjected the King harshly.

'I tell you, sir, it wasn't a case of doing that. It was as big a shock to me as it was to them when we came across the Giblite army waiting for us that far north. The first battle was a victory for us – I mean the Giblites of course. The Mitanni were beaten back, and ran. Now's my chance to go over to my own people, I thought. But no, they kept an eye on me and I couldn't escape. We followed them, that is the Giblites followed the Mitanni, me still being a prisoner, but that was the mistake, to go after the Mitanni on to the open plains. I reckon if General Zayin had been there he wouldn't have allowed it. Once in the open, the reinforcements came up, chariotry, of course, and our lot – the Giblites that is – was split up and cut to pieces – they didn't stand a chance, foot soldiers against horse on the plains.' There were tears in the sergeant's eyes as he said this.

'Well, then we regrouped and marched south – the Mitanni that is, and me their prisoner. I swear I didn't help them, Your Majesty! As soon as I started recognizing the ground I gave them the slip one night in the mountains – and here I am. Lucky it's slow going for chariots down the coast and I kept ahead of them. If I've had two hours' sleep the last five nights call me a liar! But I'm not *that* far ahead, Your Majesty. They'll be on us any time now, and there's not a Giblite soldier between them and the city.'

The King pulled at his beard and spoke as if to himself. 'How do I know you are telling the truth? How do I know you are not sent by the enemy to spread tales to alarm us? How do I know who you are?'

'I am no spy, Your Majesty!' the soldier protested. 'Where's General Zayin? He knows me! Ask him!' And at that moment a man strode into the room and the soldier looked hopefully into his face, thinking to recognize the features of Zayin. But it was not Zayin, though the face bore some resemblance. It was Nun, the sailor.

Nun made his obeisance to the King, and before he rose the King asked flatly, 'Well, what is the news from the sea? Is it victory or defeat?'

'Neither, as yet, Your Majesty,' said Nun. 'You know we set out with a small force of ships to patrol the coast to the north and south. Much as we expected, I spied the Cretan ships lying up for the night in a safe bay. They are a strong fleet. We stood in to land, trying to lure them into the open sea to do battle, and three fast rowing galleys came out to engage us. But night was falling and only one had the courage to brave the sea and the darkness. We boarded her and took prisoners. They say their fleet carries many soldiers, and their intention is to attack our city and destroy it without mercy. Your Majesty, they may be here within hours. We must have all the ships and all the troops available, and we must meet them at sea and fight there!'

The King looked grimly out to sea. 'You may have the ships. As for the men, I think there are none left in Gebal.'

There was the sound of approaching feet in the corridor, and Zayin arrived, breathless and sweating.

'Is it victory or defeat?' the King asked, not waiting for Zayin to kneel.

'Victory, Your Majesty!' reported Zayin. 'We repulsed the Egyptians with many casualties. But why have you ordered us to retire?'

The King looked no happier, and seemed to be talking to himself. 'So, many Egyptians have been killed. It might have been better to have received them with open arms, and had Pharaoh as our friend.'

Zayin stood dumb, incredulous that the news of his victory should be received in this way. 'But, Your Majesty!' he said at last. 'They came to destroy us! Your orders were to –'

The King was on his feet, looking out to sea, with his back to the men in the room. He interrupted Zayin's words. 'The Egyptians have come to destroy us. The Mitanni have come to destroy us. The Cretans have come to destroy us. The gods know whether these three great empires have conspired together to annihilate our city, or whether it is only a cruel joke of Fate that they come all at one time. But what can one city do against an empire, let alone three! We cannot sit and await destruction. We have fought, and shown our mettle. The time has now come to talk terms. Send for the High Priest.'

The High Priest had been lurking near by and it did not take long for him to come. The King turned to him. 'High Priest, the three great empires of the world are set on destroying us. What is *your* counsel?'

The High Priest had his plan ready. 'Your Majesty, we must, of course, make peace with Pharaoh, as I have always said. His gods are ours, his learning is ours. He will protect us against our other enemies.'

Zayin interrupted, 'How can you make peace with an army of soldiers who want nothing but vengeance for their defeat?'

'There are customs,' said the High Priest. 'They must be met by an embassy of peace. Gold and jewels must be sent as gifts, and before them must go the maidens of the city and of the Temple, singing and dancing to show that they mean peace.'

Nun spoke slowly, 'So we are to send our maidens to take the brunt, since our men cannot do so? And do we ever see our young women again?'

'Have you seen the desert wolves that make up the army of Pharaoh, High Priest?' cried Zayin. 'Our soldiers were frightened to look at them. Are we then to send our sisters to cope with them?' Both Zayin and Nun were thinking of Beth.

'It is a custom,' shrugged the High Priest. 'If we seek peace, we must purchase it.'

All looked at the King for a decision, but the King was looking out to sea, and his face told them nothing. Nun's eyes, too, turned to the western horizon, expecting the sight of Cretan sails. Zayin moved to catch a possible glimpse of his army returning from the coast and perhaps of the pursuing Egyptians. The sergeant looked grimly northwards.

What they saw – and not one of them at first believed his eyes, for each thought it was only an image of his sinking hopes – what they saw was the sea in retreat from the coast.

Quite smoothly and quietly, the calm sea was sinking. On the coast, great stretches of sand and weed-covered rocks were appearing, which had never emerged above tide-level before. The water of the harbour was running out of the harbour-mouth like a river, leaving a sight never previously seen on this almost tideless coast: ships lying over on their sides in the mud, timbers of sunken vessels and broken stone columns emerging from the green slime.

The four men turned and looked at each other, and knew that they had each seen the same thing. And then for a few moments it seemed as if a giant hand had taken the whole palace and shaken it until it quivered, so that pillars rocked upon their pedestals and great stones in the walls ground one against another. Each of them stood petrified, only their eyes turning from face to face. And then they saw that beside the High Priest was standing another bearded, priestly figure, the Chaldean. It was he who spoke first.

'It is the sign! It is the sign for which I have been waiting. Lord of Gebal, men of Gebal, the day of destruction is here. Flee from your city! Flee to the mountains! Flee, O Giblites, you have but a little time to save yourselves from destruction fiercer than the arms of your enemies!'

The King turned, glaring at the intruder.

'This is the Chaldean sage I spoke of, Sire,' said Nun hurriedly.

But he was vehemently interrupted by the High Priest. 'Is it not enough that the earth is shaken and the sea flies from the coast?' cried the High Priest. 'Must we also suffer false prophets and impostors in our hour of peril?'

Once again, the Chaldean spoke in a level but urgent voice. 'I foretold doom to the Cretans. They put me in prison for my pains and I vowed not to speak again. But, King of Gebal, I must speak now for the hour is already upon you. Your one hope is to abandon your city –'

'And leave it to our enemies from the North and West?' hissed the High Priest. 'Who paid you to speak thus?'

The Chaldean spoke back calmly. 'What means the destruction of your people and your city to me, High Priest? For myself, I have little fear of death, but I feel no need to seek it within your walls. Those who will take to the mountains with me, let them come. To those who choose to stay, I say farewell, for I shall not see them again.' And he bowed to the King and walked from the chamber.

When all men are in doubt, they will listen to one who seems sure of what he is saying. And for Nun it was the behaviour of his element, the sea, and the sickening sight of the ships in the harbour abandoned in the mud that decided him. Besides, he had faith in the sage with whom he had shared such strange experiences. 'Zayin,' he cried, 'I go to summon our family and take them to the mountain, and all who can may follow me.' He ran from the room, and to the crowd of amazed palace servants and courtiers who were milling around the courtyard he cried out in the words of the Chaldean, 'To the mountain! To the mountain! Abandon the city! Abandon the city!'

Remembering just in time that Beth was to be found not at home but at the Temple, he ran to the quarters of the Temple maidens. Ignoring the shrieks of 'Sacrilege!' at his irruption, which seemed to cause as much panic as the earthquake itself, he found Beth, took her hand, and pulled her after him. They hurried back together through the courtyard. As they did so another terrible shock rocked the ground and the tall obelisk with the inscription to Abish-ram toppled from its plinth and broke on the stones of the yard. They ran from the palace gates and down the narrow streets to their home, calling all the time to their amazed neighbours 'To the mountain! To the mountain! There's no safety here!'

Standing before the house, bewildered, they found Resh and their aunt and the other women. Nun looked at Beth. She was pale and out of breath, but she seemed to be more in command of her senses than the rest of the family. 'Beth,' he said urgently, 'see that they pack a few necessities – just food and some wraps, nothing else – and lead them out of the back way towards the mountain. Can I trust you to do that?' Beth nodded, and giving her hand a squeeze he rushed off to the harbour. It was his duty at least to warn the crews of the ships. As he ran along the quays he saw that the water was now returning, not wave by wave as when the tide turns on ocean shores, but welling up over the rocks and pouring back through the harbour mouth in a great surge. He found his own crew, and others standing in consternation at the sight. 'Abandon everything!' he commanded. 'Save yourselves! There is nothing we can do here.'

'The sea's returning, Master.' It was his boatswain who

spoke. 'Can't we put to sea – I'd trust it more than this shivering soil!'

For a moment Nun felt the man might be right; but he had lost his usual faith in the sea. 'Look after your families, men,' he cried. 'Take them to the mountain. Those are your orders. Save the people of Gebal! The rest must look after itself.' And as they ran from the harbour they saw to their horror that the water was not stopping at the high-water mark, but was gradually and with a deadly calm lapping the quays and swamping the warehouses.

As Nun passed through the poor quarter round the docks, yet another fierce shock made him stagger in the street and brought many of the roofs of the houses tumbling down. Everyone was now out of their houses, and he did his best to calm the panic and direct them, by families, to the mountain. Farther on he heard another voice raised above the wails and shrieks of the bewildered citizens, repeating the same message: 'To the mountain! To the mountain!' To his amazement it was the Chaldean, standing prophet-like on a flight of steps, urging the population to seek safety.

Nun made his way through the throng to the Chaldean. 'Come, sir,' he cried. 'Surely you have done enough for the people of Gebal. Save yourself! Follow your own good advice! Let me accompany you to the mountain.'

The streets were so crowded that Nun decided it would be quicker through the open spaces of the palace and the Temple courtyards. The guards had long since abandoned their posts at the palace gates and no one stopped them, but standing in the middle of the great court, by the side of the sacred pool from which the water now flowed, was a solitary figure. The High Priest!

'Will you not save yourself now, Your Reverence?' Nun called as he tried to intercept their flight. The High Priest said nothing as he planted himself squarely before them, his eyes flaming with fury.

'This is no place to stay, Your Reverence,' said Nun. He cared little whether the High Priest saved himself or not, but he could not ignore him.

'This place,' hissed the High Priest, 'is the holy place of El, of Reshef, and of Balaat-Gebal. Though all the city, the King included, may choose to abandon it at the word of a traitor, for me it *is* a place to stay. When all is done, this is but an earthquake. I have known them before during the many years the gods have permitted me to live. Three shocks, and it's over, and the work of rebuilding must begin. But this time our enemies will be in possession, because you, Son of Resh, have listened to one who was sent from the East to betray us. May they pay you well for it, Chaldean!' And the High Priest turned his back.

For a terrible moment Nun doubted, and wondered if the High Priest might not be right. He looked at the face of the Chaldean beside him, but in it he saw the last thing that he expected. He saw compassion, and when the sage spoke there was sorrow in his voice. 'Farewell again, High Priest of Gebal,' were the Chaldean's words. 'Pray to your gods that you may be right. But I fear we shall not meet again.'

Together Nun and the Chaldean made for the land gate of the town, and then up the track among the olive orchards and terraces. As the track became steeper he began to realize what an old man his companion was. He moved slowly and painfully, and Nun, who was no mountaineer himself, had often to help him. But whenever they met families who had settled themselves on the lower slopes, the Chaldean urged them to go higher, higher. Where the pine-woods began, they came upon Resh and the aunts resting at the base of a great rock, while Beth stood anxiously looking out from the top of it. Nun was relieved to see them, but the old man cried urgently, 'Bid them climb higher, bid them seek the tops of the foothills, the level spaces! There is no trust in the rocks and cliffs now.'

Nun began to protest. 'Surely this rock has stood for ages above Gebal! What can be safer?'

But the sage said, 'Indeed, that rock may have stood for ages, but when the hour of destruction comes, who knows what rock will stand?'

So Nun urged his family and the other Giblites upwards to the rounded tops of the foothills and the flat lands before the mountains themselves began. He settled Resh and the older women on a gentle slope that gave a view of the city below and the sea coast to the North and South, and told Beth that he was going to search for Zayin, and the King.

As he scrambled across the face of the hill towards the South, his heart stood still as he saw a line of hundreds of figures winding across the other side of a valley, with the sun glinting on their armour and weapons. An army! Then he realized it must be Zayin's army coming up from the direction of the Dog River. And yes, at the head of them was a figure mounted on a horse. Zayin must have ridden down the coast and diverted the army up into the hills.

Nun went ahead to meet his brother, meaning to advise him as to the safest places on the hills. In the glaring heat of the afternoon, the population of Gebal was sorting itself out, family by family, over the bare hillside. Mothers were still anxiously asking after children they had mislaid in the exodus from the city, crying children were being led from group to group, looking for their parents. Old people were being settled comfortably on the ground, babies were being fed, women were already wandering in search of water, young boys were running and climbing over the rocks, carried away by the excitement of the moment and pursued by the angry cries of their parents. But those families that were already quietly settled, and lonely individuals who had nothing to do but sit and wait, eyed Nun as he passed among them and asked, 'What next, Son of Resh? What is going to happen?' But Nun himself had not yet had time to consider the question.

Zayin was already disposing his troops when Nun came up to him; but on Nun's advice he ordered them to move on up to the level ground, and to make his headquarters with the remainder of the family from where there was a view of all the terrain below. And on their way back they saw, among the late-comers from the city, another party of armed men, accompanied by some grey heads, and carrying a litter.

'Palace guards!' exclaimed Zayin. 'It must be the King himself.' And meeting him they directed the litter-bearers to the hill-top where the King was ensconced on a throne-shaped rock.

Then a silence seemed to fall over the hills, on which the entire population of the city of Gebal were spread in the hot, still afternoon. The persistent voices of the grasshoppers, crickets, and cicadas seemed to be asking, over and over, 'What next? What next?'

Beth, sitting between her brothers, looked anxiously at Nun, and murmured, 'There have been no more shocks since the three we felt in the town.' Her voice sounded a question that must have been in many minds. Had all this alarm been over a few minor tremors? Who was going to be first to admit a false alarm? They looked at the Chaldean, but he seemed to be watching the western horizon with such intensity that there was no room for doubt in his face.

Then a mutter seemed to run through the crowd on the northern side of the hill, and people began to crane their necks and point excitedly up the coast. Zayin and Nun stood up to look in that direction. Round the foot of the farthest headland to the North they could just make out a black line, but what really caught the attention were intermittent flashes of reflected sunlight.

'Armour,' said Zayin briefly. 'The enemy from the North.'

'What are we going to do?' asked Nun, aghast.

Zayin merely looked at him. At the very same moment a breathless soldier came running up from the direction of the southern wing of the army. 'General Zayin,' he gasped. 'They come! They come!'

'I have seen the army of the North,' said Zayin curtly.

'No, my lord, the Egyptians! They are advancing from the Dog River. You may see them from that hill.'

The messenger looked at the General, as if expecting an order. Zayin looked at Nun. They both looked at the Chaldean, who still seemed to be standing in a trance, his eyes fixed on the West.

'We are to stand here, like spectators at a ritual, and see our city occupied?' asked Zayin with a set face. There was no one who could reply.

'The participants are not yet ready for the ritual,' said Nun, his eyes, too, on the western sea. 'We await the Cretan fleet.' With his hand he shaded the sun from his eyes. Were they deceiving him, was he imagining what he expected to see, or were there tiny grains scattered over the taut blue silk of the sea, moving imperceptibly from the hazy horizon towards the shore?

As they stood there, frozen immobile in the hot afternoon, it was Beth who broke the spell. Leaping to her feet she cried, 'Zayin, Nun! you *can't* stand there and do *nothing*!' And the two brothers were both on the point of giving way to the same impulse to hurl themselves down the mountain-side, had not there come at that moment a great cry from the Chaldean sage. He was standing erect with both arms outstretched towards the western sky.

'BEHOLD! IT HAS BEGUN!'

The sun stood half-way down the sky, in the dead middle of the afternoon. But out of the horizon-haze, a little north of west, there was climbing a dense black cloud in the form of a towering Giant. With monstrous speed it reached the height of the sun, solid black from base to head, then continued to spread as quickly across the sky to north and south, until the sun itself was glaring through a reddish-yellow mist, and then was blotted out completely by a blanket of intense black. Now all the western sky was black, and the sea was black beneath it. As the hot rays of the sun were cut off, a deathly chill seemed to fall over the mountain-side, and a great wail of terror arose from the Giblite multitude as they flung themselves to the ground and cowered before the awful spectacle.

Then came the earth shock, compared with which the previous tremors had been the slightest twitches of a sleeping Giant. Prostrate against the solid rock, the Giblites felt repeated blows shaking the roots of the mountain, as if monstrous limbs were striking upwards through the earth's crust, hacking their way through. All minds were numbed, but what was left of Nun's recalled the western isle and the Giants that were said to be imprisoned beneath it. Indeed, the very mountain chain seemed to be breaking up: cliff faces and escarpments were wrenched loose, and great crags rolled over and over into the valleys or into the sea, and the Giblites who had been unwise enough to settle on hanging rocks or shelter beneath them were carried down to their deaths or crushed in their headlong course.

After the cloud, and the shock waves, came the sound, and this was like all the thunderstorms a man might hear in his lifetime, rolled together in one incredible moment.

Below, the face of the sea was almost indistinguishable in the darkness, but if anyone had eyes left to see and mind to register, there was still enough light from the eastern sky to see the next messenger from the cataclysm in the west. At first a line of white foam detaching itself from the black horizon, it revealed itself as a gigantic wave rushing with unbelievable speed towards the coast. It seemed to break, to those whose horrified eyes took in the sight, not against the rocks of the shore but against the very slopes of the mountain range, so that the watchers had a mad fear that it would climb and wash them from the hill-tops where they lay. The city of Gebal was lost in a smother of darkness and foam, like a child's sand-castles swept by the advancing tide.

Then the wind reached them. The Giblites pressed themselves against the rocks, fearing to be lifted and hurled into nothingness by its force, which was indeed the fate of many who were on exposed crags and peaks. In the pine belt, the trees lay down once before the blast, and did not rise again; they had been uprooted or snapped off short in their thousands. The wind continued unabated, and spread the black cloud across the sky even to the farthest East. And after that all sense of time was lost; no one could tell when the darkness of day passed to the darkness of night, no one indeed could ever say whether it was for only one night, or two, or many, that the survivors of Gebal clung helpless to the mountainside while chaos returned to the waters and the firmament, and all light was extinguished save a ghastly red glow from the West that had nothing to do with the sun.

Beth opened her eyes. She saw a grey world – grey skies, a grey sea, grey ashes falling from the sky and covering the rocks. There were other forms around her, stirring from what might be sleep.

She tried her tongue: 'We are alive!' she said doubtfully.

'Are we?' came a voice. It sounded like one of her brothers.

'Impossible!' said another voice. It sounded like her father's.

She rubbed the sleep and the ashes from her eyes.

'Father! Nun! Zayin!' she said. Three other forms sat up, and a fourth, which she recognized as the Chaldean's.

'We have been sleeping,' said Beth. 'Wake up! We are alive.'

'How can you be sure?' asked Resh, his voice also full of doubt.

'I am here. You are here. Nun and Zayin, we are here, aren't we?' Beth said.

Resh tried to collect his wits. 'But what use is there in being alive, when the world has come to an end?'

A great sadness came over Beth. 'Has the world ended, Father?' she asked.

'Surely it did,' Resh said. 'Is not this the afterworld, where spirits eat mud and ashes?'

Beth recognized that part of her sadness was only hunger. 'Eat, did you say, Father? Are you hungry? I am, but we brought food from –' She did not want to say, 'From the world.' 'We brought food. Here!' she rummaged in a bundle lying near. 'Cheese, and olives. And bread – see, it is quite fresh, as if it was baked yesterday. Yesterday! Is that possible?'

'Certainly it was in another world that it was baked,' said Resh. 'But let us eat. Zayin? Nun? It is well we took food with us to the afterworld. We need not eat earth yet.'

Zayin accepted the food, but he was standing up and looking around him as he ate.

'What is this talk of the afterworld?' he said at last. 'It seems to me that this is the side of the mountain above Gebal where we came before –' He could not finish the sentence. 'Look, here are the people of Gebal around us. There are my soldiers. Wherever we are, we are not alone.'

They realized that other families were stirring round them; people were talking in low voices, babies were crying, children were calling for food and water.

'All souls that ever lived meet in the afterworld,' muttered Resh. 'We cannot expect to be alone.'

'My body feels as it did,' Zayin said musingly. 'I feel – I feel that this body should ache with pain, with the blows it has suffered. But I feel well. More bread, if you have it, please, Beth! I am certainly thirsty. We must find water.'

Then Nun spoke. 'Zayin, Zayin, what of the armies, the invaders? And what of the city?'

Zayin struck his head. 'Ah! If the world has not ended, what is happening there? Our city!' He strode to the edge of the slope and looked down. They waited in suspense until he returned the short distance.

'Well?' asked Nun.

Zayin's voice in reply sounded distant, baffled. 'I can make nothing of this grey world and grey sea. And the ashes!'

'The city, man, the city!' repeated Nun. 'Is it still there?'

'Yes,' replied Zayin, sitting down and taking another mouthful. 'It is still there. But it seems – dead.'

'The world is dead,' said Resh. 'It came to an end.'

'I think I am alive,' said Nun. 'I know this bread, cheese, and olives are delicious. Have we survived – survived whatever it was that happened, and are we to go on living in a dead world? Chaldean, eat, pray! Prove that you, too, are alive. But tell us. Tell us what happened!'

Just then a Giblite came over from another group, carrying a water-skin. 'We have water to spare, Resh and sons of Resh. Drink, I pray you. And tell us what we are to do, for no one knows.'

They thanked him, drank, then Nun turned again to the Chaldean. 'You who foretold the future, interpret to us poor ignorant ones who cannot rightly remember the past or understand the present. Tell us what happened, then perhaps we shall know what we must do next.'

The Chaldean finished eating, drank, and began to speak

slowly. 'To explain the present may be harder than to foretell the future. To decide what to do is always hardest. You say I foretold what has happened. Indeed, what I read in the stars, together with a voice within me, my foreboding, predicted a great calamity. The stars suggested a time. I travelled until I felt I had found the place. Nun the Seafarer, you will remember the island north of Crete?'

'The island without water, where they entertained us with wine and told of the buried Giants?' said Nun. 'Thira. Can I ever forget it?'

'That was the place,' said the Chaldean.

'Then their story of the Giants was true?' asked Nun, beginning to understand.

'Certain it is that, buried beneath the crust of earth we live on, lie forces that were free at the beginning of time and are now imprisoned, call them Giants, monsters, Titans if you wish.'

'And from this place,' said Nun, 'they escaped?'

'That is what I believe must have happened,' said the sage. 'If ever you voyage again to the isles of the west, do not look to be entertained again by our former hosts. My vision tells me that they were burned, by the first great outbreak of heat, into the ashes which are now falling over the world. Do not even look for the mountain of Thira. It, too, was consumed in an instant, and you will not see it again.'

The listeners were silent for a while, trying to comprehend the disintegration of a mountain. Then Nun spoke.

'The sign, Chaldean, what of that? The waters receded from the shore before our eyes, and you said that was the sign for the destruction to begin. Where did the waters go?'

'Who can say?' replied the Chaldean. 'But we know when the earth quakes, great chasms may appear in the land. May not this happen under the sea? May not the waters of the sea pour down such gulfs until they encounter the unquenchable fire of the underworld? Then, when one inexhaustible element meets another – what struggles must follow, what release of inconceivable forces?'

'Speak to us of Giants,' said Zayin. 'I cannot understand your philosophy of elements and forces. But a Giant we saw, a Giant in the form of a cloud, rising in the west. I can believe that the Giants have escaped and conquered the world. Tell us, Chaldean, are all the kingdoms of the earth destroyed?'

The sage's eyes took on a distant look as if he were trying to see beyond the grey horizon. 'For great Knossos, court of proud Minos, the destruction I foretold must have come to pass – yet Knossos, among its mountains, may rise again. Mallia and the cities of the Cretan coast have been overwhelmed, and for all its great wealth Crete cannot remain a power among nations for long. We all beheld the great waves that sped across the sea from the central eruption, like ripples from a stone cast into a pool. Wherever these reached the shore, the dwellers on the coast must have been swept away –'

'The armies!' cried Zayin. 'Our enemies that were marching from north and south to attack us! They must have been carried away like ants in a torrent!'

'The Cretan navies too,' said Nun. 'They are certainly destroyed. No ships could have lived in that sea.' He paused, and then added, 'Our ships in harbour too. What can be left of them? And our city? Before we rejoice over our enemies, Zayin, let us know what is left for us to rejoice over. Chaldean, you say that even Knossos may rise again. This is not the end of all things, then?'

'The end of all things? No,' replied the Chaldean. 'In my country and in Upper Egypt it may be that they have only looked upon this darkness and wondered. By the same token, I must soon return to my own people and relate these disasters.'

'But what of our future?' said Nun. 'Will you not prophesy for us? Is the nation of Gebal to rise again, or are we to die here on this ravaged mountain-side? What do the heavens hold in store for us?'

'How can I read the secrets of the heavens, when night and day they are still wrapped in the clouds of this catastrophe?' asked the sage. Then he rose to his feet and looked at the group of Giblites that had gathered around him, and went on. 'Nevertheless, I shall speak of your future – what any child among you could speak. People of Gebal, if you sit here on this mountain-side and do nothing, you will surely die. If you descend to your city, to your farms, and your shipyards, you will find your buildings overthrown, your crops and orchards devastated, your ships smashed to pieces. You may wish then that you had been wiped out on the first day of this calamity. You may feel that you might as well have stayed to starve on the mountain. But mankind is not so easily released from its penance, its commitment to toiling, striving, building. You may have to start from your beginnings again, fashioning your simplest tools from what you have to hand, like the most primitive tribes. Yet, one advantage you do have over primitive peoples. Your material possessions may be lost, your written records destroyed, but each of you carries in his mind the patterns of your civilization. And you may learn from this disaster that what you carry in your minds is of far greater value than your material possessions. General Zayin, you have only a remnant of your armies, your military stores may be destroyed, your sources of armaments cut off – yet who knows, the future may see the armies of your nation crossing deserts and mountains in lands you have not yet heard of, if its leaders retain the spark of military imagination I discern in you, though the gods know I am no man of war. Nun, Captain of Ships, I fear you have no ships now to command, and your very harbour and shipyards may be unusable. But a few generations to come may see ships from this coast penetrating to unknown shores and islands, to seas which at present have no name, thanks to the skills of navigation which now exist in your mind alone.'

The prophet's gaze fell on the face of Beth, solemn and open-eyed, and he permitted himself a gentle smile. 'Even your daughters, people of the coast, show signs that they may be the forebears of queens who shall become legendary in times to come for their wit and wisdom.' Beth blushed and smiled back shyly, and the Chaldean's eyes wandered over the rest of the assembly. 'Bear witness, Giblites, I read this not in the stars but in your minds and faces. And, indeed, there may be one among you, whose face I do not know, and who carries in his mind a secret of even greater worth, a secret seed that, planted here and now, may grow and spread over the face of the earth, beyond the farthest marches of your armies or the longest voyages of your ships. And this seed may be something which seems at present no more important than a childish game –'

And, unaware that she was doing so, Beth spoke aloud. 'Like the twenty-two letters! I wonder where Aleph is.'

A traveller was descending the slopes of the mountain above Gebal. He had passed through the belt of the cedar-forest, and had observed with wonder and dismay the tangle of uprooted trunks and splintered limbs. Only the smallest seedlings and most pliant saplings were still growing, with a few ancient trees of great girth and low growth in sheltered places. He lingered for a time in a clearing where trees had been felled some time ago by the hands of men and still lay waiting to be carried away; then he continued on down a track until he came to a place of bare rocks. Here there were great wounds in the side of the mountain, where crags had been torn away and left raw, red unweathered rock behind.

He came to the pines. Every one of them lay flat against the
ground, their tops pointing away from the West. The traveller
closed his eyes: he was faint from hunger, and his head swam
in the hot sun. He listened to the sounds of the pine-wood:
the cicadas sang their senseless song, just as he remembered
it, among the withering branches, but he missed the music of
the wind that used to play in the swaying pine-tops.

The traveller's heart was full of dread and his body was
very weary after much solitary journeying and great priva-
tion, but he forced himself on towards the city. He came to a
point where he knew he would be able to look down on
Gebal, but he was afraid of what he might see, or fail to see.
He reached the edge of the rocks and looked down. Hundreds
of feet below in the sun's glare, the promontory of Gebal
could be clearly seen. To the right, the blue indentation of
the harbour was as it used to be. The traveller screwed up his
eyes and blinked, trying to interpret what he saw; the outlines
of the city wall, the palace, the temples, and the houses
seemed to be just as he remembered them. His heart lifted
with relief – and then he began to distinguish what was
lacking from the remembered picture. The neat nutshell-hulls
of boats were missing from the harbour. The rectangle of the
palace was not sharp and bold as it had been. It was perhaps
only the empty husk of a building. And, try as he might, he
could not make out any sign of life. He tried to convince
himself that he was still too high to distinguish human figures.
He did not wish to think he was looking down on a deserted
city.

He felt he must keep going, or he would collapse from
weariness. He came to the olive orchards. They, too, were
bare, splintered, stripped of their leaves and fruit, though the
gnarled black trunks and roots still seemed to clutch the
rocky soil. As he reached the lower terraces, the walls of
which were all scattered and crumbled, he thought his ex-

haustion was playing tricks with his senses. It was still half an hour's walk to the harbour or the shore – yet there was a ship, wrecked in a tangle of olive trunks, its anchor cable trailing out behind it through a plantation where the stumps of fig trees were swathed in rotting seaweed.

The sun was setting now beyond the city. Every sunset since the time of the darkness had coloured the whole sky with flaring hues of red, orange, and violet, and so it was this evening. But the traveller did not stop to admire them. He must reach the city before dark. If he could encounter sea-going ships in an olive orchard in broad daylight, he was afraid to think what he might see in the city after nightfall. A people of ghosts?

Picking his way in the gathering dusk over pebbles, sea-sand, and rotting weed he approached the city walls. They still stood high and black against the sky, but their tops were jagged and crumbled like the walls of a ruin. At the landward gate, two soldiers barred his way. They were gaunt and famine-stricken, living spectres – but they were living.

'Who goes there?' came the challenge. 'We admit no strangers to Gebal. We've scarce enough to keep ourselves alive.'

'I have come a long way,' said the traveller. 'I am fainting with hunger.'

'There is no food here,' said the second soldier. 'Be on your way, stranger!'

'But I am a Giblite,' persisted the traveller.

'A Giblite?' repeated the first soldier, coming close to the traveller to scan his face in the dusk. 'I don't recognize you. What's your trade?'

'I am a scribe,' said the traveller. 'Apprentice scribe,' he corrected himself.

'Gebal has no scribes,' said the second soldier curtly. 'They all stayed with the High Priest and got drowned. I shouldn't linger here, stranger! You might get skinned and eaten. There's famine here.'

The traveller leaned weakly against the stone of the great gate. 'Who is left alive here?' he asked. 'My father was Chief Mason, my brothers were General Zayin and Nun, the sailor.'

The second soldier came near and examined the traveller's face in the thickening light. 'Lucky you got here before dark! We've no oil for lamps here, and we'd have made short work of you. I remember you, though. You're old Resh's son, aren't you. Used to be tally clerk at the Temple. What's the name? Aleph, isn't it?'

Aleph nodded. 'Are they alive, my family?'

'I reckon you'll find them in the same place where you used to live,' said the soldier. 'Mostly we're living in the ruins of the old houses and digging around for what we can find. Come on in. Another mouth to feed, but I dare say they'll be glad to see you.'

Wearily, but with lightened heart, Aleph made his way through the rubble-filled, barely recognizable streets. On every side families were settling themselves for the night in makeshift tents or lean-to shacks propped against whatever walls were left standing. Some were sharing out meagre rations of food, but everyone seemed subdued with the quietness of hunger and exhaustion. He even passed neighbours who smiled and saluted him wanly, unaware that he was returning from a long absence. He did not stop to tell his story.

He came to the northern slope of the mound on which the city stood, where he estimated that their house used to stand. But he could distinguish no landmark. He stood uncertainly, listening to murmured conversations of the citizens around him. Then as he stood he realized that his ear had become attuned to two, three, four voices that he knew. The voices of his family, raised in familiar argumentative tones.

'Men cannot work without food.' It was the voice of his sister Beth.

'Send the army on foraging expeditions.' It was Zayin. 'Let them bring back food from neighbouring states.'

'Keep the army here to clear the city and rebuild. Let us build ships too. Then we can trade and bring food,' came the voice of Nun.

'We can build neither ships nor houses without timber. We must fell timber and bring it from the forests,' said the voice of his father, Resh.

Beth was about to bring the argument in full circle by saying 'Woodcutters cannot work without food –' when Aleph interrupted in the darkness.

'There are twenty-nine felled trunks on the edge of the forest,' he said clearly. There was a dead silence. 'I counted the trees, Father,' he added.

His family emerged from the shack in which they were sitting and surrounded him. Beth and his father were both trying to hang round his neck, Nun was shaking him by the hand, and Zayin was thumping him on the back. It was all too much. He would have fallen to the ground in a faint if they had not all held him up and carried him in to what was left of their home.

When he came to himself, he could just see their faces by the light of a little wood fire. Beth spoke: 'We found an unbroken jar of wine and some parched corn in the rubble of the house. We were saving it, but you must eat, Aleph dear, you are not well.'

'We had given up hope for you, my son,' said Resh. 'Where have you been?'

'I was in Sinai, in Pharaoh's mines –'

'Yes, yes, we know, we know,' said Beth soothingly. 'We got your message.'

'My message?' said Aleph in bewilderment. 'You mean the bird . . .? It came back, and you understood?'

Zayin spoke as though something had just struck him. 'If that bird had not told us about Pharaoh's army, the Egyptians would have captured the city —'

'Before the destruction came,' put in Nun. 'And they would not have let us take to the mountains and —'

'And we would not be here now,' finished Beth quietly.

'Tell me what happened,' said Aleph. 'They sent me from Sinai, northward with a supply column. There was darkness and confusion, and I escaped —'

'We shall have plenty of time to tell our stories,' said Beth. 'Now you must eat.'

Aleph took the wine and the water-gruel. 'I am sorry to be just another mouth to feed,' he said.

'Nonsense, my boy,' said his father. Resh turned to the others, 'Aleph is now the only scribe in Gebal.'

His father spoke proudly, but Aleph felt all his shame returning. He turned his head away. 'You know I never learned all the six hundred and four signs, Father. Now there is no one to teach me. I am no use to anyone.'

'Aleph,' Beth said. 'You have your twenty-two letters. They seem to be enough. One day all our story will be written with them.'

A Final Word

Historians do not know how the alphabet was invented, what ship was first navigated by the stars, or who introduced mounted cavalry. So the names of people in this story are not historical: Aleph, Beth, Nun, Zayin, and Resh are taken from the names of letters in the first alphabet. The first two, of course, are contained in this word. The name of King Abishram was formed by combining the names of two known kings of Gebal, Abishmu and Ahiram.

We do know, however, that the prophecies put into the mouth of the Chaldean came true. Gebal, or Byblos, became one of the cities of the Phoenician nation, whose merchant fleets traded all over the Mediterranean and reached as far as Britain and perhaps much farther. Armies based on the Phoenician colony of Carthage threatened Rome. Dido, Queen of Carthage, was one of the first great queens of history and legend. And the simple alphabet of twenty-two letters, which as far as we know was invented and developed in Gebal-Byblos, was the basis of all writing systems used in the modern world, except the Chinese.

If you go to the island of Thira, just north of Crete, you will find a great crater filled by the sea and used as an anchorage for ships. The eruption of the original volcano must have caused the greatest explosion that has yet taken place in civilized times. It is possibly because the results were so catastrophic that its history was never written.

Bebal is now a peaceful little town on the coast of modern Lebanon, where you may see excavations representing every period for the last ten thousand years – including the King's tomb in dark and white stone, an anchor offered in a Temple, the great walls and the huddled houses, and some of the twenty-two letters.

TABLE OF THE TWENTY-TWO LETTERS

	Egyptian Hieroglyph	Meaning	Phoenician Alphabetic letter (circa 1000)	Name	Modern letter
1		Ox		Aleph	A*
2		House or Courtyard		Beth	B
3		Throw stick		Gimel	G
4		Door		Daleth	D
5		Exclamation		He	H
6		Prop		Waw	W
7		Arrow		Zayin	Z
8		Hank of rope		Kheth	Kh
9	?	Ball of twine		Teth	Th
10		Hand		Yod	Y
11		Palm		Kaph	K

*glottal stop which evolved into the written A

TABLE OF THE TWENTY-TWO LETTERS

	Egyptian Hieroglyph	Meaning	Phoenician Alphabetic letter (circa 1000)	Name	Modern letter
12		Peasant's crook		lam	L
13		Waters		mem	M
14		Sea serpent or Cobra		nun	N
15		Fish		samekh	S
16		Eye		ain – no equivalent in English	
17		Mouth		pe	P
18		Monkey		quoph	Q
19		Head		resh	R
20		Hills		shin	SH
21		Mark		taw	T
22		Grass-hopper		sade	TS

THE LOAD OF UNICORN
Cynthia Harnett

Bendy Goodrich had a problem of divided loyalties. His father and brothers were scriveners, who earned a living by copying books laboriously by hand, yet he was apprenticed to William Caxton, the master printer. Apart from the excitement of this story, life in London in the fifteenth century is well portrayed.

GOODNIGHT MISTER TOM
Michelle Magorian

Powerful first novel about a young city boy evacuated during the Second World War to live with a lonely old countryman. It is a very moving account of their growing relationship, which won the *Guardian* Award and was highly commended for the Carnegie Medal.

CUE FOR TREASON
Geoffrey Trease

Peter Browning runs away from home and joins a band of strolling players. He becomes involved with Robert Cecil's secret service and a plot to kill Queen Elizabeth.

THE BOY WITH THE BRONZE AXE
Kathleen Fidler

An imaginative reconstruction of the way the Bronze Age probably spread to outlying Stone Age settlements.

GOLDEN PENNIES
Graeme Farmer

A gripping adventure story set in Australia in 1851. Jack and Lucy go with their parents to Ballarat, where gold has just been discovered, and their story tells of the troubles that surround the family. Then things start to improve when Lucy finds three nuggets.

JOHNNY TREMAIN
Esther Forbes

A story built around the unrest in the American colonies that led to the Boston Tea Party and the American Revolution.

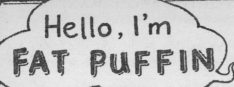